# DARK HOUSE, MANY ROOMS

## HORROR STORIES BY
## P.D. WILLIAMS

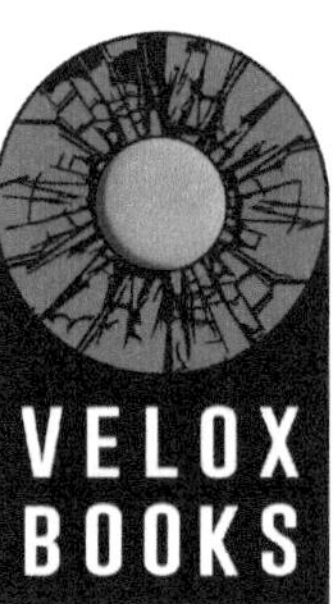

VELOX
BOOKS

# YOU'RE READING ANOTHER TERRIFYING COLLECTION FROM

**FOLLOW VELOX TO KEEP
THE NIGHTMARES COMING:**

# CONTENTS

# INTRODUCTION

S ome writers have a gift for making you laugh. Others excel at making your skin crawl. P.D. Williams does both with a masterful touch that leaves readers checking over their shoulders while wiping tears of laughter from their eyes.

Case in point, P.D.'s infamous Craig and Lorna stories—a series that proves horror and humor can do more than coexist; they can dance together in perfect, terrifying harmony. Craig and Lorna are the kind of characters that feel so real you'd swear you've met them at a small-town gas station or a backwoods barbecue, right before they stumbled into their next supernatural misadventure.

Our journey together began with "Black Wolf's Sedan," the first of P.D.'s stories I had the honor of narrating for my podcast, Drew Blood's Dark Tales. That initial collaboration sparked what would become an enduring creative partnership.

As I've continued to narrate P.D.'s work, I've developed a deep appreciation for his ability to craft tales that defy simple categorization. Each story is carefully constructed with that signature blend of spine-tingling horror and wit that has become his trademark.

We've built a working relationship that continues to bring these haunting stories to life.

Now, with *Dark House, Many Rooms*, P.D. Williams invites us into his most ambitious work yet. This isn't just a house—it's a labyrinth of nightmares, each room holding its own dark promise. But knowing P.D.'s work as I do, I can guarantee that even in the darkest corners of this house, you'll find moments of unexpected levity that make the horror hit even harder when it returns.

As you turn these pages, remember: P.D. Williams doesn't just write stories, he creates experiences that blur the line between laughter and screams. And sometimes, in those moments when you're not sure whether to chuckle or gasp, you'll find yourself doing both.

Welcome to the dark house of many rooms. And whatever you do, don't assume that strange sound you hear is just the house settling. It just might be the supernatural sneaking up on you...or gas.

Drew Blood
Host of *Drew Blood's Dark Tales*

# FOREWORD

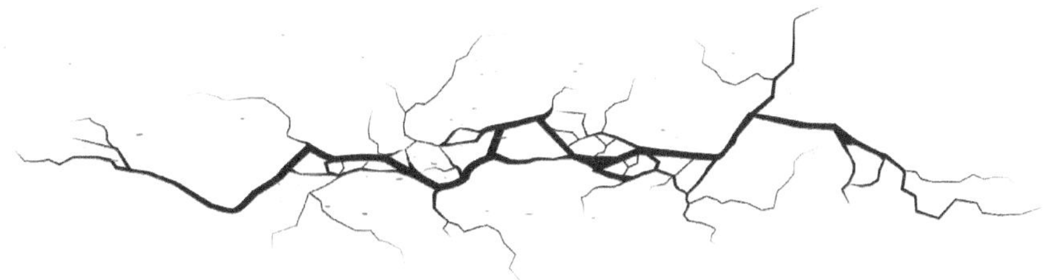

Welcome, curious guest. My name's P.D. Williams. I built this dark house of many rooms for fearless visitors such as you. Feel free to look around, unlock sealed doors, and open dark closets—there's no telling what you'll find in there.

Oh, and don't be afraid to ask questions about the rotting wooden casket displayed in the parlor—instead, be afraid of the answers.

Each room you'll visit holds within it a tale of blood-chilling terror. Don't linger too long. You wouldn't want to lose your mind—your soul.

You're looking a bit anxious, so I'll send you on your way. I suggest you begin with the first room on the left—that one's very creepy. When you're done with each room—or when each room is done with you—come and meet me at the front door. I'll be waiting there... with your straitjacket.

# JELLY

Bertram couldn't be sure how long Emeline had been dead. She'd been in the bathroom, taking one of her late afternoon soaks. He hadn't heard a peep out of her since she'd turned off the faucets over an hour ago. He didn't think much about it. After all, they were both in their early 70-s, and as you got older, things naturally took longer.

Bertram was kicked back in his time-worn recliner watching baseball. It was now well into the fourth inning when the thought hit him to check on her. *Lord, what if she's fallen and knocked herself unconscious?* He had sat through enough of those medical alert commercials to know that it was relatively easy to end up on the kitchen floor or—and this was when the disturbing mental picture took hold of him—a bathtub full of water.

He got up, walked to the bathroom, and banged on the door. "You okay in there?" She didn't answer, so he opened the unlocked door and stepped inside. Emeline was sitting in the tub, her head tilted to the side. She appeared to be napping.

"Emeline? Emeline, honey?" He inched closer to the tub. The knot in his stomach grew tighter as he reached down and pushed her shoulder. She slumped down to the waterline. He jumped back as if the tub had sent an electrical shock through him. Bertram's quaking hand felt her neck for a pulse, but found none. He stared at her chest for any movement. It was still. "Oh, Lordy Lord! Emeline? Aw, Jesus, no!" He backed out of the bathroom until he bumped into the wall in the hallway. He turned and staggered to the living room and dropped down onto the recliner. Bertram was shaky and confused.

Once he collected and arranged his thoughts, he realized that the first thing he needed to do was contact the authorities. He shut off the TV, turned, lifted the receiver of the landline phone on the small table next to him, and began dialing 9-1-1. Then the voice called from the bathroom.

"Bertram! Are you there?"

He froze, his finger still hovering over the 1 button on the phone's receiver. He reminded himself there were no such things as ghosts. He dialed the 1, then he heard the water stirring, followed by the faint sound of feet sliding over the tile floor toward the bathroom door. In his mind's eye, Bertram watched the doorknob slowly turning, heard the telltale creak of the door hinges. The wet footsteps squished as they dragged down the hall and toward the living room.

Bertram laid the receiver on the table and stared straight ahead at the darkened TV screen. He could see his own reflection and the living room around him. His peripheral vision detected the form stepping out of the hall. He stayed focused on the TV mirror. He might lose what little sanity he had left if he looked directly at her. He panted as the body wrapped in a white bathrobe sauntered past him and sat down in the chair next to him.

"Bertram, I feel funny," she said. "I hope I didn't have a stroke or somethin'." Emeline looked over to him. "Bertram, what's wrong with you? Look at me when I'm-a-talkin' to you."

Bertram worked up enough courage to swivel his head toward her like a wobbly animatronic. When he saw that his wife was very much alive, and not some revenant haunting him, his body relaxed, and his heart rate returned to near normal.

"Baby?" he asked with more relief than fear. "God of Moses, darlin', I thought you'd gone and died in the bathtub."

"Died in the bathtub? What's gotten into you, ya old fool?" She smiled and snickered at him.

"You was in the tub for a while, so I went to check on ya. You weren't breathin', or movin', or nothin'. When I touched ya, you slumped over like a loose fence post. Are you sure you're all right?"

"Yes, Bertram, I think I might remember dyin'. I probably just fainted. Them new blood pressure pills Doc Melbourne has me on has been givin' me the woozies. I'll call him tomorrow and get that straightened out." She shot a quick glance at the antique clock on the mantle and said, "Good gracious, would you look at the time? Have you eaten anything?"

"Well, of course, Emeline. The first thing I thought of when I figured you was dead was to go in the kitchen and stuff my pie-hole."

"Oh, Bertram," she mewed through one of the loving smiles he always found endearing. "You must be starved. I'll whip you up some fried cubed steak and mashed potatoes."

"Ain't you hungry, too? You know how much dyin' can wear a body out."

"Ha ha, ain't you a riot? Ya know, for some reason, I ain't hungry."

"Well, how 'bout you get on to bed and rest yourself. I've got more of a hankerin' for a peanut butter and nanner sandwich."

"All righty, then. I am feelin' pretty run down. I'll see you in the mornin'."

"I sure hope so."

Emeline got up from her chair, stood over him, and kissed him on top of his balding head before heading off to bed. *Sweet Jesus, how her lips are cold.*

A good half hour before even God himself was set to awaken, the rooster crowed. Bertram sat up in bed, rubbed his eyes, and swung his legs over the side. He drew in the familiar fragrance wafting in from the kitchen. Bertram loved the smell of freshly brewed coffee and bacon in the morning. He threw on some fresh overalls and made a beeline to his breakfast.

He leaned over the stove in the kitchen and sniffed the frying pans that created what he liked to think of as the Morning Miracle. He poured himself a mug of hot, black coffee and sat down at the small table by the kitchen window, where he was greeted by the glorious sight of one of Emeline's life-altering breakfasts. He was about to place the napkin in his lap when it dawned on him that Emeline wasn't buzzing around the way she typically did. His stomach lurched at the thought that she may have passed out again.

"Hey, honey, where you at?"

"I'm down here!" Emeline hollered from the root cellar, where she stored her delicious homemade jellies. Soon, the cellar's two heavy doors slammed shut. Bertram heard her grunting as she climbed the steps of the side porch.

"Darlin', are you okay? Do you need some help?"

"No, I'm good. Just needed to grab a fresh jar of jelly," Emeline replied.

Bertram started loading up his plate with scrambled eggs. He heard the squeal of the long spring on the screen door stretching. "Come on, old woman, or I'll start the blessin' without ya!"

Emeline scooted past him as he saturated his eggs with Tabasco sauce. He was stretching for the bacon just as she was sitting down. She reached across the table and placed the jelly at the center, next to the biscuits' covered bowl.

The jar was her strawberry blend. Bertram read the personalized note on the label affixed to the front: Strappin' Strawberry, Main Ingredient—LOVE. He smiled as if he were reading the sentiment for the first time.

"I don't know what's up with me this mornin'. My joints feel so stiff," Emeline complained.

"Oh, now, Emeline, you know neither of us is exactly a spring chick—" Bertram looked at her. She had dark circles under her slightly milky eyes. Purple veins crisscrossed her upper torso.

"Bertram, what is it? Are you all right? You look like you've seen a ghost."

Bertram swallowed hard. "Emeline, baby, have you looked in a mirror?"

"No, I just threw on my dress and got about my business. I didn't have the energy to go comb my hair or brush my teeth. 'Sides, who's there to try and impress way out here anyways? Speakin' of teeth, my jaw feels tight. It's makin' it hard to talk. Do you think I might've gotten a tick bite? Those things can cause all kinds of bad symptoms."

Bertram didn't feel like eating anymore. "I think we ought to get you in the truck and go to the ER over in Campbell."

"That's nearly an hour from here! Just let me see if I can stomach some food, then I'll go take some aspirin and lie down. I'll be all right."

"Here, let me see if you've got a fever first." Bertram felt her forehead. He snatched his hand back.

"Bertram, what is it? Do I have a temperature, or not?"

"Sweetie, you don't have no temperature at all. You're colder than an Eskimo's nose. Are you sure you don't want me to rush you to the hospital in Campbell? There's no tellin' what you might've caught."

"No. I'm too tired to even walk out to the truck. Just help me get back to bed. I don't think I can hold anything down after all. We'll see how I feel later."

"All right, if you're sure."

Bertram took her arm. He nearly yelped. It felt as if her arm had turned into an unyielding rubber. When he finally got her to the bedroom, he began unbuttoning the back of her dress. He noticed it was damp, and her skin had a slight sheen to it. After he lowered her onto the bed, he covered her up and kissed her frigid forehead before heading to the living room to give all of this a good think.

Throughout the morning and early afternoon, Bertram checked on her four times. Each time, she was sleeping. Worn out by questions and concerns, he nodded off in the recliner. A while later, he awoke with a start and saw the early evening's faint shadows beginning to take shape on the living room's wall. He had drifted off earlier in the afternoon, which meant Emeline hadn't been checked on for hours. Bertram gave a slight grunt as he hauled himself up and out of his chair. He was just beginning to get acclimated to alertness when he heard a gurgling voice cry out from the back bedroom.

"Bertram!"

Her voice sounded like it was underwater. Bertram was running down the hall when the odd smell hit him. It was like rotten fruit and spoiled meat. He charged through the bedroom door, flipped on the light switch, and blocked his howl with his palm.

"Bertram," she asked, "do I look odd to you? I feel different from this mornin'. What do you think's goin' on?"

Bertram had no response for the waxy corpse sitting on the side of the bed. Then his attention shifted to the stomach-churning stench emanating from the oozing, pus-filled blisters covering her body.

"I feel sick. Will you help me get to the bathroom?"

Bertram stood there, gawking at her. He didn't know if he should run screaming from the house or call an ambulance.

"Bertram, help me," she pleaded.

He walked to the bed. Emeline held up a water-logged arm, and Bertram grimaced as he took hold of it. He began lifting her up to a standing position and felt the top layer of her skin slip a little. His repulsion made him pause.

"Bertram, get me to the toilet!"

It was enough to snap him back. After helping Emeline up, he stepped back a bit but held his arms out to catch her if she fell, though he dreaded having to touch her again. Once he'd directed her into the bathroom, she shuffled toward the toilet. She bent forward slightly and vomited up copious amounts of blackish blood and small, chunky pieces.

Feeling his own gorge rising, Bertram said, "I'm so sorry," as he dashed from the bathroom and out to the side porch, where he did some puking of his own. As he was finishing, it gradually dawned on him that he had left his ailing wife alone in the bathroom, dealing with her own fear and discomfort. Wiping his mouth with the back of his hand, he composed himself as best he could and ventured back inside.

The only thing worse than Emeline's hideous appearance was the horrendous smell of decaying flesh that now permeated the back of the house. He grabbed a handkerchief from a pocket in his overalls and covered his nose and mouth. "Emeline, where are you, sugar?"

"Bah-room," the croaking voice replied. She was hunched over the porcelain sink, her darkened hands gripping the sides. A few nails were peeled away from her fingertips. "Oh, Ber-ham," she whispered.

Bertram approached the sink. He couldn't see Emeline's face; her oily hair had fallen forward over her brow. Bloody teeth clogged the drain. *I think we might be lookin' at more than some tick bite or faintin' spell.* The conclusion he was coming to unleashed a bevy of goosebumps all over his body. She wasn't merely ill—she was a withering corpse. Bertram had seen enough dead farm animals. Emeline was just as gone as they had been.

He had no idea what to do, think, or say. Then the small crumb of rationality told him that the first thing he needed to do was become more practical—crying and confusion would not help. He could no longer think of Emeline as his beloved high school sweetheart and wife of over fifty years—she was now a body he had to deal with. His first course of action was to get her out of the house.

"Emeline, sweetness, let's get you on the porch. I think we both could use some fresh air."

She remained still at first and then made four small turns to her left until she was facing the bathroom doorway. "Do you want me to help you?" Bertram asked. He was relieved when she didn't answer.

Once she made it to the porch, Emeline managed to bend her knees enough to lower herself down onto one of the rocking chairs. Bertram attempted to conceal the look of disgust on his face about her joints' loud cracking as she sat down. Foamy blood leaked from her mouth and nose.

Bertram attempted to conceal the look of disgust on his face about her joints' loud cracking as she sat down. Foamy blood leaked from her mouth and nose. He felt the need to cover her wretched body with something. "Sugar, would you like a blanket?"

Emeline nodded ever so slightly, her neck making the cringe-worthy cracking sound again.

Bertram pulled in a deep breath. Holding onto it for as long as possible, he jogged to the bedroom closet for the blanket. Once he was back outside, he tenderly wrapped the blanket around her and sat in the other rocking chair. Neither said a word. They stared out across the yard at the fading springtime sun as it slid softly and colorfully behind the tree line.

Bertram rocked back and forth. He tried desperately to direct his mind toward any other place, but the porch he was sharing with a dead woman. Bertram let his gaze wash over the front property, corralled by a long stretch of wire fencing. He was rapt as he took notice of the straight rows of neatly planted corn. They reminded him of a battalion of soldiers standing at attention. *God, how I love the country life: it surely does agree with me.*

But the merciful distraction dissipated as his thoughts circled back to Emeline. He recalled fondly the acreage portion that she had claimed: the magical place that ran along the north side of the house that gave the fruit bushes their first breath of glorious life. She used the berries she grew to create her wondrous and delectable delights. His lips trembled as he remembered the unique labels she made for each jar. She'd give each flavor a catchy name, like Big Bad Blueberry, Betcha Like 'Em Blackberry, or Really Red Raspberry. And just as she had done on the label for the strawberry jelly she'd served at breakfast, she always finished out the stickers with the affectionate phrase: Main Ingredient—LOVE.

As the hours wore on, Emeline's wet breathing slowed. Her once bold eyes grew dull and distant. Despite his effort to stay awake with her, Bertram eventually fell into a deep and uneasy sleep. He was so drained that he slept past the rooster for one of the very few times in his adult life.

He was awakened by a loud buzzing. Emeline was still gazing well past nowhere; her eyes had receded deep into their sockets. The buzzing that Bertram heard was the numerous flying insects rushing in and out of her open mouth, invading her nose and ears. Her greenish body had bloated; it looked as though her stomach was set to burst. The gas that had accumulated inside her was loudly escaping through the various orifices of her disintegrating vessel. *They say that there's dignity in death,* Bertram thought, *but there ain't nothin' dignified about my wife right now.*

For Emeline's sake, Bertram tried to remain stoic. It would be cruel to let her witness her husband's revulsion. His disordered mind made it difficult for him to decide on what he should do for his wife at this awful moment. He did know that he would never leave her with the relentless flies and their maggots. More important, he would never allow anyone else to see her in her current ghastly state—the authorities be damned!

"I'm fadin', Ber-ham," she mumbled.

"What can I do, darlin'? Tell me what I can do for you."

She struggled mightily to make herself understood. "Put me back in da tub. Please, let me twy and wash tiss mess off of meee."

It was hard for Bertram to watch the filthy insects pushed out of her mouth as she spoke. It seemed evil and profane, and it brought about a wave of anger. "I'll go and get the bath ready," he said. "I'll be back in a jiffy."

When he returned to the porch, he had his handkerchief tied around the lower half of his face. He went to Emeline and gently peeled off her gooey blanket as if it were a Band-Aid. Then he placed one arm under her knees, now stiff with rigor mortis, and the other across her shifting shoulder blades, and carried her to the bathroom.

The muscles in his lower back strained as he placed her down into the water's warm comfort.

He stood up straight to loosen up and noticed that his arms were sticky and stained. "Do you want me to help wash you off?"

"No. Juss leave meee."

Bertram shuddered as he realized that this was likely the last time he would ever hear his wife's voice. "Call if you need anything."

He went back out to the front porch to clear his head and allow the tears to purge his heart. He waited there for a very long time, but Emeline still hadn't called for him. When he couldn't take the silence and worrying any longer, he re-covered his mouth and nose with his handkerchief and returned to the bathroom.

Emeline was slumped over, just as she had been the first time he found her. Her skin was turning black, and there was a slimy film on the surface of the water. Worse yet, her body was beginning to liquefy. The odor that ripped through his mask was the worst by far. Bertram opened a window and then bolted back outside to retch.

"Lord, please help me! What in the world am I gonna do?" he shouted. But Heaven was silent. Should he now call the authorities? And if he did, what would he tell them? What might they make of his wife's decomposed body? Would they think him a ghoul and lock him away?

There was going to be an investigation and many questions he couldn't possibly answer.

Bertram needed a place to think. He walked around to the side of the house and stood near Emeline's garden, where her prized crop flourished. He paced anxiously, frazzled and useless, hoping for an idea. Then he abruptly stopped. As Bertram gazed upon the columns of ripened berries, an inexplicable feeling of calmness enveloped him. The garden's peacefulness brought clarity, allowing him to ponder a few simple ideas rather than trudge through a complicated maze of elaborate plans. The decision he made felt not so much correct as it did proper. For Bertram, this was now a sacred place of remembrance—a place where a woman's love nurtured the rich, brown earth that had yielded so much sweetness and beauty. Now, he knew what in the world he was gonna do.

He let her sit in the tub for over a week, so nature could finish the job it'd screwed up before. Then, he dug a hole out by her garden and began pouring her gelatinous remains into it. When he got down to the last of it, Bertram picked up the small jar he had brought with him and filled it. He screwed on the two-piece metal lid, took a pen from one of his overalls' chest pockets, and scribbled some words on the blank label.

Bertram carried the jar down to its final resting place. There, it would serve as a small monument to a love that would continue far beyond its fifty-plus years of earthly existence. He said a few words of prayer, then solemnly ascended the stairs of the root cellar. He lowered its doors as if they were the lid of a coffin. There in the darkness, on a row of tall racks, sat a jar of dark jelly. Written on the white label were the words: Amazing Emeline, Main Ingredient—LOVE.

# WRATH OF SHADOWS

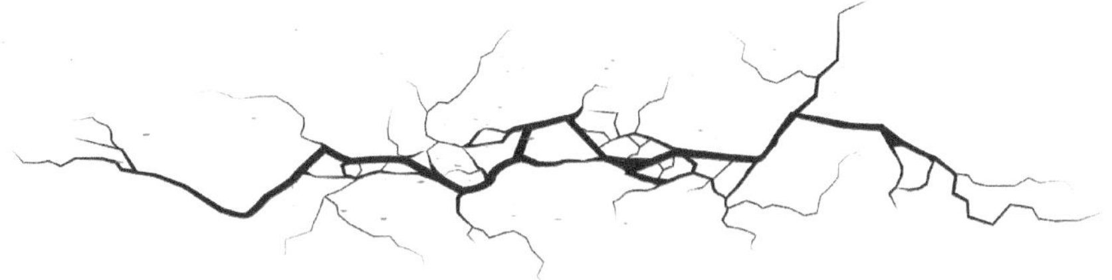

I saw my first shadow person when I was ten years old. It terrified me then, and it terrifies me now. My name is Travis Burke, and you can believe me if you want to.

It started one night at bedtime. I was lying in the dark, trying to ignore the battle sounds bleeding through the flimsy wall. The tension between my mom and George, her newest louse of a husband, was stifling. Their arguments didn't care if it was a school night or not. So I learned to focus on the quiet things: the swish of tree limbs outside my window, the occasional rain on the rooftop, or the soft glow of my Avengers' wall clock and the peaceful ticking of its second hand.

As I was nodding off, something moved across the clock. The form was so black that it stood out from the darkness itself. It drifted through the shadows like a murky mist. I lay there, frozen and breathless. Watching... listening. The vein in my temple pulsed with every heartbeat. I braced for an icy touch or the hissing of my name. Easing my arm from beneath the covers, I turned on the Captain America lamp on my nightstand. There was no lunging monster, no ghoul grasping. There was simply no one there.

I checked the usual hiding places where all monsters dwell—under the bed, inside the closet—but found nothing. Still, I shivered. At age ten, ghosts and monsters were still a frightening possibility to me. I lay in bed with the lamp on until I couldn't stay awake any longer.

When I woke up after a few hours of fitful sleep, the sun had risen. The first dull moments of wakefulness temporarily erased the previous night's episode from my mind. But the lamp was still on, and I remembered why.

Getting dressed that morning, I debated whether I should tell Mom about the dark object. She'd probably just chalk it up to a bad dream and move on. Then there was the other part of the decision. I didn't want to add weight to the heavy emotional bundle she was already lugging around. The poor woman was working two part-time jobs and bowing before a three-pack-a-day habit. She was depressed and angry; she didn't need any more problems. Besides, we already had a demon to deal with. So I kept it to myself.

The next few nights were uneventful. Could've been the lights I kept on as a precaution, but I was starting not to think so. Maybe there'd been no specter in the first place. It was conceivable that it'd all been a trick of my tired eyes. I was glad that I hadn't told Mom; I felt a little embarrassed about the whole thing. I turned off the lights and closed my eyes. Curled up on my side, I listened to the clock's ticking, my breath keeping time with the steady beats. Soon, I felt the gentle tug of sleep.

Noises came from inside my closet: wire hangers tinkled, shoes tapped. My stomach was tight, my jaw trembled. The doorknob creaked as it turned. Slowly, the door dragged over the carpet. I sat up and looked at the closet. A chill ran through me like an electrical current as I watched four inky fingers curl out and grab hold of the outside edge of the door. Whatever was on the other side shot out and landed on my ceiling like a fly. It was directly over me, so I had my first sight of the strange being: it resembled an adult human shadow. Suddenly, two white, beastly eyes sprang open and glared down at me. Horror seized me, constricting my lungs, preventing me from screaming. Though terrified, I couldn't look away from the creature. Soundlessly, it dropped from the ceiling and locked me in a cold embrace. A rush of blackness filled my head. And then... I can't remember.

The following morning, I was startled awake when Mom yelled at me to get ready for school.

I'd been so worked up at bedtime that I'd forgotten to set my alarm clock. The first thing I noticed was that my pajamas were soaked in sweat. Then the hazy memory of the creature slithered through my mind, its image sharpening with every wriggle. I searched the room for something out of place—my ceiling in particular. There was no sign that anything had been there. And I couldn't remember what had happened after I'd blacked out. It was like trying to make sense of a past dream. But there was something different about me. Something was... off.

I went through the morning routine like a robot. Somehow, I faked my way through the day and the couple of weeks that followed. Sleep was hard to come by, but when I was able to, it was with the ceiling light, my superhero lamp, and my old Scooby-Doo nightlight on.

Soon, it was early January, and Old Man Winter started throwing his weight around. Our small, drafty house was locked up tight to keep out the cold, so it always reeked of alcohol and nicotine. If that wasn't bad enough, the winter months brought out the worst in George and Mom. They were like two feral animals cooped up in a tiny cage.

By now, Mom probably realized that marrying George had been a mistake. Some women marry men hoping to change them, but George did not subscribe to this plan. For one thing, he liked to drink, and when he did, he darn well didn't want to be bothered. Sometimes, all it took to set him off was my leaving toys out. I can still feel his belt on my back. I recall times when Mom and I would have to run to the bathroom and lock the door during one of his drunken outbursts. We'd cower in the bathtub until he gave up and went to pass out in the living room.

One evening after dinner, I was on my bed doing homework. The overhead light gave me a headache, so I turned it off and used the lamp. As I perused my history book, I felt like someone was staring at me. I jerked my head up—no one was there. I waited for a bit before returning to my textbook. A few minutes later, I saw movement out of the corner of my eye. When I turned to it, I began trembling.

In place of the usual shadows of my room, the figures of a man and woman were on my bedroom wall. They stood facing each other, their mouths moving. A few seconds later, the man slapped the woman. When she tried to fight back, the slaps became punches. Then the man choked her until she went limp. He maintained his grip on her for a while longer. When he finally let go, the woman's body dropped in a heap at his feet. Gradually, the figures morphed into the original shadows of my bed, my dresser, and me.

My body was like a slab of ice. Was I hallucinating? Crazy? I was afraid I'd crossed over to a foreign, forbidding place from which I'd never return. An overwhelming wave of distress washed over me. Whom could I turn to? Not Mom—certainly not George. There was no one to save me. I was helpless and alone in a realm of dark thoughts, scared and isolated.

But then, I'd always felt that way. I was an odd duck with few friends, a loser always on the outside looking in at kids who had a chance at something better. As I settled down and thought more about it, my fear gave way to curiosity. What were those shadows? Why hadn't they hurt me? And why were they communicating with me?

The answer came the next day.

There were police cars and an ambulance in front of my house. From the sidewalk, I could see George sitting in the back of one of the cruisers. Flashing blue lights cast a pulsating glow on his pale, sweaty face. His empty eyes stared forward into nowhere.

As I stumbled toward my house, our neighbor, Annie Miller, rushed up beside me and threw her arms around me. She was crying. "Oh, sweetie," she said, "you don't want to go up there. Just wait here with Annie for a bit."

Standing there next to Mrs. Miller, I watched the scene unfold with everyone else on the block. After a while, two men in uniforms eased a stretcher through the front door. On top was a bulging black bag. My heart began pounding to the point of bursting. I started sobbing. No one needed to tell me who was in that bag. I knew it was my mother. George had killed her. It had all taken place on my bedroom wall.

Anguish pierced my soul like a white-hot blade. The most important person in my life was gone. Memories of Mom crowded my mind. The way she gushed over every crappy picture I drew in kindergarten. Pawning her jewelry so she could give me decent a Christmas. She was my world. Now that world had ended. What was going to happen to me?

Aunt Gertie and Uncle Harry didn't hesitate to take me in after Mom's murder. Aunt Gertie was Mom's older sister by two years. She and Uncle Harry had always done their best to help us out. Their home was a haven for us whenever we fled from George. They had no children of their own and had always treated me as if I were theirs. Their unconditional love and kindness relieved some of the torment.

The emotions that pummeled me during that time left a permanent stain on my spirit. First, I missed my mother. Second, I felt like a stupid coward for seeing the shadow people as scary monsters instead of what they were: harbingers. I could've saved my mom, could've warned her, but I didn't understand. Last, there was my overwhelming urge to kill that animal, George. Rage devoured me. Forgiveness, mercy, and empathy evaporated like dew under the sun.

Over the next several weeks, I was subjected to police questioning, court testimony, and grief counseling. I was exhausted.

Late one evening, I was lying in my new bed with the lamp on, unable to turn off my brain. Something stirred on the wall. After a long break, they were back. I was hesitant to look, but what if it was another message? My first thought was *Oh, God—not Aunt Gertie and Uncle Harry!*

There was a lone shadow facing sideways. I could tell by its size and shape that it was George's silhouette. Standing behind bars, he took off his shirt and began tying one end to the top grid of one of the bars; the other he wrapped around his neck. He walked forward a few steps and then fell backward. And just as before, once the shadows completed the scene, my wall went blank again.

I probably should've been petrified. Instead, I enjoyed a sublime sense of satisfaction and a peace I hadn't known since before George invaded our lives. I turned off the light and slept like a baby.

The next morning, we got the news of George's suicide. Uncle Harry said, "That's too bad. Pass the pancakes."

I was in awe of the shadows and their strange abilities, grateful for the vengeance they'd exacted. It was as if they were mine and I was theirs, forever joined in thought and deed. I decided that I'd keep their existence, as well as their specific purpose, my special secret.

The recent performance of the Terror Troupe filled me with questions. Why had they chosen me? Had they sensed my pain, my anger, my fear? I'd wanted George to die, and he had. I wondered about the first shadow, after it pulled me into itself. Had the experience given me special power? I needed some answers, but I knew I'd have to go to a dark place to find them. In the end, it wasn't that difficult. All I needed was a lab rat. For that, I chose Adam Wentz: the terror of Westland Elementary.

Because he'd been left behind twice, Adam was bigger and older than the rest of us. He was meaner, too. The kids he slapped, shoved, and threatened were legion. Like me, he came from a broken home, the difference being that it had never occurred to me to blame others. Who knows what it was about me that attracted his hatred? I was small for my age, nerdy, and painfully shy, so he probably found me an easy target. Once, during recess, he punched me in my stomach so hard that I threw up. Of course, there were no teachers around. The only thing worse than the physical abuse was the delight he took in humiliating me. He'd taken to calling me Baby Boy, a nickname that caught on much too quickly. It was as if the other kids had figured that the best way to escape his notice was to join in. I hated going to school; dreaded it, in fact. It always left me feeling small, weak. Worthless.

After another awful day at school, I returned home and ran straight to my room. Most times, I went there to cry and think about harming myself. However, that day was different. That day offered possibilities. Answers.

Laying on my bed, I closed my eyes and filled my thoughts with every cruel thing that Adam had ever done to me. After a while, the effort tired me to the point that I slipped away into an easy sleep. I dreamed about him. I don't recall how long I was out, but when I woke up, the room was beginning to darken, and Aunt Gertie was calling me down for supper.

After devouring another of her amazing Swiss chicken casseroles, I watched TV until she and Uncle Harry told me to get ready for bed.

When I got to my room, I put on my pajamas, climbed into bed, and waited. I was eager to see what kind of payback my defenders would unleash on Adam—God, how he deserved it. My arm was still sore from the previous day when he'd twisted it until I yelled, "I'm a baby boy!"

I stared at my wall for a long time. When the shadows didn't appear, I figured the experiment had failed. I was disappointed. Who was I kidding? There were no special powers—certainly not for me. I reached over to turn off the light...

An image of someone reclining in a bathtub materialized on the wall. It was a bit hard to identify, but it could only be Adam. There was a small rectangular object at the foot of the tub. Adam's feet were tapping, and his head was bobbing. His foot nudged the object, and it tumbled into the water. His shadow flopped around for a while, then stopped and slumped until his head disappeared. The moving shadows melted into familiar ones.

I was dumbfounded. Could it be true? Did I have the ability to mete out retribution? Did this mean that I would no longer be the victim, but the victor? Relief settled over me. And just as I'd done after George's execution, I turned off the lamp and went straight to sleep, smiling.

The news of Adam's death passed through school the next day. Chatty teachers whispered innuendos about his dysfunctional family. An indifferent janitor removed Adam's personal effects from his locker. None of the students seemed upset; some were likely relieved. As for me, I was exhilarated. Ten years old, and I had power over life and death. It was as though I'd become a superhero. Oh yeah, there was a new sheriff in town, and he was lookin' for justice.

Over the next several years, I worked my magic on a few other people: a cheating girlfriend (decapitation), another bully (broken neck). And the weird neighbor who hung around the playground? Struck by a car. I was so drunk on power I was staggering. I was also getting sloppy.

One day, Paul, my college roommate, asked, "Say, Travis, doesn't it creep you out that you knew all those people who died?" Poor Paul (Rottweiler attack). I regretted that one. Paul was my friend, and I'd offered him up to the shadows for nothing other than convenience.

Seeing Paul's shattered family at his funeral caused a seismic shift. It brought back all the brokenness I'd gone through after a selfish thug had taken away my heart and soul. I was ashamed, convicted. It was time to stop. I'd taken more than my pound of flesh. I needed to move on before becoming a monster far worse than those I'd encountered growing up. Problem was, there were still other monsters roving around.

Not long after I graduated, I began working as an administrative assistant for a major banking firm, which meant being nothing more than a glorified gofer. At the time, I was the assistant to Mr. Marcus T. Connor, an up-and-coming financial wizard, and first-rate jerk.

Marcus treated me like a stupid animal in constant need of a good, swift kick. He even had a nickname for me: Monkey. It wasn't quite as bad as Baby Boy, but it hurt just the same. Marcus took great delight in humiliating me in front of others. Sort of a *hey, look what I can do* power trip. Most of my co-workers felt bad for me. But just like those cowardly kids in grade school, some of them ragged me about it. It was common to find a banana lying on my desk.

Marcus's bullying destroyed what little was left of my self-esteem. My stomach constantly churned with nerves. And the nightmares? Horrific. Finally, I pulled together enough courage to do something about it. But like so many of my plans, all my efforts to transfer to other departments failed. When Marcus caught wind of it, he waged a personal terror campaign against me: cleaning up the coffee he'd "accidentally" spilled on his office's floor or having me come in on weekends to change out copier ink. Life was miserable again.

He summoned me to his office one day and chewed me out for not having filed a report on time (which I had). He swore at me and intimidated me just like Adam and George had done all those years ago. I felt their fists all over my body; their terrible words squirmed through my brain like earwigs. A wave of old, familiar anxiety rose inside me like bile. My hands shook; my mouth was an arid pit. Never having been one for physical confrontation, I broke eye contact. My vision moved about, to the left, to his right...

On top of a credenza in the corner of the office were some photos of Marcus and his family on vacation: a beach, a ski lodge, a cruise ship. But what caught my eye was the young boy in the pictures. He had such a sweet, happy smile. They all did. As Marcus raged on, I smiled a bit myself.

I rambled around my apartment that night, trying to convince myself that I was no longer a killer. Marcus was a despicable person, but he had a family who loved him—had a child, for pity's sake! I wanted to surrender my pride to those feelings, but I'd come too far to go back to being less than nothing. I threw back several Jack and Cokes. The more I drank, the weaker my conscience became. Who'd that creep think he was to screw with me? I controlled a shadow army, the agents of my wrath! I paced back and forth like a panther in a cage. Drunk and exhausted, I collapsed on the couch and fell asleep.

The following morning, the alarm on my cell phone roused me. I rolled off the couch and crawled to the bathroom, managed a cold shower, and got dressed. I was so hungover that I barely made it to work.

When I arrived, I found a yellow Post-it that Marcus had attached to my PC monitor: *Get yourself in my office five minutes ago!* After a couple of slow, deep breaths, I walked over to his office and rapped on the door.

"Come in!" he yelled.

He was sitting on the front edge of his desk, glaring at me. "Know why you're here?" When I told him I didn't, he pounded his fist on his desk hard enough to make me jump. As it turned out, he was furious that I hadn't come in early enough to pick up his dry cleaning. He'd had an important meeting to attend, and he'd wanted to wear his power suit. The louder he got, the sicker I felt.

I looked at the pictures of his son—his charmed, grinning son. His image taunted me. Once again, I was staring at another of the blessed few who got to enjoy a better life than I'd had or would ever have. Call it hopelessness or self-pity, but at that moment, I felt like a non-person—a wasted opportunity to become someone valuable and respectable. After all this time, I was still a loser, on the outside looking, always destined to be a doormat.

My face grew hot as cruel memories assaulted my mind:
*Shut up or I'll kill you and your stupid mother!*
*Look, it's Baby Boy!*
*Clean up that coffee before it stains my carpet, Monkey!*
Adrenaline roared through my veins. I gritted my teeth so hard I thought they'd shatter. Then, for the first time in my life, I became the angry one, the one who did the shoving. I grabbed Marcus by his lapels, spun him around, and threw him over his desk.

My co-worker, Albert, who was working outside of Marcus's office, rushed in to see what was going on.

Marcus clambered to his feet. "This idiot just tried to kill me! Call Security!"

I pushed past Albert and ran.

I sat at home, waiting for my cell phone to ring, but neither Marcus, his lawyer, nor the police called. I thought about contacting some friends at the office and asking for intel. Bad idea? I didn't know. My nerves were making me squirrelly and paranoid. To keep it together, I lay down on the couch and threw back more Jack and Coke.

By early evening, I was kicked back and watching trash TV. I'd become quite relaxed—filthy drunk. My mouth tasted stale. I squinted at the TV, trying to sharpen the images that flitted about like blurry moths. Then the wall behind the TV became a canvas of shifting light. I thought I was seeing things. I wasn't.

The figures were two men. Judging by the animated body language, one of them was upset. It didn't take long to recognize the shadows of Marcus and me. I looked on as they recreated the fight scene from earlier that day. Once it ended, the shadows returned to normal.

Watching my shadow take on a life of its own that way gave me a cold chill—it was like staring at my ghost. When it came to the shadow soldiers, I hadn't experienced this level of unease for quite some time. Why had they shown me the re-enactment? It was all past now. As if someone were reading my thoughts, my cell phone rang.

It was Albert, the referee from the office smackdown. "My God, Travis. I can't believe you're home," he said. "I thought they'd have you downtown for questioning by now."

As I was two sheets to the wind, it was hard to focus. "What are you sayin', Albert?" My head was beginning to throb. I wanted to pass out. I wish I had.

"It's Marcus," he said. "He's dead. They think he may have hit his head harder than anyone realized when you two were going at it—like maybe his brain swelled up or something. He's dead, and they think it's a direct result of you assaulting him."

That's all I could stand to hear. I hung up. I didn't make a move or think a thought for the longest time. When the police arrived and started pounding on my door, I couldn't get up to open it. Eventually, Mr. Inez, the building super, had to let the two detectives inside.

Detectives Andrews and Marsh had likely dealt with more cooperative suspects than me. I was like a mannequin throughout the interrogation, arraignment, and trial. I mentioned a little something about supernatural beings to my sad excuse for a lawyer, but he dismissed it. It didn't help that my co-workers testified that I'd been miserable working for Marcus, that I despised him.

But the worst part was watching Marcus's family in the gallery. His wife was glassy-eyed and expressionless, as if she had no more tears, no more heart. And his son—my God, that poor little boy. He looked like he'd been broken into a million tiny shards. I knew that look. I had the same one when they carried my mother away.

I found no joy in Marcus's death. I failed to understand why the shadows hadn't alerted me to their violent prediction and the role I'd play in its execution. Eventually, it came to me. How arrogant of me to think I was the only one deserving of strength and mercy.

I wonder if the kid was as scared as I was when I first witnessed the shadows. I'm sure he had no idea how to process the macabre performance. By the time he could, it was already too late. I understand how he felt when he learned that I was the one who'd robbed him of his father. I know his guilt, his rage.

Everything wrapped up just a few weeks ago. I'm agonizing over how I'm supposed to get through the next five years in this cramped metal cage until I'm eligible for parole. Marcus's death was a horrible accident. But the justice system doesn't always go out of its way to split hairs about homicide.

As for the shadow figures, I'm awaiting a visit from them most anytime now. My first experience showed me how they deal with killers. A child will dream about me. Then one evening, he'll detect movement on a wall. The dark ones will perform a scene featuring a lone figure in a cell. Perhaps it will stab itself in its dark throat with a handmade shiv or fashion a noose from prison clothing. I wonder if I'll have a say in my suicide or if I'll be helpless in bringing about my death sentence.

It's hard to fall asleep here. There's no glowing Avengers clock hanging on these filthy walls, no second hand lulling me to sleep, carrying me far away from the barren terrain of my life. The only sounds in this human zoo are snores and whispers. On nights like this, when I plead with the angels for sleep, I often look back to that night when I'd first searched for a monster under my bed and a ghost in my closet but discovered the shadow instead. It terrified me then, and it terrifies me now.

When my final scene concludes, I fear they will absorb my shadow—my soul—and count me among their own. Who knows? Maybe I'll be coming to a wall near you.

My name is Travis Burke, and you can believe me if you want to. But if you do, you might want to turn on the lights... it's starting to get dark.

# NEW BONES

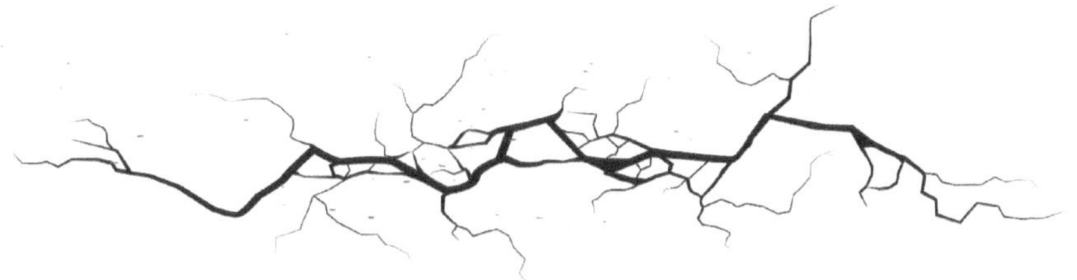

## 1

R yan and Nicole Sullivan parked their SUV in front of the badly weathered Victorian house. As successful home-flippers, they knew a good investment when they saw one. They had purchased the old home sight unseen at a bank auction for pennies on the dollar. Unbeknownst to them, the price reflected the house's curious history.

The Haycock House had been painstakingly planted almost a century before by an eccentric painter named Reynolds Haycock and his wife, Abigail. Unlike the other homes in the area, the house had exuded no charm, warmth, or life. Because the newly planted vegetation had yet to take root, the yard was devoid of color and form, accentuating the bleakness of the property. At the house's peak were two red-stained attic windows that resembled a pair of fiery eyes: always open, always burning. The home's ominous presence unnerved anyone who walked near it. It was like a spider's web disguised as a house. It didn't welcome—it beckoned.

From the start, the Haycocks kept to themselves. They'd offered their neighbors little more than harsh glares and unreturned waves. Their window shades remained drawn day and night as if they were trying to keep secrets in. The neighbors seldom saw them anywhere beyond their property. The couple had milk and groceries delivered once a week and left on their front porch. To maintain the upkeep of the property, they hired transients via an ad that they posted at the rail yard offering free room and board. Several months elapsed before anyone noticed that of all the hired hands who had entered the house, no one could recall seeing any of them come out.

Rumors of foul play began to circulate about the odd and mysterious couple regarding the disappearances. Then, amidst the growing threat of police scrutiny, the Haycocks inexplicably vanished. No one noticed them moving out. They told no one where they were going, and no one saw or heard from them again. Their belongings, too, had vanished. All that the authorities had found was an oil painting of the couple left hanging in the drawing room. A subsequent investigation had turned up no evidence regarding the vagrants.

Over the years, at least a dozen people had purchased the house to sell or to inhabit. None stayed there for more than a month. Like the original owners, they simply up and left, each leaving the vacated house to fall into foreclosure.

And now, here were the Sullivans, the enterprising young couple who believed more in a reasonable return rate than they did in scary stories.

2

Ryan and Nicole leaned against the side of their SUV and stared up at the house for a moment, taking in its full measure.

Ryan was grinning like a big kid, full of excitement. He marveled at the imposing house with its period architecture, ornate wrought iron fencing, and fully matured yard.

Nicole was wary. She saw an abandoned property with peeling paint and a battered roof that was going to suck their budget dry. "I don't know, babe. I'm starting to think we might've bitten off more than we can chew with this one. Something feels off about it. We may have just bought ourselves nothin' but a big ol' headache."

"Well, you know what they say, shug: Go big or go home. Speaking of big, let's hitch up our big kid pants and go see what we're dealing with." Ryan gave Nicole a quick peck on her cheek before bounding up the walkway to check out his newest toy.

3

The sun-cracked, wrap-around porch creaked in time with their steps. Cobwebs and wasp nests hung down like warped chandeliers. Nicole put the key into the lock and pushed open the heavy front door.

A musty odor greeted them. It smelled like an old trunk that had been opened after many years. Dust motes danced in a brilliant sunray that was concentrated through a window like a theater spotlight.

"Hell's bells on an Easter bonnet," Ryan remarked as he surveyed the old-fashioned grandeur of the aged house. He craned his neck to take in the fifteen-foot-tall ceiling that topped the spacious entrance. Dark mahogany floors flowed as far as they could see.

Ahead on the left, Ryan and Nicole admired a spectacular winding staircase. It resembled a decorative vine as it snaked its way along the wall. Its carpeted steps paused at a small landing before winding their way upward again.

The neglected floors that had welcomed them continued beyond a solid oak archway that looked as if it'd been pulled from an artisan's dream. Nicole couldn't resist running her fingertips over the masterful carvings. "Hell's bells, indeed," she muttered to herself. She turned to Ryan and said, "I'm gonna go check out the rest of this level. You take the other ones."

"Roger that."

As Ryan ascended the handsome wooden staircase, Nicole walked forward under the archway and into a large dining room.

The big, open area was surrounded on three sides by floor-to-ceiling windows, which allowed the entire space to be bathed in rich sunlight. A posh wrought iron light fixture dangled from the ceiling's center. Its many curled arms supported frosted globes, making it look somewhat like an elegant octopus juggling bright orbs of light. Despite the chamber's shabbiness, Nicole pondered its promising potential.

The dirty worksite surrounding Nicole was incongruous among her mental pictures of a sophisticated setting. Tools and building materials that the last flipper and his crew had left behind were strewn everywhere. The scene resembled a worksite where the crew had left for lunch and never returned.

From there, she entered a kitchen painted a dreary gray. Judging by its sad condition, Nicole figured it was probably the original color. The gritty floor crunched under her feet as she inspected the cracked and faded cabinetry. Out of nowhere, a cold blast of air kissed the back of Nicole's bare neck. She touched the spot and turned around. When she didn't see an obvious source for the draft, such as an open window or air duct, she shrugged it off and moved on from the kitchen.

The last room she visited was a drawing room. It was the most opulent space yet, with its hand-carved oak wall panels and an intricately patterned tin ceiling, from which hung a beveled glass chandelier fit for a castle. Six stained glass windows were divided evenly among three walls.

A pair of French doors opened out to the back portion of the wrap-around porch, which gave view to the unkempt backyard. The long-neglected area was thick with grass and saplings. Nicole thought it looked like a dying cornfield that someone had left to fend for itself.

The room's focal point was a large stone fireplace. It was crowned with a sturdy, hand-hewed, wood plank, adding to its grandiosity. Nicole imagined the powerful fires that had filled the stately room with great light and warmth. Its majestic presence enthralled her. Then she noticed the picture hanging above it.

It was a large oil painting of an older man and woman. They were dressed in period clothes that looked to Nicole to be from the early 1900s. They sat stiffly in two beautifully upholstered wingback chairs. With facial expressions that lacked any sense of love or joy, the duo exuded an austere countenance. At the woman's feet laid a fluffy, white cat that looked as indifferent as the couple. The signature on the bottom right-hand corner indicated that it was a self-portrait.

"So you're the infamous art freaks," Nicole said. "Ain't you the party animals?"

Upstairs, Ryan discovered similar scenes of abandonment. There were wooden floors that had been sanded but never finished. He found several doors stacked neatly in the hall.

Ryan entered one of the bedrooms to look for damage. As he poked at a deep hole in one of the walls, a shadow of a man appeared beside it, causing him to jump back. He turned. No one. When he looked at the wall again, the silhouette was gone. Ryan's arm hair stood on end. "Easy does it, dude; lots of shadows in this old place. Let's just get outta here."

Ryan trotted out of the room and into the hallway. Suddenly, another form stepped in front of him, causing him to skid to a halt.

"Cripes, Nicole! You scared the Keebler Fudge out of me!" He was breathing hard and sweating.

"I scared *you*? Good Lord, Ryan, you nearly steamrolled me. What's wrong with you? You're whiter than an albino in a snowstorm."

Ryan took a few seconds to recover. Once he regained his composure, he became embarrassed and defensive. "Nothing's wrong with me. I was trying to get away from a couple of wasps." He quickly changed the subject. "What'd you find downstairs, or should I even ask?"

"Well, we'll have to check the basement, the foundation, the plumbing, and the wiring. But as far as I can tell, it's got good bones; it just needs a few new ones. I have to tell you, though; it looks like one of those Wild West ghost towns down there. This place was bustling with construction, and then *poof,* it's deserted."

"Yeah, same thing up here. Guess the guy ran out of money—no pay, no workers."

"Okay, but if the construction crew isn't getting paid, why would they leave their tools and building supplies behind? Those things ain't cheap."

"Who knows? Wanna check out the rest?" he asked.

"That seems only proper," Nicole replied with a hokey, old west accent.

As they headed downstairs, Ryan cast a nervous glance over his shoulder.

4

After completing the initial inspection, their next task was to set up a temporary camp upstairs in the main bedroom. With a project of this magnitude, they preferred to stay onsite because it saved them the expense of a lengthy hotel stay and allowed them to keep the place secure.

It only took them a couple of days to bring in a contractor familiar with projects such as theirs. Todd Blake came highly recommended by some of the top-tier realtors from the area.

After meeting with Ryan and Nicole, he agreed to take on the lengthy and arduous renovation. He explained that he was at least two weeks out with his current job. Still, he offered up some suggestions for easy tasks that they could knock out in the meantime.

Nicole had a group of chores already nestled in her head. For herself, she planned some mowing, pruning, and the planting of a colorful flower bed along the front of the porch. She decided to place Ryan in charge of doing something about the awful gray paint that made the kitchen look like a monochrome monstrosity. Nicole had something perky in mind, such as a vibrant yellow.

Ryan obeyed Sergeant Nicole's order to paint the kitchen. The following day, he drove to Pinehurst to check out a newly foreclosed property on a parkland golf course. Such premium real estate didn't come on the market often, so he wanted to get first dibs.

Nicole stayed behind to keep an eye on things at the Haycock House. With Ryan gone, the place was too quiet. The air felt cold and thick, and many of the rooms were dark, despite their oversized windows. Also, seeing the rough condition of the house's interior left her feeling overwhelmed and defeated. The pall over the place made Nicole's decision to work outside an easy one.

5

The anxiety that Nicole had experienced inside of the foreboding residence dissipated once she stepped outside into the fresh air of the peaceful morning. The sounds of the birds and the swishes of the undulating tree limbs filled her ears. The day was warm, the ground was moist, and the shade felt exquisite. It was early morning, so she had most of the day to work on the new flowerbed before the summer sun worked its way around to the front of the house. As she enjoyed the peacefulness of it, Nicole became lost in the motion of the work. She checked her watch and realized that she had been toiling for hours. *Geez, Louise; no wonder I'm hungry.*

Nicole stood, bent her achy knees, and dusted the potting soil off the front of her shorts. As she rose, there was a flash of something in the corner of her eye. She glanced back toward the house. A large cat perched on the top step of the porch was leering at her.

"Hey there, pussycat." The cat narrowed its eyes and hissed at her like an angry cobra. "Shoo!" Nicole yelled. The cat rose and snarled at her. Suddenly, it turned and ran through the open front door of the house. Nicole took off after it.

Once inside, she proceeded through some of the first-floor rooms, watching and listening for the furry intruder. "Where'd you go, you little jerk?" Nicole heard a growl nearby.

She stepped cautiously through the freshly painted kitchen. She stopped to peek into one of the open cabinets.

"Here, kitty, kitty."

Nicole froze at the voice, the cabinet door half open. Its tone was distinctly feminine. It had echoed from the drawing room. Nicole hoped that the call was from the cat's owner, who'd tracked it into the house. *Please, don't be an intruder; of all the times for Ryan to be gone.*

Nicole's jaw quaked with nervousness. "Who's there? Hello?" The lack of response made her fearful that someone might be lying in wait for her. Realizing that she couldn't hide out in the kitchen indefinitely, she worked up the courage to go and investigate the sound.

Nicole followed the haunting call into the drawing room and found it empty. Despite being alone, she was skittish, as if someone might attack her out of thin air. She trembled. *The porch,* she reasoned. *Maybe the backyard.* She tiptoed to the doors that led out to the porch. Cautiously opening them, she leaned out and looked around. Seeing no signs of the interloper, she relaxed a bit. She hoped that whoever had been in the room when she called out from the kitchen had fled.

Her adrenaline ebbing, Nicole blew out a cleansing breath. As she was doing so, she happened to glance up at the portrait of the Haycocks. Something about it looked different, but she couldn't quite—*YOAR!* Nicole jumped a foot as a streak of screaming fur blurred past her feet, heading straight for the front door.

Nicole braked when she got to the top step of the porch. The cat had vanished. She left the porch and searched the yard, but saw no sign of it. Once she was satisfied that the cat had moved on, she decided to go back in and dig up some lunch.

When she reached the foot of the porch steps, she saw that all of the new flowers were dead. It was as if the soil had poisoned them. Despite the heat of the day, Nicole shivered.

Although she'd rationalized the phantom voice, she had no answer for the inexplicable demise of the once colorful blooms. *What's happening around this place?* The implications chilled her.

6

Ryan had gotten back earlier than expected, much to Nicole's relief. He'd picked up a pizza, two salads, and a bottle of pinot grigio on the way home, so they wouldn't have to go out and leave the house unattended. On his way in, he noticed the wilted flowers. "Who planted these? The Angel of Death?"

As they stood over the makeshift sawhorse table eating their dinner, Ryan brought Nicole up to date on the property in Pinehurst. Nicole typically asked a host of questions, but tonight, she was shaken and distracted.

"Somethin' up, hon?" he inquired. "You're not saying much. Did anything happen while I was gone?"

Nicole picked at her salad and considered the question.

"Nicole?"

"Uh, yeah... I mean, no." She paused. "Okay, maybe something weird did happen. It's probably nothing—nothing worth talking about anyway."

Ryan set the slice of pizza down and then took a sip of his wine. "I think it might be worth talking about. I've never seen you this quiet and tense. Talk to me. What happened today?"

Nicole related the entire cat incident to Ryan. She could tell by the way he was staring at her that he wasn't taking her seriously at first. But could he be blamed? As she spoke, even she became increasingly unsure of her story. To Ryan's credit, he listened to everything she was sharing. It gave her hope that, even if he thought she was beginning to get spooked in the shadowy old house, at least he might try to work through the events with her and to make some sense of them.

"Are you sure you heard someone speaking?" he asked.

"As clear as I'm hearing you now. And then, there's the flowers I spent the morning planting."

"Yeah, I caught sight of 'em on the way in. What happened there?"

"When I couldn't find the cat, I walked back to the porch. I found them looking the same way you did. It totally freaked me out. So, what do you think? Am I starting to lose it here?"

"That's a weird one, all right. I might walk around and talk to some of the neighbors, find out who owns the cat. What'd it look like?"

"It was all white and fluffy; a Persian, I think."

"Oh, like the one in the painting."

Nicole's face slackened as it came to her why the portrait had looked different.

She left the dining room and went directly to the drawing room, ignoring Ryan calling behind her. There, above the fireplace, was the portrait, with the white Persian properly in its place.

7

The mid-July heat in the Carolinas was relentless, the night air stifling and humid. The Sullivans' bedroom windows were wide open, and they'd set the ceiling fan to *STOMP!*

Nicole was lying in bed, replaying the events of the day. Each recollection was like a ghostly hand trying to pull her down into a dark lake. But even as the disturbing thoughts kept threatening to overwhelm her, Nicole remained emotionally tethered to her intense feeling of annoyance with Ryan. Despite everything, he'd still somehow managed to fall asleep effortlessly. It reminded her that he always got to play the charming, laid-back role, forcing her to be the hardline negotiator. *That's right. You sleep well like you always do. I'll just keep on lying awake nearly every night, worrying about what'll happen when one of these investments blows up in our faces—that and ghost cats.*

As the night flowed onward, her resentment gave way to envy. *How the heck can he sleep on this crappy air mattress, in this sauna, with that ancient ceiling fan, while I lie here sweating like a whore in church?* She flipped back and forth on the mattress as if she were a strip of meat, trying to be cooked evenly on both sides. But it meant that she wasn't dreaming when she heard the footsteps downstairs. *Oh, dear God! There's a crackhead in the house!* The sounds seemed to be coming from the foot of the stairs. She nudged Ryan. "Ryan," she whispered.

When he didn't respond, she shook him. "Ryan, wake up."

Nicole could tell when the intruder had made it as far as the landing by the creak of the third floorboard.

"Ryan? Ryan! Get the hell up!" At this point, she didn't care if the prowler heard her or not.

"Whut... whut," he mumbled.

"Don't you hear that?"

The footsteps were coming down the hall toward them. It didn't sound as if the burglar was in a hurry to get to their bedroom—there was at least a full second between each plodding step. As he drew closer, they heard his shoes squeaking.

"What in hell?" Ryan said as he awoke to the realization that they were in danger. He propelled himself off the air mattress and rushed to lock their bedroom door. Then he ran back to Nicole, who was now on her feet.

The footsteps arrived at their door. "I have a gun in here!" Ryan shouted. "Leave, or I will shoot. You. Dead!" All he heard was the squeal of the ceiling fan. "Hey! I'm counting to three, and then I'm coming out blazing!"

"What should we do?" Nicole whispered.

"Grab the phone and go lock yourself in the bathroom. Call 9-1-1. I'm gonna go check things out."

"Are you insane?" Nicole asked, punching him on his shoulder for emphasis. "Stay here with me. He may still be outside that door."

"Babe, if I don't hold this guy off, the only thing that the cops are gonna find is the two of us dead. Now go hide in the bathroom."

Nicole started to cry. "Ryan, baby, please stay here with me."

"Nicole, for once, let me handle this. Now go."

Nicole grabbed the phone and tiptoed to the bathroom, locking the door behind her. Her hands were shaking, making it difficult to press the numbers. As soon as someone answered the call, she said, "Hi. I'm calling to report an intruder. He's just outside our bedroom door." She waited for the dispatcher to ask for her name and address, but the person didn't say anything. Nicole was anxious and impatient. "Hello? Is this 9-1-1?" The only sound she heard on the other end was raspy breathing. She gasped and hung up. She tried twice more and got the same response.

Meanwhile, Ryan looked around for something to use as a weapon. The only thing he saw with any heft was the large flashlight by the air mattress.

Weapon in hand, Ryan crept to the door and put his ear against it. His spine tingled as he listened to the gruff wheezing on the other side. The sound reminded him of his uncle, Jerry, who had struggled with emphysema. It was how he had sounded at the end: like dry death.

Ryan stepped back and braced himself for a confrontation. He took a couple of deep breaths, raised the flashlight, and yanked the door open. The doorway was empty. He stuck his neck out, looked up and down the dimly lit hall, and found it equally empty. *Like a vanishing cat,* he thought.

"Ryan? What's happening out there?"

Ryan had never heard such terror in anyone's voice before. "It's okay, hon. Just stay put." Then, for the benefit of the trespasser, he added, "I think the cops are nearly here!" His proclamation yielded no results: no running, no crashing, no sound.

Ryan turned on the flashlight and shined it up and down the passageway but still saw nothing.

His head drooped as he let out a shaky sigh. He lowered his eyes and caught a quick shimmer on the floor near his feet. He stared. Footprints. They led from the top of the stairs to the bedroom door. Ryan stooped to touch the light-colored tracks and found them sticky. He stood and began tracing them, following them down the hallway to the stairs.

Ryan descended the dark staircase. The powerful beam from the flashlight illuminated the phantom imprints. The more he tracked them, the more slippery the flashlight became in his hand.

He continued following the trail down to the main entrance. From there, he worked his way through the dining room, then the pitch-black kitchen, before ending up in the drawing room.

The point of origin was the fireplace hearth. Goosebumps sprang from Ryan's flesh, and his teeth began chattering. He slid his socked feet across the floor until he was standing in front of the fireplace. He lifted the flashlight's ray to the portrait. At first glance, the painting looked as it always had. He wanted to get a better look, so he inched forward until he was standing directly under it. That's when he saw the yellow paint around Reynolds Haycock's shoes.

*I need a drink.* Ryan shuffled to the lightless kitchen. He groped around until he located the wall switch and flipped it on. Someone had somehow removed the fresh yellow paint from the kitchen walls.

8

The series of macabre events left Ryan feeling rattled. It took some time for him to collect his thoughts.

"Ryan, where are you?"

Nicole's loud voice startled him.

"In the kitchen, hon."

She was about to walk in when Ryan stopped her. "Babe, I want you to prepare yourself. Please, try not to freak out."

"I'll do my best," she promised.

Nicole said nothing during her tour of the kitchen and the drawing room. She walked as if she were trudging through mud. When she finally spoke, she said, "Oh my God, Ryan; what have we gotten ourselves into? I'm really, truly terrified. We have to get out of this house. I can't stay here another second. Let's go to a hotel or rent an apartment; I don't care which."

"Nicole, honey, we can't afford that. We've got everything tied up in this house. Outside of living in the SUV, we have zero options. And there is *no way* we're living out of that stupid SUV!"

"Like hell, we're not!" Nicole grabbed Ryan by his wrist, led him outside, and directed him into the SUV. Ryan's pride was slightly sore, but at least Nicole had gotten them out of the house of horrors.

A short time later, Ryan attempted to appeal to Nicole's sense of reason. "Babe, what are we supposed to do now? That surprise real estate I checked out in Pinehurst looks really promising.

But you know this business: we can't grab hold of any other opportunities while we're still holding on to this one. If we unload this house now, we'll get our heads kicked in. Nicole, I know we're scared, but we have no choice; we have to make this work.

"Ryan, how bad will this get? This isn't some elaborate prank. All of the terrifying things that have happened to us are real. Think about it: the contractors, the work crews, previous owners.

Why do you think we got this house so cheap? It's because everyone else took the loss and got as far away from this place as possible."

"Look, I'm no expert on the paranormal, okay? But maybe we can find a priest, or a shaman, or even a voodoo doctor who'll come and bless the place. Ooh, ooh, how 'bout a TV show that'll send some crackpots out here to stink up the house with loser sweat while they pretend to gab with ghosts?"

Her emotional temperature was rising. She resented Ryan's condescending tone, so she decided to give him a taste of his own medicine. "Just to make sure that an idiot like me can understand you, you're saying we should advertise that we have ghosts in this house? Oh, yeah—that'll prompt some genius to buy it!"

"All right, Nicole. What do you suggest?"

She mulled the question over. "Everything that's happened has a common denominator: that creepy portrait, right? Why don't we just try getting rid of it? Let's burn the S.O.B. like they do in the movies. If nothing else, at least we won't have to look at it anymore."

Ryan perked up. "I've got the matches if you've got the fuel. You go around back and find a safe place to burn it. I'll be the hero and go in and get it."

"Works for me, Sir Dunderhead."

"Aaand she's back," he said.

Nicole retrieved the two-gallon gas can from the rear of the SUV and hurried toward the backyard.

When she got there, she waded through the knee-high grass until she got to a worn-down area that someone had used as a scrap pile. She picked through the trash for something to use as a digging instrument. Eventually, she found a jagged piece of two-by-four that she used to dig a shallow hole.

Ryan emerged from the drawing room and onto the back porch. He was holding the sinister portrait as if it were covered in poison ivy.

"Hurry! Bring it!" Nicole instructed.

Ryan used the picture frame to push through the overgrown yard. As soon as he arrived at the impromptu fire pit, he plopped the painting down into it and soaked it with the gasoline. Then he tossed in a lit book of matches.

As the picture burned, they could feel the stress gradually leaving their bodies. They watched the cursed object curl up at the edges as the ravenous flames consumed it. Once the fire had reduced the portrait to glowing ash, they took hold of each other's hand and reluctantly returned to the house.

9

As soon as Ryan and Nicole stepped inside, they sensed a change. The air that used to press down on them felt lighter, and everything looked sharper as if someone had adjusted an unfocused lens.

"Do you think it's finally over?" Nicole asked. "I have to say something feels right about this place now. It's different from before, don't you think? It feels... healed."

"Yeah, I suppose so. I just hope that Gomez and Morticia have moved on."

"Guess they just didn't want strangers changing their house around," she said. "I can't say as I blame them. After all, they meant this house for themselves. They poured their souls into it: every nail, every brick. That painting was probably all that was left to anchor them here."

Then Nicole looked at Ryan, who had suddenly become lost in thought.

"I can't help but wonder," he said, "if anyone else ever thought of destroying the painting."

"If they did, they sure didn't stick around long enough to try it. So, whadaya say? Should we try another night?"

"Are you sure? An hour ago, you wanted out of here."

"I know what I said, but I just want to know if this nightmare is finally over, so we can move on."

"Agreed," Ryan said.

10

Though the night had been uneventful, neither slept very well. Every minor noise had sounded to them as if it were heralding another march of the undead. They'd been glad when the sun had finally risen to rescue them.

"We better get started on the cleanup. Todd's work crew'll be here next week," Nicole said.

"Why don't we just let them fix it?" Ryan asked, yawning.

"Money, sweetheart. Money. We can do this. Listen, I think we still have some cereal downstairs. Grab the milk from the cooler, why don't cha?"

Ryan and Nicole got dressed and then followed the ghostly road map downstairs. They checked out the drawing room, hoping and praying not to find the painting there waiting for them. Notwithstanding the yellow footprints, they were relieved to see that the portrait was still out of their lives, unlike in the movies.

They entered the kitchen and enjoyed a relaxed breakfast.

"I'll be so happy once we get all that paint off the floor," Nicole said. "It's what's creeped me out the most. Oh, and speaking of paint, you know that you're going to have to paint this *entire* kitchen. All. Over. Agaaain. Any thoughts on color?"

"I think I might go with yellow. It stands out so well, don't cha think?"

"You do, and I'll be repainting it with your brain matter, wise guy. Now come on, let's get this knocked out. We've got a lot to get done today."

They had only walked a few feet into the drawing room before they stopped cold. They were astonished to see that the footprints were gone.

"Where'd they go?" Ryan asked.

Frigid sweat slid down Nicole's bare back like cold, skeletal fingers. She was pale, her body limp. "Ryan?" Her voice quivered. "Do you see it?"

"Oh my God," he whispered.

With great trepidation, they walked further into the room. Ryan took hold of Nicole's moist hand. "I'm right here, babe." His breathing was fast and irregular. With each pant, he could feel his heartbeat through his temples as if it were keeping time with a funeral dirge.

They turned together and faced the imposing fireplace, the source of their blind terror.

The painting was hanging over the mantle, and it had changed. The Haycocks were posed in a standing position by their respective chairs. Each of their faces was a horrifying rictus of rage. In a blink, they were closer to the frame. Their cracked lips were pulled back grotesquely, baring small, jagged teeth. Then, like a flash of lightning, the savage creatures were at the very edge of the frame. Their eyes were crimson red, just like those belonging to the white Persian hunched up behind Ryan and Nicole, snarling.

11

The front door opened, and the real estate agent led Frank and Helen Morganstern into the vestibule of the musty house. "And here we are," the agent announced with a grand flourish.

"Wow," Frank said.

"I hope the rest of the house has this much potential," added Helen.

The agent took that as her cue. "Now, as I told you, there have been some attempts at renovations over the years, but it's still in need of some T.L.C. Nevertheless, with what the bank's willing to let it go for, it would make a terrific investment for folks like you, who are thinking about converting it into bed and breakfast. Now, follow me. I want you to check out the focal point of the whole downstairs."

The couple strolled around the impressive drawing room, taking in its regal décor's richness, along with its exquisite fireplace.

"So, who's this?" Helen asked as she stood before the long, rustic mantle.

"Oh, them. Yes, I believe that's the Haycocks, the people for whom this house was built. Now then, let's see if I can remember their names. That's Reynolds sitting on the left and Abigail on the right. As for that young couple holding the cat, I don't know who they are, but they sure don't look very thrilled to be there."

# BLACK WOLF'S SEDAN

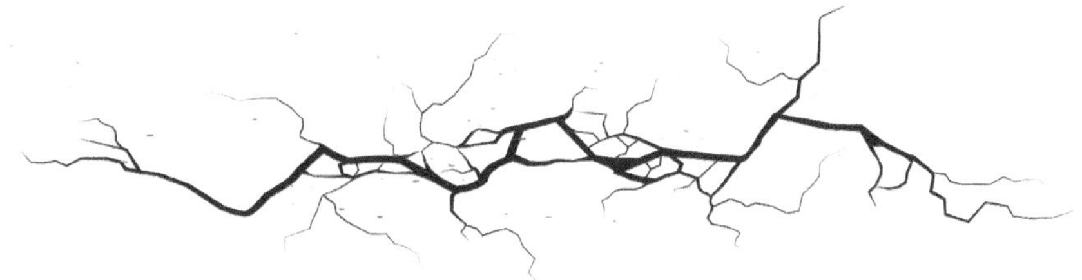

1

Taking out the old man had been simple for Black Wolf: locate, break-in, kill him, and secure the body for transport. The job had been clean and bloodless, leaving no evidence. Once he'd finished the hit, he placed the target in a thick canvas bag and fastened the four restraints to hold the body in place. Satisfied that he'd completed the most challenging part of the job, he looked around outside to make sure he wouldn't be seen. It was two in the morning, so he figured he was safe. He threw the bag over his shoulder and took it out the back door and into the alley.

After Black Wolf dumped the body in the car's trunk, he poked it a couple of times to be on the safe side. It didn't move. *Thank God.*

He climbed in the front seat of his luxurious black sedan. *I'll be glad when this job is over. There's some bad juju goin' on with this one.* He lit a cigarette, tuned the radio to a classical music station, and drove away.

His orders were to deliver the cargo to the nearest wet room. The site was hidden in some woods just outside the rearview town of Wyattsville, a three-hour drive. The team there would handle the final disposal. Black Wolf had made the trip many times. It was the perfect place for a drop: dark and secluded. He hoped that the others would have things ready to roll when he arrived with the former Erik Werner. He didn't like spending any more time in the woods than necessary. Even for a man with his background, the place was creepy. Unholy.

Black Wolf had been driving for two hours—one more and he'd be near the site. It typically took about five hours for things to turn dangerous, so he was glad to find himself safely ahead of schedule. He decided to use the extra time to relax and put his mind on better things than the body in the back. He turned up Vivaldi's *The Four Seasons* and allowed its lightness to carry him away. He'd always enjoyed the elegance and complexity of classical music. It helped to bring order to the chaos around him. As he conducted the orchestra with his free right hand, his stomach growled along, reminding him that he hadn't eaten in hours.

There was an all-night gas station about ten miles before his destination. He was so hungry that he was willing to roll the dice on an ancient wiener from a greasy rotisserie. He'd dropped in at the store he'd nicknamed the Stop 'n Rob on many occasions and had gotten to know Jack, the old man who ran the place.

Jack was a three-time loser with felony convictions. He didn't burden himself with suspicions about the mysterious man with the sleek automobile that made occasional trips to the middle of nowhere.

Black Wolf pulled up to one of the gas pumps, threw the car into park, and climbed out. The night air was thick and humid, coating his skin like warm mud. Smells were absorbed by its immensity, creating a dank fog, but he could just identify the pungent scent of the two young men loitering outside.

Black Wolf sized them up. *Greasy losers.* They looked like a couple of twenty-somethings with no luck and very few prospects. Their gangly necks and arms were home to cheap tattoos, their clothes ratty. He knew their species well, had been there himself once upon a time before the military straightened him out.

When Black Wolf neared the gas station's entrance, one of the men stepped in front of him, causing a collision.

"Sorry, mister."

Black Wolf didn't want any trouble this late in the game, so he just gave the scrawny stranger a glare of disapproval.

*Ding!* Black Wolf walked through the smeary Plexiglas door. The overly sweet stench of floor disinfectant made him queasy. He winced as his eyes adjusted to the uncomfortable brightness of the store. The harsh fluorescent lighting emitted a low hum that made his eardrums vibrate and gave everything a washed-out appearance.

"Hey there, Jack."

"Sup, young fella?"

Black Wolf checked out the encrusted rack of revolving franks at the end of the counter and decided to peruse the snack aisle instead. He settled on a bag of pretzels, some beef jerky, and a Red Bull from the wall cooler.

Jack began ringing up the items. "That'll be six thirty—"

*VROOOM!* Black Wolf's car roared as it rocketed out of the small lot, leaving behind a veil of gravel and dust. He slapped his jacket pockets. Empty. *Why that little...* Angry and embarrassed, he turned to Jack. "Those two punks who were loitering outside, do ya know 'em?"

"Sorry to say I do. One of 'em's name is Curtis, I think. Can't remember the other one. Should I call the po-po?"

"No. I'll handle this. Any idea where they might be heading?"

"If I had to guess, I'd say that ol' abandoned farmhouse a couple of miles up the road. Druggies sometimes use it as a shootin' gallery."

Black Wolf had an ace in the hole: the car's tracking device. He took out his cellphone, accessed the app, and waited. Soon, the car's location appeared on the screen. It hadn't traveled far. Suddenly, the dot turned left and slowed down. "Gotcha," he muttered. He looked at Jack. "Looks like you were right. They're somewhere just up the road a ways. That'd be the farmhouse, correct?"

"Yep."

"Don't suppose you've got a car I can borrow."

Jack pointed out the window at a rusty riding mower.

"Seriously?" Black Wolf asked.

"Too many DUI's."

*Guess I'm jogging.*

"Ya know, there's two of them and one of you," Jack said. "Are you sure you don't want me to call the cops?"

"I think I got this."

"So, you gonna kill 'em?"

"Nope. I'm gonna save 'em."

2

As Black Wolf huffed up the highway, Curtis and Razor were maneuvering the car down the narrow lane that led to the farmhouse.

"Where should I park it?" Curtis asked.

"Pull around to the back. We can put it in the barn," Razor replied.

Curtis eased around the dilapidated two-story house and followed a worn dirt path about thirty yards to the rickety barn. Razor jumped out and swung open its large wooden doors.

He entered first, using the car's headlights to light his path as he peered through the semi-darkness. "Anybody in here? We ain't the cops. Just wanna know if it's cool to come in." No one answered.

"Hey, Raze! Can I pull in or not?"

"We're clear!" Razor stood near the entrance and guided Curtis inside. Once the car was entirely in, he pulled the doors shut, then lit the four lanterns they kept stashed around the barn.

Curtis sprang from the car and began circling it like a bird of prey. He ran his nicotine-stained fingers through his long, stringy hair, a huge smile stretched across his face. "Dude, I am so jacked right now! Can you believe this? Oh, man, what a score!"

"We gotta get Li'l B out here to check this mother out. He'll probably give us top dollar for it," Razor said.

"Shoot him a text. Let him know that—"

*BANG! BANG!*

. . . "The hell was that?" Curtis asked.

Equally startled, Razor said, "I think it came from the trunk."

They moved towards the rear of the car with the same stealth they used when breaking and entering.

"Hello?" Razor asked. No reply. He lowered his head to the trunk and listened for movement.

*BANG!*

The two jumped back.

"Dude, I think somebody's locked in there," Curtis said.

The sedan rocked back and forth, its shock absorbers yelping.

"Should we let him out?" Razor huffed.

"Hell no! What's wrong with you?"

"Okay, okay. Let's just go outside, roll a couple joints, and figure out what to do next."

"Yeah, okay. Ain't nobody around to hear no noise, so we're good."

They'd walked about ten yards when a metallic explosion rang out from the barn. A few seconds later, there was a heavy thud.

"Whoa! What just happened?" Curtis asked.

"I ain't sure, but we need to go check on the car. Somethin' might've fallen on it."

"Like what?"

"I don't know. Maybe somethin' fell out the loft. Li'l B ain't gonna be interested in no beat-up ride. Let's go together. It might be we need to mess somebody up."

They returned to the barn. The trunk hatch had been blown off and hung over the edge of one of the lofts, fifteen feet up.

"I don't know who was in that trunk, but they sure wanted out," Razor observed.

Curtis retrieved one of the lanterns and raised its wick. He inched toward the mangled opening of the trunk and looked inside. "Yo, check this out."

A shredded canvas bag covered the bottom of the trunk. Shattered metal buckles dangled from its thick straps. The whole space was dripping with thick, red slime that smelled like oil and rotting meat.

"This is messed up, Raze. Let's get outta—"

*EEEEEEE!*

The shrill sound was deafening. Heavy footsteps moved around the loft. Then they heard something drop into the shadows.

They didn't wait to find out what. The two ran from the barn and sprinted toward the dark farmhouse.

"Run! We're dead meat out here in the open!" Curtis yelled.

They busted through the back door and into the dark, grimy kitchen. Having participated in numerous parties and minor drug deals, they knew the layout of the house well.

Curtis was holding the lantern in a death grip. "Check them drawers for a knife."

The wooden drawers fell to the floor as Razor yanked them from the base cabinet. All were empty, save for dust and dead bugs. "No luck."

From there, they went to the living room at the front of the house. Broken furniture was strewn about. The water-damaged ceiling sagged and cobwebs coated the corners of the ravaged room. They pushed a musty, mouse-infested couch away from the wall and hunkered down behind it. The damp, moldy material coated their lungs with every pant.

"Do you hear anything?" Razor asked.

"Shhh... be quiet."

The tall grass that ran along the side of the house rustled. There was a sniffling and snorting.

"Is that thing tryin' to sniff us out?" Curtis whispered.

The noise stopped. They waited. *CRASH... CRUNCH... CRASH...* Something was climbing up the side of the house. They could hear chunks of wood being ripped away and dropping to the ground as the thing clawed its way to the second floor. An upstairs window shattered. Glass tinkled and feet thumped across the room directly over them. They froze, barely breathing.

Wide-eyed, Curtis and Razor stared at one another as the thing clomped down the stairs, grunting and sniffing. The floor vibrated as it stomped around the living room. When it got to the couch, it stopped. Silence.

Curtis extinguished the lantern, his muscles prepared to run.

The thing gave a loud grunt as it grabbed hold of the couch. Cool air swept over them. The couch flew across the room and smashed into a far wall. A rancid stench assaulted their nostrils. A shadowy form crouched before them. As it rose, glass cascaded off its outer shell, and two dull, bulging eyes swiveled towards them. With its bony frame and grotesquely long arms and legs, it resembled a human-sized praying mantis. Thinly stretched human skin covered most of its spindly body. Its wrinkled head was that of an elderly man, the scalp punctuated with tufts of white hair. Its gaping mouth was an enormous, pink, pulpy maw with a flapping tongue in the middle.

The two men screamed as the thing reared back. When it fell forward, it grabbed Razor with its hooked hands and flung him against the wall. His limp body dropped to the floor.

Then the thing turned to Curtis. He was numb all over. The thing drew its arm back, preparing to strike. He closed his eyes, wondering how bad his death would hurt. He lamented his foolish life choices. "I'm so sorry, God... for everything."

Suddenly, there were two sharp pops. The creature cried out and Curtis's eyes popped open.

Curtis saw someone standing just inside the doorway in a shooter's stance. He recoiled as the shooter fired two more explosive rounds at the thing. Pieces of its shell clattered to the floor as it screeched and jumped upward, attaching itself to the ceiling.

The shooter closed the distance until he was directly under the thing. He fired several more bullets into its body. The dripping man-monster clawed at the ceiling, raining plaster upon Curtis and the towering figure. It finally tore through and pulled itself up and into the room above them.

In the gloom, Curtis couldn't recognize his savior right away. But as he dusted the plaster from his face, he realized it was the man whose elegant machine was now parked in the barn. "Please don't shoot me, sir. I'm sorry 'bout the car, okay?"

"Forget about the car," Black Wolf said. "I need to kill that thing, or a lot of people are gonna die—starting with us."

"What ta hell is it?"

"It was still a man when I threw it in the trunk. But there's a short window of time before it morphs into *that*," he said, pointing up. "I was well on my way to the disposal site when you and your idiot friend decided to go *Grand Theft Auto* on me. Now, I'm gonna need your help. It's too much to handle on my own."

"You got the wrong guy, mister. Look, my friend needs—"

"Leave him! He's dead!"

Curtis halted. The man was serious. If the man didn't kill him, the bug would.

Black Wolf surveyed the battered room. He picked through the busted furniture until he found a table leg. He moved around the room, tapping on the ceiling and listening.

"What're ya doin'?" Curtis asked.

"I'm monitoring its movements." After a few more pokes, they heard scuttling above them. Then it stopped.

"It seems to be taking its time, regrouping or hiding—I can't tell which," Black Wolf said. "I don't think it's through with us yet. It likely sees you and me as an immediate threat to its escape. We need to contain it."

Curtis shook his head. "Uh-uh; no way!"

"Listen, boy. If you've got the stones to steal my car, then you've got the stones to help me kill that freak before the worst happens."

"The 'worst'? As in it ain't happened yet? What is that thing?"

"Five hours ago, that thing was Dr. Erik Werner. A microscopic piece of alien DNA outwitted him, some other dumb scientists, and a few pompous generals. Werner and his so-called geniuses studied it, experimented on it, did some other sci-fi crap. Of course, they immediately saw dollar signs and military applications. But they didn't consider what that tiny group of cells might evolve into. It's like looking at a strange egg and not knowing what's gonna pop out of it. Well, now we do. It's making up its mind."

"About what?"

"The most efficient way to kill us. Unless we kill it first. That's the choice I prefer."

Curtis gulped. "Are you outta your damn mind? Let's just get outta here and let some other fools handle this!"

Ignoring Curtis, Black Wolf followed the noise above him, prodding the ceiling as he went. With every jab, the thing moved.

"Who are you, man?" Curtis's voice trembled.

Continuing to track his prey, Black Wolf said, "Some other elite trackers and I were brought in to hunt and kill these things while they're still human and manageable. Once that's done, their bodies are delivered to lab wonks who know how to dispose of them. Things have to happen fast, though."

There was more movement above them.

"What happens if you don't get the body there in time?"

"First, it turns into what killed your friend. Then, that 'worst' I mentioned comes next."

"Do you... think you can kill it?"

"Don't know; haven't dealt with one in this stage of development." Black Wolf stabbed the ceiling hard and the thing ran. They heard it enter another room, slamming the door.

"Bingo! We got it," Black Wolf said.

"How many of those things are out there?"

"So far, we've only located a handful of infected outsiders and lab folks. We took them out before they'd advanced too far. Now, I've gotta somehow ice Alien up there and get it to our local disposal site before things really go south. Does that satisfy your curiosity?"

"I wish you hadn't told me. Will you kill me if I run?"

"This is a highly classified initiative. What do you think? Good news is there's a way out of this for you if you do as I say."

Curtis sighed. "Whaddaya want me to do?"

"It's closed itself off in a room at the top of those stairs. I need you to go up and get its attention. When it comes after you, lead it back down and I'll use some high-impact rounds to penetrate its skull. Questions?"

"Since this is classified, how do I know you won't shoot me when this is all over?"

"'Cause I always keep my word. But if I ever get wind that you've been shootin' off your mouth, I'll come back and kill you myself. I think we both know that the only reason you're goin' up there is to save your skin. So if this works, I'll owe you your life. Can you work with that?"

Curtis nodded. "Let's just get this over with."

Black Wolf began loading the gun's magazine while Curtis grabbed the lantern and climbed the creaky stairs. *Oh, Jesus—oh, Jesus—oh, Jesus...* Curtis's legs were shaking, his teeth chattering. Icy sweat slid down his back like cold fingers as he inched closer to the room where he did not want to go.

When he reached the second floor, Curtis stopped and listened. It'd been quiet for too long.

He wondered just how cunning the humanoid was. He tiptoed to the room where they had last heard the creature. A bedroom.

He threw open the door and stepped back, expecting an assault. When none came, he eased his head into the dusky room and looked around. In the dimness, he could make out a filthy mattress on the floor surrounded by cigarette butts, used syringes, and empty liquor bottles. Seeing nothing of the Werner-Bug, he entered.

Curtis stepped in a puddle of dark goo. *Why won't this thing just die?* He followed the goo's trail to the ensuite bathroom where he found the door ajar. *You got this, man.* He took a deep, shaky breath as if he were preparing to take a high bungee dive. When he was ready, he eased the door open and leaned inside. A thick string of drool dropped on the floor in front of him. He looked up at the bathroom ceiling.

*EEEEEEE!*

Curtis jumped back just in time to avoid being crushed. He screamed and bolted from the room. He flew down the stairs three at a time as the creature lumbered after him. The air behind him moved as the thing swung its powerful arm, giving a loud bark each time it missed. Black Wolf was at the base of the stairs waiting to fire. Seeing him, Curtis felt equal parts panic and relief.

*POP! POP!* Wet chunks of brain and bone splattered over the staircase. Curtis barely made it over the railing and out of the way of the howling beast as it tumbled down the stairs behind him.

The broken creature flopped at Black Wolf's feet. He fired three more enhanced rounds into what was left of its exposed skull. Thick blood squirted from its shattered head, the flow decreasing with every fading heartbeat. A long, fetid breath marked its end.

"Omigod! Is it dead?" Curtis hollered.

Black Wolf kicked the carcass with the tip of his heavy boot. "Yeah. It's dead. Now, go to the barn and look for anything we can use to tie it to the car. Then pull around to the front. Hurry!"

Curtis was too stunned to move, so Black Wolf went over and pulled him to his feet. "You're gonna be fine. Just let the adrenaline settle down. Now, go and get—"

A wet, tearing sound came from the dead monster.

"Oh no," Black Wolf muttered.

"Whaddaya mean, 'Oh no'? Is it dead or not?"

Black Wolf eased back over to the carcass. He turned on his small Maglite and shined it on the twisting face. Its jaws cracked apart, ripping the surrounding skin like cellophane. Three thick, spider-like legs appeared on each side of the monster's mouth, spreading it wide. An oily, black object the size and shape of a baseball pulled itself out of the ruptured opening and crawled onto the dead creature's chest. It looked like a clawless crab, with two eyes attached to short stalks. It hissed at Black Wolf.

"What's happening?" Curtis pleaded. "Is that..."

"The worst." Black Wolf raised his gun and began firing, but the alien arachnid jumped out of the way with blurry speed. It charged forward, working its way toward Black Wolf, forcing him and Curtis to back up against one of the living room's walls. Black Wolf kept firing until the gun's chamber sprang forward, and clicked.

"Oh God, this is it, isn't it?" Curtis barely recognized his own voice. *Please, let it be quick. I don't wanna feel that thing bitin' me... infectin' me.*

The shimmering creature crawled toward them, its dagger feet clicking on the warped, wooden floor. Black Wolf hurled his gun at the creature, unsurprised when he missed. He tried to move to his left and right to get around it. But by hopping from side to side, it blocked his path before he could complete a whole step. When the monstrosity was six feet from them, it reared back, exposing four dripping mandibles. It lurched forward.

*CRUNCH!*

Curtis and Black Wolf jolted. Razor came up behind the creature, hammering it repeatedly with a long, metal lampstand. Red and yellow gunk squirted out, some spraying onto Curtis's sneakers.

"Sooo..." Razor said. "What'd I miss?"

3

The two kids waited in the back seat of Black Wolf's sedan while he torched the farmhouse. Curtis figured it must be necessary to destroy all evidence of the monster. While they waited on Black Wolf to return, he filled Razor in on everything that had happened while he was unconscious. The information had Razor contemplating every possible meaning of the term "grave concern."

"D'ya think he's gonna have to kill us?" Razor asked. "This is some *Bourne Identity* kinda stuff."

"Naw. I think this guy'll cut us loose. He just seems like the type: dangerous but reasonable.

He had a job to do, that's all. And we helped him do it. So all we gotta do is convince him we'll keep our mouths shut. I think he'll be cool with that."

Curtis looked out the rear window and saw the silhouette of Black Wolf sprinting across the way as the house blazed behind him.

Black Wolf jumped in the front and slammed the door shut, then sat silently for a good long while. "So, boys, what happens next?"

Curtis was too nervous to answer him.

Razor said, "I dunno. What are our choices?"

"Well," Black Wolf began, "I can take you back to that crappy little convenience store and let you take your chances, or you can come with me."

Razor swallowed. "Where would you take us if we went with you?"

Black Wolf smiled. "I never would've thought it, but you boys showed some spunk back there. You might suck at everything else in life, but you know how to slay a dragon, by God. I figure you two now have more experience than the general public in handling freaks of science. So... you wanna join the organization? It's plenty dangerous, but as they told me in the Marines, 'It's not just a job, it's an adventure.'"

Razor and Curtis looked at one another as if to divine the other's response to the unusual job offer.

"Does it pay good?" Razor asked.

"The organization wants its trackers focused on the job. So you'll never be distracted by want," Black Wolf answered. "Anything else?"

Curtis relaxed his body, placed his hands behind his head as a cushion, and let the plush leather seat absorb his lean frame. "Yeah, I got one. Will we get a sweet ride like this one?"

"Actually," Black Wolf chuckled, "you can have this one. It just needs a new trunk."

He started the sedan's engine and backed out of the barn and up the dirt path, before stopping at the rough two-lane road. Hanging a right out of the property, he drove the two twenty-somethings with very few prospects away from the rearview town of Wyattsville.

# THE WOODEN BOX

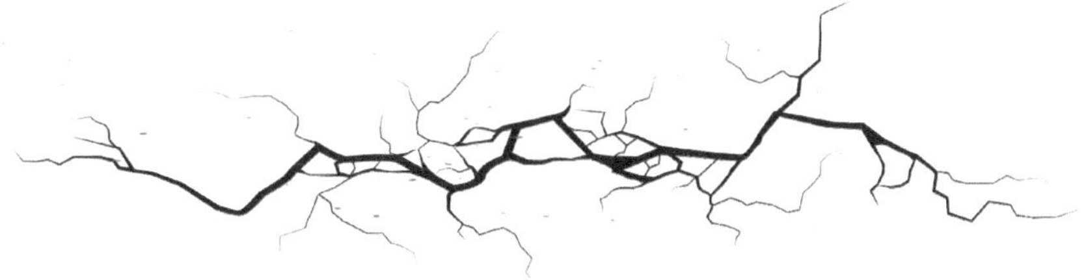

"Peter? Oh, Peter? It's time to wake up, sleepyhead." The quiet voice drifted through the blackness of the small enclosure, like a fall leaf looking for a place to land.

Peter lay sprawled across a concrete floor. His eyelids fluttered as the sing-songy voice pulled him back to consciousness. With great effort, he pushed up until he was leaning on one elbow. He was surrounded by nothingness. The pain in his head was sharp and intense, like someone was trying to break out of his skull with a jackhammer.

"What... what's going on?" he asked, his speech slurred. He was woozy and confused, as if he'd been drugged. He vaguely remembered walking to his car after work. Something covered his face (a rag?). It had a strong, medicinal smell, and then... what?

Gentle, upbeat music began to fill the lightless room. It had a bouncy rhythm, a child-like quality. A brief intro was followed by a chorus of small children singing gleefully.

*Good mornin'! Good morning'! Let's all get up and sing Shake those webs out of your head, and dance, and play, and sing Oh, good mornin'! Good mornin'! It's time to move along With a doo-dil-*

*ly-dee and a doo-dilly-doo, it's our good mornin' song* The tune ended with an abrupt thump. Peter continued to lean against the floor. *What was that? Are there children here?*

"Well, look who's finally up. Welcome, Peter." The voice was not insistent or urgent; it nudged, rather than pushed. "Please, take a few moments to acclimate yourself."

Peter heaved himself up to a crooked sitting position. He had no sense of time or location—the lack of light clouded his perception. His head swayed as he attempted to make out his surroundings, but his eyes proved useless. As he continued to suck in deep breaths of air, he gradually became more lucid. When his situation became clear to him, Peter hyperventilated. His intense fear of the dark seized control of his mind and body.

He was cloaked in impenetrable darkness. His terrified mind drew vivid pictures of phantom tendrils reaching out for him. They pulled him down into a pit with a withered ghoul whose hands could reach out at any time and drag its cracked fingernails down his naked arm. His neck muscles stiffened and tingled as he thought of the thing's hot, putrid breath caressing his neck, lingering there like a sticky web. His instinctive need to escape overwhelmed him to the point of incoherence. He hoped it was all a nightmare, something that would evaporate once the lights came on. But he knew this was real—it was happening.

He could feel the unforgiving floor beneath his quivering body. He managed to stand upright, nearly slipping. White dots danced before his eyes, and sickness churned in his belly. Despite his alarm, he did not shout for help. *That's the thing about the dark. I could be anywhere. Am I alone? Is there someone in here with me?*

He thought of addressing the unsettling voice, but he also wondered what he might draw forth from the inky expanse. He felt caught between needing to know what was happening and fearing the answer.

As if divining Peter's concerns, the floating voice again penetrated the void. "Hello again, Peter. Now that you've had ample time to adjust, tell me: Are you scared? Do you find yourself alone in the shadows, or are others standing near you? I can hear your frantic breathing. I can feel your heartbeat through the walls. Would you care to know where you are, or are you afraid to be told that you've died and fallen into the deepest hole in hell? Maybe you're wondering if this is a place from which you can escape or, hopefully, be rescued. Talk to me, Peter. Your questions pose no danger to you."

"Where am I?"

"Not as far away as your imagination and distress might be telling you. In fact, you're within ten miles of your office. And you might be relieved to learn that you're not in some large, abandoned warehouse. The room you're in only measures fourteen by ten, probably the size of your bedroom. This is a place that you likely drive by every day on your way to work and never take notice of it. Probably no one else does, either."

"Why am I here? Why have I been kidnapped?"

"Why not you, Peter? Is your life any more or less important than someone else's?"

"But I haven't done anything. What are you going to do to me?"

"I'm going to offer you an opportunity to free yourself."

"How? How am I going to free myself?"

"With something small yet important, something necessary for your survival."

"Such as?"

"A key. Well, not so much *a* key as *the* key."

"Key to what?"

"Isn't it obvious? The key to the door. You do want to get out, don't you? And no, I won't track you down or harm you in any way. Your escape comes with no consequences. All you have to do is move around the room and find that key. It shouldn't be too difficult; the room is empty. Now, keep in mind it could be anywhere. It might be hanging on a wall, dangling from the ceiling, or lying on the floor. Who knows? Once you find it, all you have to do is feel your way to the door, unlock it, and step out into the glorious sunlight."

Peter restrained his optimism. There had to be a catch—there was always a catch.

"You're leaving something out, aren't you? There's something you want. Tell me what's in this for you."

"You got me, Peter. It doesn't mean much if it's not challenging. It's okay, though. You're going to do fine."

"Just tell me what I have to do."

"With you is a small wooden box. Feel around the floor and let me know when you find it."

"And if I refuse?"

"Then my efforts to lead you toward a solution to your dire circumstances will be moot."

The threat was clear, so he stooped and began groping around. His fingertips pushed against something hard. Peter felt the rectangular object, determined that it was the hidden box, and picked it up. "Okay, I found it," he said.

"That's very good, Peter. You're one step closer to home. Now then, you'll feel a lid on top of the box. Lay the box back down on the floor and remove it. Then stand up quickly and take a few steps back."

Peter complied. He heard a faint scraping noise and something light hitting the floor. Two more of the puzzling sounds followed. Then he detected some faint scuttling. Soon after, something crawled over his shoe. He gasped, lifted his foot, and propelled whatever it was across the room.

"What was in that box?"

"Peter, listen to me carefully. In the room with you are three sizeable and highly venomous black fat-tailed scorpions. In the Middle East and parts of Africa, they are known as 'man killer.' Peter, you have to be careful here. They're nocturnal, so they thrive in the dark. They're capable of climbing rough walls, such as the brick ones in your room. They can crawl across a ceiling and drop down on you. Like all good hunters, they hide and wait patiently for their prey to wander along. As you search for the key, you'll want to tread lightly—they can sense vibrations. Their venom is fast-acting. Without prompt medical care, you won't survive. The immediate symptoms from being stung are swift, painful, and hor-rific. Do you understand what I've just told you?"

Peter stood petrified and mute.

"Peter, do you understand?"

"Yes," he croaked.

"Marvelous! It's now officially you against the scorpions. I hope you crush it—I mean that literally and figuratively. I'll be watching all the action via an infrared camera."

"How do I know you won't kill me, anyway?"

"I said I wouldn't, but I've never had to think about it before. No one has escaped yet. For now, you're the next contestant. Good luck, Peter."

"Wait! Just let me out of here. I haven't seen you. I can pull together some money. Okay, not a lot, but enough to make it worth your while."

Silence.

"Hey, c'mon! Don't just leave me here! *Please! Pleeease!*"

Silence. Peter exhaled. His teeth chattered and his body trem-bled. *Lightless room, poisonous scorpions, and a blind search for a small key—what could go wrong?*

His first idea was to try his cell phone, but his pocket's light-ness indicated it was missing. Then he considered the door. He wondered if it could somehow be forced open. Peter suspected that pounding on it and yelling for help wasn't going to do him any good—Lord only knew where he was. "Okay, you can do this, you can do this, you can do this."

He stuck his arms out into the windowless room and took a step forward. Despite trying to remain poised, he felt fear, like a frigid river, rushing through his veins. His unhelpful mind began conjuring images of dog-sized monstrosities swirling about the room, ready to snare him with over-sized pincers and squeeze him until he was sliced in two. He shuddered as he imagined the excruciating gouge of a gigantic, barbed stinger that would pump gallon after gallon of searing poison into his cracking frame.

*Knock it off! We don't have time for this now. Just focus on that stupid key so we can get out of here.*

Once Peter got himself marginally in check, he began moving again. He walked until he came to a wall and then felt his way along until he reached a steel door. It was heavy and dense, like the type used for extra security. Tracing the frame, he discovered the knob and twisted it.

Because it moved freely, Peter reasoned that it wasn't the knob securing the door but some other kind of locking mechanism. He examined further and came across the bulge of a double deadbolt lock. Now, he knew what he was dealing with—the key it would have to be.

He couldn't see the room and its contents, so that was an obvious disadvantage. But he remembered hearing that the brain could compensate for a lost sense by enhancing the other faculties. He hoped that his perceptions might be heightened enough to guide him past the scorpions and to the key.

His idea was to start with the floor, then gradually work his way upward. He followed the wall until he felt a corner. Then he got down on his hands and knees and started crawling, sliding his palms across the surface of the floor. Despite his resolve, his desire to find the key began to be hampered by his knowledge that somewhere around him lurked three large and deadly scorpions. *Scorpions. What did I ever do to deserve this?*

He wandered around for several minutes, then halted when his hand collided with something small and firm. He shot to his feet. "Oh, crap!" He immediately began stomping around the floor. He heard the unmistakable crunch followed by the sound of fast tapping swiftly moving away from him.

His body shook as the adrenaline ran its course. Once his nerves settled down, Peter lowered himself again and resumed his search. He glided his hands over the smooth surface of the floor, keeping in mind that the other scorpions could be scattered across it. He moved forward in a straight line. When he came to the wall, he made a U-turn. Crawling, unseeing and defenseless, he kept anticipating a sharp sting. His stomach hurt. Once he convinced himself that he had successfully surveyed the entire room, Peter enjoyed a palpable sense of relief.

He was about to switch his blind search to the walls when he remembered what the voice had warned: they're capable of climbing. "Okay," he mumbled, "easy does it."

He prepared himself for the fact that the walls were going to take longer because, although he could sweep his hands widely over the floor, he would need to traverse the walls in tighter quadrants.

Peter started at the lowest point and, with tremoring hands, progressed upward, then over and down again. As he moved down, his palm scraped over something with stiff hairs, and he leaped back. He heard the scorpion skittering across the bumpy bricks to his left. Peter knew that he needed to pin down the scorpion's exact location and remove it before he could safely proceed with the wall search.

He took off his thin outer shirt, rolled it thickly around his right hand, formed a fist, then turned it so that it resembled a crude, fleshy hammer. He systematically began pounding his fist, one blow at a time, against the bricks, listening for movement. After a few hits, he felt a light tugging on the cloth. Next, there came a soft jabbing sensation against the outside of the covering. He continued smashing his padded hand against the wall, hoping the scorpion wouldn't climb over the protective barrier and stab him.

Peter's heart was thumping like a 1980s techno beat. He could imagine the creature's fiery needle. He was more disgusted than satisfied when he finally heard the loud crack of its exoskeleton and felt warm fluid squirt onto his exposed wrist. "Ugh," he moaned as he wiped away the crushed remains of the scorpion before tossing the shirt aside. *Okay, that's two.*

Peter finished going over the last remaining wall space. He found no trace of the key or its dangerous guardian, so he turned his attention to the ceiling, from where he hoped to find the key suspended from a string.

Despite having dispatched two-thirds of the obstacles between him and possible release, Peter was still unnerved. He felt like an inmate sentenced to execution—time and manner of death unknown. But his terror of the dark was considerably greater than his fear of the deadly hunter maneuvering around him, waiting to pounce. His muscles locked, and his staccato breathing was like the desperate pant of a trapped animal. His mind vacillated between breaking out of the black, awful cage and the suffocating horror clinging to him like a blood-soaked shroud. *Oh God! Is the dark getting thicker? I can't breathe!*

Peter's chest hitched as he pulled in short gasps of dank air. He used the breathing technique that his psychiatrist had taught him some years back. *Breathe in, and hold it for three... two... one... exhale slowly.* He repeated the mantra until it had the desired effect. Once he regained a measure of composure, he turned his thoughts back to the key.

He began working through logical scenarios. He didn't yet know where the key was, but he now knew where it wasn't. He also knew that the third scorpion hadn't been on the floor or walls—at least not the wall he'd just beaten to a pulp—so it could be somewhere above him, along with the key. He held out hope that he'd startled it enough to send it fleeing back down to the floor or a wall, rather than remaining on the ceiling waiting for its quarry to wander by. "So, where are you, you little monster?"

As he began advancing, he lifted his arms over his head and made a forward paddling motion with his hands, hoping to graze the hanging key. After a while, he detected some quiet clacking.

But the harsh acoustics of the empty room made the sound little more than a soft echo, making it difficult for Peter to establish the scorpion's whereabouts. He shivered at the thought of the hellish creature scurrying up his leg at any second. He paused and lowered his arms. He felt the need to think things through before proceeding. *I can stay still and pray like crazy that help arrives, or I can go for the surer thing and keep looking for the key, assuming there even is one.*

Peter wondered if anybody had noticed yet that he was missing. He had no idea how long his abductor had imprisoned him. So why, when, or where would the search for him begin and end? His only tangible hope was to find the key.

Peter raised his hands high again and resumed searching the room step by agonizing step. To maintain as straight a line as possible, he walked heel to toe until he reached the room's end. He continued to listen for the final attacker. *Please, God. I can't take this much longer.*

On the one hand, he was discouraged by not yet having found the key. On the other, he was reassured by the fact that the waiting scorpion hadn't speared him. He was also becoming impatient. He wanted out now. He picked up the pace and swung his hands out further in front of him. After a couple more wide passes, he bumped into a wall, and kicked it in frustration.

Peter sensed no air movement, just the raw feeling of something dropping down onto his head. He shrieked as he felt the scorpion scratching its way across his scalp. In a frenzy, he raked his fingers through his hair, working to dislodge it before it had a chance to strike. When his right-hand fingers swept underneath the enraged arachnid, it gave his index finger a painful squeeze. Peter yelped and snapped his hand backward, sending the scorpion tumbling down the back of his undershirt. Its tiny leg bristles scraped against his goosebump-dotted skin as it slid slowly down his bare back.

At first, its sting felt like little more than a slight needle prick. But as the site of the jab began to burn with increasing intensity, Peter knew the worst had happened. His heart thumped furiously inside his chest as a primal instinct overtook him, throwing him into a mad fit of desperation. Hoping to kill the scorpion, he ran backward until he collided with one of the walls. He screamed as agonizing pain shot through his swelling back like a white-hot electrical current.

Peter groaned in anguish when he felt the sinister thing's spider-like body squirming around at the bottom of his shirt. His effort had failed. He grimaced and arched his back as the unharmed scorpion clawed its way upward toward the shirt's entry point, digging its dagger feet in along the way and slamming its stinger against his tender flesh repeatedly, like endless injections of boiling acid.

Feeling his strength waning, Peter hurled himself backward one last time. His nearly limp body crashed heavily against the rigid wall, causing the foul creature's soupy guts to explode through its shattered armor and onto his tortured skin.

Then, his legs gave way and he dropped to the floor in a paralyzed heap. He was sweating profusely, spit oozing from his mouth like clear syrup. "Help," he whimpered. "Please, help me."

He heard the turning of the deadbolt. The door opened, and a vague outline of a person filled the bright opening. Peter's eyelids began to droop; his vision blurred, making it impossible to make out the figure that had entered the room and was now stooping beside him.

"Oh, Peter; oh my goodness." The voice was serene and soothing. "I know you might find this hard to believe, but I truly did want you to figure this out. I'm getting bored with the same old outcome. Why do people have to make everything so complicated? The answer's always the simplest. That's sad, don't you think, Peter? Isn't that sad?"

Peter was finding it harder to breathe. The waves of nausea were getting stronger. Tears flowed from his eyes in a salty torrent. He didn't want to end up like this: a crumpled corpse on a filthy floor, whose body would never be found by anyone. *This is going to kill Mom and Dad.*

"Honestly, Peter, I would've allowed you to walk away. As you observed earlier, you never saw me, and I can always relocate. But here you are. The paralysis has already overtaken you: first your limbs, then your lungs, and then other vital organs. But the good news is the overall pain will lessen to a dull throb. Your heartbeat will slow down, and breathing will become much more difficult. You've got maybe a couple of hours or so, and then your soul, at least, will be free. If there's anything you want to say, you'll need to say it now while you can still talk."

"Where," Peter grunted. "Where's... key? I have to know. Please. Was it... ceiling?"

"Well, after everything you've been through, the least I can do is show you the answer. It's both logical and straightforward. Whenever something goes missing, most people tend to look all over their house for it—they turn the whole place inside out. And like them, all of you waste so much time trying to be resourceful that it never occurs to you to begin by searching the one place people eventually find most lost items."

The man reached into Peter's front pants pocket and removed a key.

# THE DISAPPEARING BOY

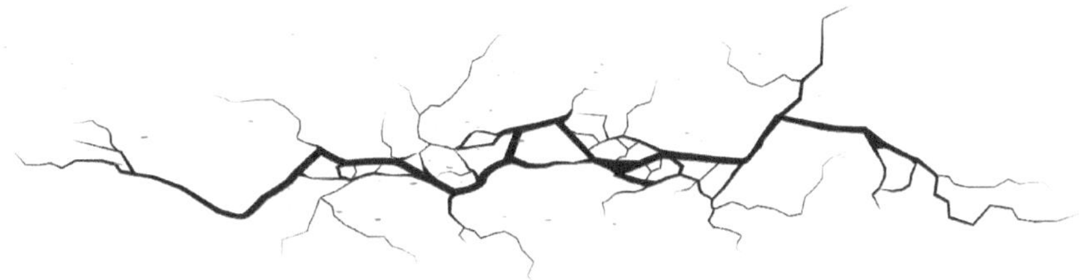

## 1

I never believed in magic until I met Tommy Naughton.

The first time I saw him was in my eleventh-grade English class at Ridley High in 2001. He looked odd, with his gapped-up haircut and baggy clothing. He always smelled like sour sweat—ugh! He rarely made eye contact, never spoke unless spoken to, and sat as far back in the classroom as the wall would allow. I was sorry for him, but pity doesn't do much to cure another's social awkwardness. Then one day, Tommy went from being a social outcast to the talk of the school. It all started when our English teacher, Mrs. Sharon, gave us an assignment.

"Okay, listen up, people. When I call on you, I want you to come up. Then I'd like you to tell everyone something unique about yourself: a special talent, family history, interesting hobbies; anything. We'll go alphabetically. First up, Larry Anders."

Let me tell you, there was nothin' special about ol' Larry (still isn't, from what I hear). A few kids had some cool things to share, like Teresa Donavan. Turns out one of her uncles was a roadie for Red Hot Chili Peppers. Skyler Murphy held the swim team record for holding her breath underwater: a whopping five and a half minutes! I dreaded my turn. For once, I was happy to have the name "Lenore Zylstra." But my dread must have paled compared to Tommy.

"Tommy Naughton," said Mrs. Sharon.

Tommy was reading a book, or pretending to.

"Tommy, put the book down and come up. I'm sure everyone else is a little embarrassed, too," said Mrs. Sharon.

Tommy lowered his book and looked at her solemnly. When he spoke, somewhere between a mumble and a whisper, no one could understand him.

"I can't hear a word you're saying," said Mrs. Sharon.

"I said I have nothing to share."

"You could tell us how you plan to kill your barber!" That was Brad Oberstrom. Butthole.

Everyone guffawed; poor Tommy looked mortified. I couldn't stand the cruelty for another second, so I raised my hand.

"I don't mind taking his place," I said. I hated going next, but anything was better than watching Tommy being humiliated.

"That's thoughtful, Lenore, but I called on Tommy, not you." She glared at Tommy. "Mr. Naughton, a weary world awaits you."

"Yes, ma'am." Tommy placed his book on his desk, then shuffled to the front of the classroom, snickers following him with each plodding footstep.

"Oh, boy. This is gonna be timeless." Brad again. Butthole.

I think Mrs. Sharon felt sorry for Tommy now. She looked remorseful, sympathetic. When the uproar died down, she gently addressed him.

"Tommy, hon. You can start whenever you're ready. I promise we'll give you our full attention."

Maybe it was my imagination, but I could've sworn he looked right at me. It wasn't a harsh stare. It was as though he was singling me out.

"I have a special talent that no one else has. Some people who practice magic say they have this ability, too, but they're lying. For them, it's just a trick. But I can make things disappear... for real. It's called teleportation. Want me to show you?"

I spoke up, surprising myself. "Would you? Make something disappear, I mean."

Tommy gave me that odd look again as if he were only going through this to impress me. "Sure I can, Lenore. I think you'll like it." Gazing around the classroom, he said, "Does anyone have a small object like a watch or a ring?"

"I got a watch," Peter Travers said, passing it forward.

"Watch closely." Tommy cupped the watch between his hands and massaged it with his palms. He stopped, then opened his hands. The watch had disappeared.

A collective "whoa" swept over the classroom. "Dude, that was cool. Where'd it go?" Peter asked.

"I teleported it to another place. I can do that: make something disappear and wind up somewhere else." He turned to Mrs. Sharon. "Ma'am, would you open your upper right desk drawer?"

The place went wild when she opened the drawer and retrieved the wristwatch. Mrs. Sharon looked like she had just pulled out a three-headed chicken. "H-How?" she stammered. "How in the world did you do that, Tommy?"

"Because I know real magic," he said matter-of-factly. "May I sit down now, ma'am?"

"Of course. Thank you, Tommy."

Poor Tina Newsome; how the heck was she gonna top Tommy's act?"

2

Typically, the kids in English sauntered in, sat at their desks, and exhaled one of those *Why do I have to take this stupid course?* sighs. But that day everyone seemed excited to be there.

Mrs. Sharon sensed the energy. "My, you guys are lively. Is there something I don't know?"

Before anyone answered, Tommy drifted into the room. His head was down, his shoulders slumped, and he was hitching up his baggy pants with every other step.

"There he goes... the magic maggot!" Oberstrom. Butthole.

You might've thought Lady Gaga or Eminem had entered the building by the jubilant faces that morning in English 101. Eager eyes followed Tommy as he made his way to the back of the room. He took no notice. I suppose he wasn't used to being the object of attention. He sat down and looked out the window. His face was full of melancholy, as if he were watching a funeral procession.

Mrs. Sharon snapped the class to attention. "Okay, everyone. Please take out your textbook and turn to Chapter Five. I hope some of you have read ahead."

As we pulled our textbooks from our bags, Mary Glover held up her hand.

"Yes, Mary?" Mrs. Sharon asked.

"I was wondering if we could wrap up a few minutes early today. I'd like—I mean, we'd like—to see some more of Tommy's magic."

"Judas Priest, Glover," Chris Sampson said, rolling his eyes. "It ain't magic. I've seen a million magicians do the same trick he did."

Others mumbled in agreement.

"Settle down, everyone!" said Mrs. Sharon. "We're not here to see magic tricks; it's still an English class. And besides—"

"It's not a magic trick," the small voice said from the back corner. "It's real. I can make things travel from one place to another."

"Teleportation," I said. "You called it teleportation."

He glanced at me. "That's right, Lenore. Thank you for remembering."

"Is that something you might enjoy doing, Tommy?" Mrs. Sharon asked with delicacy.

Tommy looked around at the pleading eyes. "Sure, I guess so.

With fifteen minutes left before the bell, Mrs. Sharon put down her pen. "Okay, fans. Let's put away our books and prepare to be amazed. Tommy Naughton, come on down!"

There were several "woo-hoos" and chants of, "Tommy! Tommy!" as he took his place at the front of the classroom. He waited for the noise to diminish. When he spoke, his voice was still light, but now it sounded more confident. *He* seemed more confident.

"Yesterday, I teleported a wristwatch to Mrs. Sharon's desk drawer. Small objects are no big deal. But what if you could move a person? Wouldn't that be something?"

"No way," said Aimee Knight.

"Then I'll prove it to you." Tommy searched the room and stopped at a large cloth banner with an amateurish painting of Earth and the words "Let's keep it green" under it. "Mrs. Sharon, ma'am, is it okay to use your banner?"

"Yes, yes," she said with childlike giddiness. "Do you need help to take it down?"

"No, ma'am; I've got it." Tommy stood on tippy-toes and removed the cloth from the wall.

Then he took his place beside Mrs. Sharon's desk. "Now, you see me," he said, concealing himself with the banner. "Now you don't." From under the covering, he said, "Are you all ready?"

"Just shut up and do it!" Oberstrom yelled.

Tommy's muffled voice began counting down. "Okay... three... two..." Everyone gasped as the empty banner floated to the floor. The screams came when Tommy appeared in the doorway. *"One!"*

We erupted in cheers as Tommy returned to his desk. Mr. Edelman, the science teacher next door, raced in. "Monica, is everything okay?"

Mrs. Sharon was breathless. "Myron, you should've seen him. He disappeared—he really disappeared!"

"Who disappeared? Should I call the office?"

"No. I'm not talking about someone going missing. I'm talking about magic, er, I mean teleport... oh, hell. That kid over there went from standing next to me to outside that doorway in an instant."

Before she could say more, the bell rang. Tommy stood first. As he crossed the room, everyone stopped moving and talking. They watched with silent reverence as he left, as though they were working up the nerve to touch the hem of his garment. I was happy for him. At first.

3

By the following day, everyone knew about Tommy's ability. I saw some kids corner him in the hall, insisting that he make something disappear. "Come on, dude, show us some magic," one of them shouted. Others chimed in. Tommy recoiled and threaded himself through the relentless crowd. Then he jogged away, pages from his notebook dropping behind him like breadcrumbs.

After a few days of hectoring, Tommy relented and began performing quick sleights of hand between classes. His popularity grew by the day. Soon, he'd gone from being nervous and withdrawn to eating the attention up like cotton candy. He became the main attraction during lunch, entertaining the ever-growing crowd of onlookers with one feat after another.

The one that had everyone talking was when he made his feet disappear. He had a beach towel he'd brought to school for the performance. He stretched it out so that it was horizontal, then stood behind it with only his legs showing from his shins down.

With each of his hands grasping an upper corner, he raised his right foot behind the towel, so you couldn't see it. He put it down and did the same with his left foot. Then he lifted both feet, so that he appeared to be floating in midair. He put his feet back on the ground, tossed the towel aside, and took a flamboyant bow.

There were over a hundred people in the cafeteria that day, all clapping, yelling, and chanting his name. After that, no one called him Tommy anymore. He was now the one, the only, The Disappearing Boy.

Tommy changed after that. He still dressed like a dork and wore that god-awful hairstyle, but he held his head up; he was confident. Teachers, students; it didn't matter. They couldn't take their eyes off him. He became the school celebrity. I became the focus of his attention.

It started out kind of cute: a wave in the hall, a wink in class. But then I started getting an eerie vibe, like I was being watched. Everywhere I went, he'd be nearby wearing that spooky smile.

One night in the shower, I had an unsettling feeling that someone else was in the bathroom.

There was no way anyone else could fit into the tiny space, so I shook it off as paranoia. I was almost undressed when I heard breathing behind me. I froze. Something cold and clammy touched my shoulder. I yelped and spun around. No one was there. I waited, but nothing happened. I turned on the water and waited for it to get warm before climbing inside the shower. While I was rinsing off, I turned toward the semi-clear curtain and saw Tommy on the other side looking right at me. My heart nearly shot out of my chest. I snatched back the curtain, but he was gone. My breaths were quick and loud, and I was shaking despite the warm shower. I set a land speed record for getting out of the bathroom.

I bolted to my room and locked the door behind me. The air was cold, and it smelled like stale perspiration. "Hello?" I muttered. I peeked under my bed and checked my closet. Seeing nothing, I settled down enough to go to bed.

I turned off my table lamp and wriggled under the covers. That was when I sensed eyes on me, piercing the shadows. I sat up on my elbows and peered into the darkness. When I saw Tommy standing in the corner leering, I screamed. I thought I'd never stop.

My dad burst into my room and flipped on the wall switch, but Tommy had vanished. When I told my dad what I'd seen, he didn't believe me.

"What'd your mom and I tell you about watching those stupid *Nightmare on Elm Street* movies? Jesus, Mary, and Joseph! You scared us half to death!"

Despite his frustration, I wouldn't let him leave until he'd searched every inch of my room. Even after he pronounced it monster-free, I slept with the light on.

4

I dreaded seeing Tommy the next day, but it was unavoidable. When he came down the hall toward me, I averted my eyes. As we passed each other, my stomach was so roiled with nerves that I thought I might throw up.

When he arrived in English class, I pretended to be looking through my backpack. The thought of him sitting near me with that jack-o'-lantern grin made my skin crawl.

It went on like that for days. Each time I met Tommy, he was bolder. He began speaking to me, something he'd never had the nerve to do before. In the hall: "Hi, Lenore." Once at the mall: "Wow, what a beautiful surprise!"

Things came to a head one day in the cafeteria. I was sitting with my friends, enjoying my favorite lunch: a PBJ, potato chips, and a diet soda. Becky Martin was across from me. She was in the middle of one of her hilarious stories when she glanced up and stopped mid-sentence.

Tommy dropped onto the seat next to me with a tray of food. "Don't stop talking on my account. I just wanted to sit by Lenore."

My face flushed.

"Um, do you guys need some privacy?" Becky asked.

I lost it. "What is your problem?" I snarled at him. "Do you think because people find you interesting that I'm gonna go all googly-eyed over you? Leave me alone!"

His eyes flashed with anger. Then he stood from his chair and spoke, loud enough for everyone to hear. "Hey, listen up! I've got another cool thing to show you. Wanna see it?"

Shouts of excitement echoed through the cafeteria.

Tommy glowed as he addressed his legion of fans. "Lenore here has some curious culinary tastes. Let's see, she's got a PBJ; how lame." Gales of laughter. "We've got chips and diet soda. Doesn't one cancel out the other?" More guffawing. I wanted to die.

"I'm gonna do Lenore a favor. I'm gonna make this junk disappear because I'm..."

"The Disappearing Boy!" the crowd chorused.

Tommy snatched my brown paper bag and crammed my lunch into it. He shook it a few times, then turned it upside down. Nothing fell out.

No one responded because they knew the best part—the *WOW* part—was coming.

With a flourish, Tommy finished his act. "That lunch is trash. And where should trash go?"

"In the trash can!" they all screamed.

Tommy pointed to a fifty-five-gallon trashcan several yards away. A tall, skinny girl was standing near it. "Hey!" he shouted to her. "Look in that trash can and tell me what you see!"

The girl peered into the container. Her mouth dropped like a drawbridge, and she gasped. "It's here! That chick's lunch is right here!"

The entire cafeteria made a beeline to the trashcan.

A big guy, some uber-jock, yelled, "You guys gotta look at this! It's the same stuff he put in the bag!"

Becky and my other friends looked flabbergasted—all but Ella Grassfield; she looked concerned. "Oh, Lenore," she said. "You've got problems."

"Hey, if you're still hungry," the jock shouted at me, "I know where you can find your lunch!"

I had all I could stand. If Tommy's goal was to repay me for the humiliation I'd caused him then he accomplished his mission. I grabbed my things and ran from the cafeteria.

I returned to the main building and entered the nearest girls' restroom. I checked to make sure I was alone; I couldn't bear being embarrassed again. When I was sure that the room was empty, I locked myself in a stall. I buried my face in my hands and cried until my eyes burned. I was distraught, at first, then I became afraid. Was he out to get me now? Was he going to show up at my house again?

5

I avoided Tommy as much as I could. I started eating my lunch in the restroom. I dreaded English class. His gaze was always on me, like an oil coating my skin.

As his fan base grew, Tommy got cockier, which means he made more enemies. The football team's left tackle, Luke Tyler, had a problem sharing popularity with the school's outcast. According to gossip, Luke confronted Tommy in the boys' locker room one day.

"You must think you're the big man on campus," the jock said. "I ought to cram your skinny butt inside that locker."

Tommy was calm as a pond. He looked up at Luke towering over him and grinned. "Tell ya what. Walk into that shower stall over there, pull the curtain, and let me transport you. If I fail, I'll walk through the school naked. If that won't make a guy humble, I don't know what will. But if I teleport you, you leave me alone. Do we have a deal?"

Luke made a hasty decision. He should've made a careful one. "Yeah, it's a deal, gooch-sniffer." He walked to the nearest stall and closed the curtain behind him. "I'm *waitiiing.*"

"Well, off you go then," Tommy said.

After a moment, one of Luke's teammates spoke up. "Luke? Hey, Luke! Quit messin' around!"

"Do you think he's in there?" another guy asked.

The teammate crept toward the stall and snatched back the curtain. Luke was gone. "Where'd he go?"

"Somewhere else," Tommy said. He finished getting dressed and left. The others searched the changing room. They inspected stalls, opened lockers, and searched hallways. They found nothing.

A couple of days passed with no sign of Luke. Detectives interviewed everyone who'd seen him last; police officers led a search team and dogs around the school and surrounding areas; they checked hospitals and morgues. Nothing. No one accused Tommy outright. They didn't want to sound like children wondering where the magician's rabbit had gone Despite Luke's disappearance, the team played the game on Friday night. Our guys won 38–17. That meant a Saturday afternoon celebration.

As was the tradition for many years, fans gathered at the school's back parking lot to celebrate the win. They called it the Victory Smash. Students took turns using a sledgehammer to pound an old junker car painted blue and white, our school colors. Each time a blow landed, a cheer broke out.

Five minutes into the celebration, a female student walked to the rear of the car to knock off the bumper. She was about to lift the sledgehammer when she stopped. Her lips curled, and her nose crinkled as if she'd come across a dead skunk. "Oh my God," she said. "Does anybody smell that? I think it's coming from the trunk."

Mr. Farnham, the head football coach, joined her. He took a whiff and covered his mouth and nose with his elbow. "Geez. I smell it, too." He turned to the girl and motioned for her to give him the sledgehammer. "Stand back," he said. Coach hammered at the bottom seam of the trunk. On the third strike, it popped open. Coach grabbed the girl and pulled her close to his chest, turning her face away from the car. "Someone, call 9-1-1, now!" he hollered.

A murmur passed through the crowd. A boy walked to the trunk, gazed inside, and blanched.

"It's Luke! He's dead!"

Some people screamed; others rushed to the trunk. Many of them retched; others puked outright.

That night, I had a terrible dream about Luke. I was walking by the junker car when I heard a scratching noise and someone yelling, "Let me out!" I opened the trunk. The lid had bloody scratch marks on the inside. Luke was there curled up in a ball. Buzzing flies streamed from his nose and mouth, landing on his dull, milky eyes. His blue lips peeled open, and his dead eyes locked onto mine. A gooey mass of fat worms cascaded from his mouth as he croaked, "Ta-da!" I woke up screaming.

6

People avoided Tommy after that. The hoots and hollers turned into worried whispers. I thought Tommy might've picked up on everyone's wariness whenever he walked into a room. But either he didn't notice, or he didn't care. The dragging of his feet had become a victory march.

Not long after Luke disappeared, I was at my locker when Tommy came up to me.

"Hi there, Lenore," he said. "Shame what happened to Luke, huh? I know everyone blames me, but the part they leave out is that he insisted I make him disappear. He never clarified where. I could sure use a friend right now. I think the entire school's against me."

"What have I ever done to make you think I want to be your friend?" I asked, trembling.

"Yelling at you in the cafeteria? The way I've been avoiding you? What, exactly?"

He looked surprised. "I don't understand. I thought we had a connection. I was only trying to impress you in the cafeteria. Everything I've done has been to impress you."

"Humiliating me in front of everyone did not impress me. Luke's death did not impress me.

Showing up at my house did not impress me. I'm afraid of you. Why don't you make yourself disappear again? And this time, don't come back!"

He looked stunned; I thought he might cry. The old sadness returned to his face. I wish I could say I was sorry for him, but I wasn't. After I stood up to him, he didn't scare me as much. He was still a timid little weirdo.

"Okay," he muttered. "I understand. Bye, Lenore." He turned and walked away, with that same pathetic shuffle.

7

I was relieved when Tommy didn't show up at school the next day. I felt like I could breathe again.

I was in my third-period Social Studies class when Principal Haynes leaned into the room and motioned to our teacher, Ms. Brown, to join him in the hall. When she returned, she was red— eyed and sniffling.

"Guys," she said, "something awful has happened and I'd rather you heard it from me." She bit her bottom lip. "We were just informed that Tommy Naughton has passed away. Please keep his family in your prayers." The poor woman seemed devastated by the news. A sob spilled from her. "I need to step out for a moment." I heard her crying all the way down the hall.

None of us said anything. What was there to say? Most of the school had never met Tommy; they only knew of him.

Over the course of the day, rumors swirled about how he'd died: a hit and run, a deadly assault, and other nasty scenarios. It turned out he'd killed himself. He'd been found hanging in his grandmother's shed. He'd left no note of explanation, only his lonely corpse.

My emotions and thoughts were jumbled together—sorrow for his family's grief, comfort from not being afraid anymore, but mainly guilt that my harsh words might've driven him to take his own life. I thought back to the morning when Tommy had shown up out of nowhere, of the bizarre events that led up to his departure. *Now you see him, now you don't.*

8

Tommy had made me anxious and fearful, but that didn't mean I shouldn't show some compassion. That's more than I can say for his so-called fans. The funeral service was depressing enough, but the lack of attendees made it even more tragic. Only a handful of students came. Not even Principal Haynes bothered to show up. I was grateful that Mrs. Sharon and Ms. Brown were there.

An elderly woman sat up front with a couple of other adults. I heard someone say that she was the grandmother whom Tommy had moved in with after his mom had died. She was bent by grief, hitching with despair. The most heartbreaking thing about burying her grandson must've been that so few people mourned him.

They had laid Tommy out in a cheap, no-frills coffin. He looked odd wearing an oversized gray suit, his gapped-up hair slicked back. A rent-a-priest pretended to know about the kid he'd never met. After the service, two funeral home attendants shuffled to Tommy's coffin and began lowering the lid. *Now you see him, now you don't.*

I skipped the graveside service. Several folks were driving in the opposite direction of the cemetery, so I figured I wasn't the only one. I thought about going home, changing clothes, and returning to school. Maybe doing something normal would help take my mind off Tommy. But when I got home, all I wanted to do was to go to my room and nap. I fell asleep right after my head hit the pillow.

I didn't wake-up until after dark; my parents let me sleep. My stomach growled; I hadn't eaten anything since breakfast. I didn't know what was being cooked for dinner, but it smelled terrific. I couldn't wait to get downstairs.

I went to the bathroom and took a long shower to wake up. As I returned to my bedroom, I found the lights were off. I was ninety-five percent certain that I'd left them on.

As soon as I entered, I froze. Tommy, dressed in his funeral attire, stood next to my bed, wearing that awful grin. I took off like a bullet, screaming. My parents attempted to calm me down, but I couldn't stop shaking.

We all went upstairs to my room to look for Tommy, but I knew he wouldn't be there. Mom and Dad exchanged worried looks. They tried to convince me that the recent events had left me overwrought and that the hallucinations would stop. But I knew it wasn't the last time I'd see The Disappearing Boy.

9

It's been decades since I sat in Mrs. Sharon's English class looking at the nerdy kid hiding behind a book. I remember how acceptance by his peers hadn't encouraged him, only corrupted him. Tommy had a gift. Most of us believed that. But the naysayers were always trying to figure out how he'd pulled off his illusions. They never did. Tommy said that what he did wasn't a trick, but real magic. That's the thought that haunts me.

I see him now and again around my house, at the office, or somewhere in the distance. He mainly shows up in my nightmares. Forever sixteen, he looks like he did at his funeral.

Sometimes he's gloomy. Other times, he has that horrifying grimace etched into his thin, pale face. I shiver every time. I've considered going to a shrink, hoping they'll tell me it's all just a guilt-induced fantasy. But then, I think, *If a person can disappear and wind up someplace else, couldn't he teleport himself from a buried casket?*

Over the years, I've become accustomed to his appearances. My husband claims to have seen him from the driveway. He looked up and there was Tommy, glaring at him from one of the upstairs windows. That's my Mike. The thought of the Carolina Panthers having another losing season terrifies him more than seeing the ghost of a long-dead teenager.

But my eight-year-old, Stella, is another story. She started seeing him a few weeks ago. The first time, she woke up screaming about the scary boy standing at the foot of her bed. I wasn't ready to tell her his story, so I convinced her it was all a nightmare. Then I curled up next to her and held her until she went back to sleep.

The other night, she caught him looking over her shoulder while she was watching TV.

Remembering the awful horror of her screams still makes the hairs on my arms and neck stand on end. Finally, I decided to be truthful with her.

"Oh, Mama," she said, "can't you just tell him to go away?"

I felt so impotent. How do you tell your child that you can't protect her from a ghoul in her home? Or that we now share a common nightmare? I just pray that someday, somehow, I can help her find some peace and acceptance. Deep down, I wonder if I ever truly found either.

It's late. The lights are out. Mike and Stella have been asleep for hours. I'm waiting, listening. Trembling. I smell sour sweat. I'm not surprised by the sound of Stella's closet door squeaking open.

*Now you see him...*

# CRAIG'S CHAIR

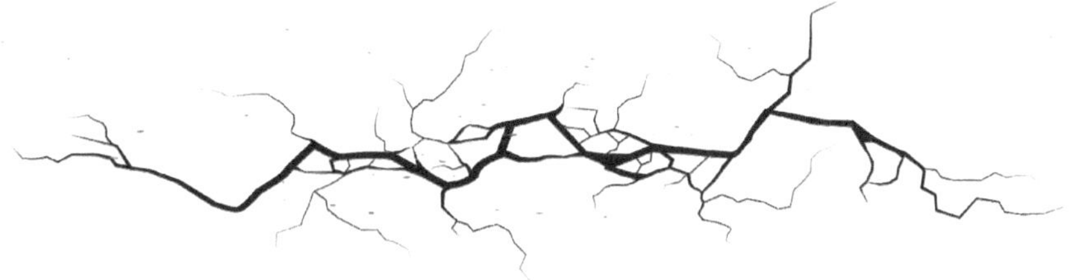

## 1

*The night shrouds the upstairs bedroom in darkness and shadows. Growling thunder rolls through the nighttime sky, punctuated by flashes of summer lightning. He's using his full body weight to hold her down on the bed. The pillow he's pressing to her face muffles her screams. She fights for her life, but he is relentless. After what seems like an eternity of horror, her body goes limp. The pillow lands on the floor. He didn't want to do this—murder his wife—but he had no choice. Its will was too great. He'll do anything to please it.*

*He hears a sound—a melody, perhaps. As though he's floating through a dream, he follows the sweet siren's call downstairs to his office where it waits with open arms.*

## 2

It was early April in the small southern town of Claxton, Georgia. The upscale neighborhood of Collinwood brimmed with vibrant flowers and small, white cherry blossoms that danced through the air like springtime snow. Old oak trees lined both sides of the narrow streets, their outstretched arms providing a lush canopy that shielded the residents from the sunlight like gentle green hands.

It was time for the annual citywide pickup of bulky items. Furniture, exercise equipment, and other large items covered the curbs and sidewalks. They were ripe pickings for poor people with trucks and vans; people like Craig.

Craig scoured the neighborhood looking for scrap metal—copper items were the best—and anything else that he might use or sell before the city hauled it away. *Yeah, baby!* he thought to himself. *There's money to be made, and beer to be bought!* Then he saw it: an attractive, brown leather chair that someone had placed near the curb with a few other odds and ends.

Craig parked his four-wheel rust bucket in front of the beautiful, whitewashed brick house with the For Sale sign and got out.

**TAKE!** That's what someone had written on the small sign taped to the chair's headrest. It astounded Craig that anyone would toss out such an amazing piece of furniture. *Are they serious?* he wondered. Then he took notice of the vacant house.

Although the artful exterior was stylish and attractive, its unkempt yard, with its tall grass and overgrown hedges, made it appear neglected, abandoned, and unloved. On the small stone porch, yellow police tape crisscrossed the front door. *What the hell happened here?* thought Craig.

He then went about inspecting the chair that someone had abandoned like a baby at a fire station. Save for a few worn spots on the armrests, it was in good condition. The thick, hand-stitched leather looked expensive. But Craig didn't much care for leather—it accentuated the loud detonations of butt bombs. He was partial to cloth upholstery, as it absorbed more of the blast. But there was something about this chair; something he felt he needed.

Craig wanted to take it on a test spin before putting it in the F-150. However, the thought of being seen sitting in it embarrassed him; he was poor but proud. He looked up and down the street for potential witnesses. Not seeing any, he lowered himself onto the seat. "Aaaaaah," Craig sighed, as the chair relaxed him to the point of sinfulness. He closed his eyes and let the world go crazy without him. The sensation had a transcendental effect; he felt weightless and calm. He smiled with satisfaction as he thought, *I wouldn't get up out of this sweet seat if Sofia Vergara came over, dropped her top, and begged me to motorboat her.*

Craig heard a garage door opening a few houses down and thought, *Crap! Let's get outta here. I'll look cheap and desperate.* He felt a twinge of resentment when he recalled that "cheap and desperate" were the words used by his first wife to describe how he'd looked on the night she met him.

After pulling himself up from the chair, he lifted it and hauled it to the truck, its lightness surprising him. He placed the leather prize in the truck bed and strapped it down with some of the bungee cords he kept in the cab. Grateful for his good fortune, Craig fired up his chariot of rust and headed for his double-wide castle on the hill.

3

Craig couldn't afford to park the double-wide in a trailer park, so he was thankful for the small plot of land his uncle, Bradley, had lent him. Without his generosity, Craig and Lorna, his second wife, would still live in the rent-by-the-hour room at Motel 666.

"Lord, Craig," moaned Lorna, "what have you drug home now?"

"Found it sittin' out front of one of them big houses in Collinwood. It'll give us somethin' better to sit on than that beat-up sofa and them two rickety lawn chairs."

"Maybe if you hadn't let Belinda take everything in the divorce, we wouldn't have to live in this dump. Hell, you're payin' child support for five young'uns, and one of 'em ain't even yours!"

"Which one?"

"I'm guessin' the Asian one, Craig. You got any more insightful questions?"

Craig let the hurtful remarks go. The reason he was in this mess had less to do with his ex-wife's vindictiveness than it did with his prolific marital infidelity. Lorna had a way of forgetting that. "It is what it is, Lorna. Now howzabout holdin' the storm door open?" Craig unhooked the bungee cords from the chair and lifted it out.

"Need some help?" Lorna asked halfheartedly.

"Nah, it's lighter than it looks." Craig bear-hugged the chair and toted it over the threshold of the trailer, as if it were a spring bride. Then he put it down and surveyed the small living area.

"Where ya want it?"

Lorna snatched up the two lawn chairs under the living room window and tossed them toward the wall. "Here's as good a place as any."

Craig did as instructed and placed the chair where Lorna had chosen. "Here, try it out. You won't believe how comfy it is."

Lorna dropped into the chair, prepared to be impressed. Instead, her smile evaporated and her eyes broadened. She catapulted herself out of the chair as though it had bitten her. "Oh my God!

This thing's freezin'! Just look at my nips—it looks like I'm smugglin' a pair of thimbles!"

"What the hell are you talkin' about, woman?" Craig took her place, preparing to have his butt cheeks turned into a couple of frozen fish sticks. It pleased him that the chair was still soft and agreeable. The differing experiences confounded him. "I don't understand your problem. This puppy feels like a hug from heaven."

Lorna pursed her lips in annoyance. "Get up and let me try it again."

Craig stood and let her have another go at his posh leather trophy.

The instant Lorna's butt connected with the seat cushion, she sprang from it as if she'd mistaken a bear trap for a toilet seat. She glared at Craig. "Can you not feel that? You mean to tell me this thing didn't turn your pecker into a popsicle?"

Craig was confused. It made him think back to a recent New Year's Eve party.

He'd gotten so drunk that he wandered off down the street, pissing his pants, and staggering around like Hunter Biden on his birthday.

He touched the seat of the chair—still toasty. "I don't get it, Lorna. It feels fine to me. Are you gettin' your period? Could be a woman thing."

Lorna gave him "The Look" to remind him she didn't get periods—she got exclamation points. "Period, shmeriod!" she barked. "This is officially your chair. I hope your ass and that cushion have a happy life together!" Then she stormed off, grabbed the keys to her orange 2002 Ford Fiesta—made in America, *by God!*—and headed out the door.

Craig followed her outside as if he'd tethered himself to a train. "Lorna, where you goin'?"

"To get some damn groceries. You drank almost all the PBR. And don't tell me you ain't been smokin' my cigarettes!"

Shame coursed through Craig's rail-thin body. He'd been sought, caught, and convicted. In the tense moment, he hated asking for anything, especially something embarrassing. "Could you pick up some Preparation-H? My butt's got company over and they're gettin' kind of rowdy. I'd like to be comfortable in the new chair."

Lorna threw her head back with a grunt. "Yeah, I'll get it. Anything else, your ass-holiness?"

Craig also wanted some Pop-Tarts, but he wasn't about to put his pecker on that power line again. "Nah, it's all good."

Lorna jumped into the pumpkin car, turning the engine over on the fifth try. Then she roared away, slinging gravel and dust in her wake, while the fan belt squealed like a hog in a wood chipper.

After watching her leave, Craig ambled back inside, wondering to himself, *If they call it Preparation-H, how badly must Preparations A—G have burned?*

4

Craig searched the kitchen for something to eat. It was now well into the early afternoon hours, and he'd had nothing since the stale Captain Crush cereal he'd eaten for breakfast. He hated the generic food that Lorna always got on the cheap at Costco. The brands had names that skirted the edges of copyright infringement: Dr. Popper soda, Aunt Geronimo syrup, Chef Homeboy-ee Spaghetti.

He settled on one of the freeze-dried turkey sandwiches that his Aunt Pauline had given him back in January. Stupid woman had gotten one of those freeze-drying machines for Christmas. Now, she freeze-dried everything, including one of her cats, who'd died from choking on a dead mouse. Craig still cringed at the memory of how the poor creature looked after Pauline had caved in its body using the Heimlich Maneuver. *More like the Heineken Maneuver, considering how drunk she was,* he thought.

After nuking the sandwich, he grabbed a can of Mountain Drew from the fridge and sat down at the wobbly table decorated with cigarette burns and water rings.

The sandwich was tolerable, the drink cold and delicious. The satisfying meal, along with the trailer's warmth, lulled him into a state of heavy drowsiness. Craig likened it to whenever he took three fingers of Nyquil; or, as he thought of it, the poor man's crack. He rose from the table and set upon the arduous five-yard journey to the living room.

Craig usually took his power naps in the bedroom, but today he wanted to break in the new, used chair. "Whoa, sweet mama," he moaned, as he nestled into the bosom of his dark leather lover. Then he closed his eyes and allowed the gentle pull of slumber to spirit him away.

5

*The music wakes him. He can't quite place the booming rock song. A voice breaks in as the tune is ending. "That's the new one from Loverboy: "Everybody's Working for the Weekend." "Stick around for—"*

*He switches off the stereo receiver. The room is hazy, and he feels as though he's walking through thick, swampy water. He doesn't recognize the house. It's bigger than the trailer; more opulent. The decor looks dated: late '70s, early '80s.*

*He enters the kitchen. It looks high end with stainless steel appliances, mahogany cabinets, and a granite-topped island at the center. He wanders around, looking for something; for what, he doesn't know. He walks to a cabinet and opens the second drawer from the top. It's full of kitchen utensils: spatulas, wooden mixing spoons, clips for chip bags. After moving the contents around, he finds what he's searching for. He pulls the corkscrew from the drawer and walks to the bay window over the porcelain farmhouse sink. He turns the corkscrew in the sunlight cascading through the window. It glitters in its golden rays.*

*"Honey, what are you doing?" a woman asks.*

*He turns to her and smiles.*

*"John, are you okay?"*

*He continues to smile as he goes to her and rams the corkscrew into her eye, twisting it until he feels it enter her brain. She drops to the floor in a lifeless heap, as he continues smiling.*

*Something unseen is pulling him, calling him. A gentle sound echoes from the wood-paneled den. There are no words, just a melody—and it's intoxicating. He must go to it. He cannot wait to fall back into its soft arms; arms of comfort, of dark dreams. He closes his eyes and—*

6

"Holy moly, rock 'n' rolly!" Craig hollered. He fell out of the chair and landed face-first on the cheap carpeting littered with corn dog sticks and toenail clippings. Peeling a stick off the side of his face, he muttered, "What the hell just happened?" He jumped to his feet and willed his heart to be calm, as adrenaline surged through his veins like jet fuel. He held his hands to his face and saw that they were pale and shaking. He was relieved to see that no blood and goo were on them.

He spun around, looking at his surroundings. He was happy to see the stack of dirty plates and bowls in the sink, along with the empty beer cans and eggshells on the kitchen counter. They never looked so good.

Craig plodded to the bathroom on wobbly legs and opened the closet door. Then he lifted the stack of towels in the left-hand corner of the upper shelf, grabbed the box of Marlboro Lights he'd pilfered from Lorna's secret stash, and shook out a cigarette. He pulled his Harley Davidson lighter from his pocket, lit the cig, and took a long drag. He blew the smoke through his nostrils and sighed. "Sweet child of mine; talk about a nightmare from hell."

Craig looked at the official NASCAR wall clock featuring Chase Elliott and saw that he'd been out for almost an hour. *Where's Lorna with the groceries?* he wondered. He fished his cellphone from his back pocket and called her. When she picked up, he said, "Where you at, woman? You've been gone forever."

"I had to run by work. Jade called from the hair salon and said Vonda showed up drunk again. She got woozy while she was cuttin' some gal's hair and puked all over her head. They needed help cleanin' up the mess before the cops came and the lawyers called."

Lorna was a hairstylist—code for a barber with boobs. The Snappy Snip was in a small, sketchy strip mall, next to a business that sold discount cigarettes. Lorna preferred the name brands. Since they cost more, she figured they were better for you. And with all the dumb crap going on at the shop daily, she needed them to keep herself calm and sane.

"So, when do you think you'll get home?" asked Craig "It shouldn't be too much longer. Why?"

"I need to take some stuff to the recycling center. I just didn't wanna miss ya."

"Can you get back by four?"

"No problemo. Actually, I'll probably beat ya there."

"See ya later, then."

Craig put the phone away and set about loading the scrap metal under the carport into his truck bed. Then he headed out, his Kenny Chesney CD blaring as he went.

7

A couple of hours later, Craig was heading back from the metal re-cycling center. He'd gotten twelve dollars for the beat-up barbecue grill and seven bags of soda cans. *Every bit helps,* he thought. It still bothered him that Lorna was the breadwinner in the marriage. But she was, after all, the brains of the outfit; no question there. It was just something he knew he'd have to make peace with.

When Craig got home, he stripped down to his drawers, grabbed a freeze-dried pickle to suck on, and plopped onto the chair. He shivered when he recalled the nightmare from earlier. *Second time's the charm*, he hoped.

He turned on the TV and found a show that didn't feature post-prison love affairs, rich social media influencers, or Mama June's big, sweaty ass.

Craig loved everything about the show, *Deadliest Catch* but the theme song: "Wanted Dead or Alive" by Bon Jovi. He had no respect for cutesy male bands that used more haircare products than his wife. Discovery Channel was running a marathon on the fishing show. However, not only could Craig not run a marathon, he couldn't stay awake for one on TV either.

Before you could say, "Alaskan king crab," he was floating on a tranquil river of dreams.

8

*He's awakened by the TV. The news is on. There are images of people running through clouds of dust, crumbling buildings, and New York City first responders scrambling. The voice on the news is describing a horrible plane crash—two, in fact.*

*It's dark outside. He looks at his watch and sees that it's after midnight. His wife and kids are asleep by now.*

*He rises from his chair. He doesn't recognize the room. He feels compelled to go to the garage. He's not sure why, but he knows it's important.*

*Now, he's standing in the dark garage. His fingertips brush over the wall and soon he finds a light switch and flips it on. An overhead light bulb blankets the space in a dull, yellow glow. Like a nail to a magnet, he's pulled to his workbench. He's not yet sure what he's looking for. He waves his hand over the many tools affixed to a swath of pegboard. His hand stops at a ball-peen hammer, like a divining rod when it locates water. Lifting it from its hook, he grips it hard and re-enters the house.*

*The narrow hallway has doors on either side. The one where his children are sleeping is where he enters. They don't stir, despite the door creaking. He's standing over the older boy, watching him, hating him. He doesn't know why. He wonders if it's love causing him to hesitate.*

*The child wakes up.*

*"Daddy, you scared me. Is everything okay? You look angry. Did I do something wrong?"*

*If he doesn't do it now, he never will. He lifts the hammer high, then—*

## 9

"Craig! Get your tail up and help me with these groceries!"

Craig jolted awake, hyperventilating and terrified. It took him a while to realize he was in his own home again. For once, it was nice to hear The Sarge yelling at him.

Lorna looked at him, her gaze filled with curiosity more than concern. "You all right? You look like you're on somethin'."

Craig struggled to speak. He felt as though he'd been stuck underwater, but had surfaced. When he caught his breath, he said, "I think so... I ain't sure. God, that was an awful nightmare."

"Tell ya what: Help me with the groceries, then you can tell me all about your nap-mare."

Craig shook some alertness back into his head like a dog shaking water off its coat. "Yeah, let's do that; let's grab the groceries." Then the unexpected happened: Craig did something that Lorna wanted him to do without complaining.

## 10

Craig helped Lorna unload and store the groceries. As he was placing the beer in the refrigerator, Lorna said, "Why don't you keep a couple out of them out? Let's hear about that bad dream you had. Was it the one where you realized it was it time to get an actual job?"

"That ain't funny, Lorna. That's twice today I've had a bad dream about killin' somebody."

"Killin' somebody? Killin' who? It better not be me or else you're gonna wake up on fire!"

"Did I say it was you?" Craig paused before sharing his story. He wanted to tell it plainly, accurately. "In the dream, I wake up in that chair, but in somebody else's body. I get up and notice that I'm in somebody else's house, too. Everything's takin' place in the past.

I can't explain why, but I feel drawn to certain rooms and things in 'em."

"Like what?"

"The first time, I murdered somebody with a corkscrew; a woman, I think. The next one..." Craig's emotions welled up inside of him, threatening to spill out, something he never wanted Lorna to see. "Lord, help me. I think I might've killed a child."

A part of Lorna wanted to laugh at Craig; another part made her afraid for him—of him. "Baby, they're just dreams. I'm pretty sure you ain't been goin' out and murderin' people."

"But they seemed so real. I could hear the sounds of the place; smell it, touch it. You don't think it's got anything to do with the chair, do ya?"

Lorna was skeptical. "How could it be the chair? It's just an old piece of furniture. Where'd you say you found it? Wasn't it sittin' in front of one of them nice houses in Collinwood?"

"Yeah. It was just sittin' there like it was waitin'."

"Waitin' for what?"

"Maybe for somebody to take it home. I know that sounds weird, but there's somethin' off about that dang chair."

"What d'ya mean?"

"Remember how cold it was when you sat in it? It was as if it didn't want you there. But for some reason, it welcomed me."

Craig followed Lorna's eyes to the chair. "Have you touched it again?" she asked.

"Not since I got up to help you with the groceries. Should we test it?"

Lorna nodded. "Go on, try it."

Craig put his beer down and walked toward the chair. He moved like a condemned man heading to the gallows.

He cautiously lowered his hand to the armrest as if he were checking a stove burner for heat. "It's still warm. Come on over and feel it."

Lorna joined Craig. She touched the cushion and exhaled sharply, the cold alarming her. "Whoa! I think you might inadvertently be right—this thing ain't normal."

"Should we get rid of it? I can dump it on the side of the road somewhere."

"Alrighty, then. You open the door and I'll tote it to the truck." Craig bent over and put his arms around the chair. Suddenly, he stood and yelped—the chair was freezing. He waved his arms, trying to shake off its icy sting.

"What happened?" asked Lorna.

"Thing's colder than a polar bear's balls!"

Lorna gave things a quick think. "You don't suppose it's startin' to hate you, too, do ya?"

"More reason to get rid of it." A 20-watt lightbulb snapped on in Craig's head. "Go fetch me a blanket."

It was Lorna's turn to follow orders, something she didn't mind doing right now. She went to the hall closet, retrieved a thick blanket, then returned to the living room. She tossed it to Craig, who wrapped it around the front of the chair. "You need help to lift it?" she asked.

"Nah. I remember it was pretty light. Just hold the door open, and stand back."

As Lorna went to take care of the storm door, Craig squatted and wrapped his arms around the chair.

"Okay, let's try her again." This time, his hands slipped off—the chair had become heavy. On the next attempt, he tightened his grip. Then he pushed his leg muscles to their limit, grunting from the effort. The chair remained adhered to the carpet, like a boulder resting in cement.

"How come you can't you lift it?" Lorna asked.

"It's like pullin' on the leash of a dog that won't come. I ain't sure, but I think we pissed it off. Let's see if we can raise it together. I'll drape the blanket over it, then we'll get on each side and lift."

Lorna locked the pneumatic bar on the door to keep it open and joined Craig. Although she dreaded touching the chair again, she resolved to help him remove it. They knelt, preparing themselves for the heavy task. "I'm ready when you are," she said.

"Okay, when I say go, we'll pick it up and carry it outside to the truck. Ready... GO!"

They gritted their teeth as they strained to rise; sweat trickled down their overburdened bodies in salty rivulets. After great exertion, they raised the chair and carried it out of the trailer, fighting the weighty beast toward the truck.

Once it was loaded, Craig, panting and exhausted, wiped his wet forehead with his shirtsleeve. "Praise the Lord, and pass the nachos! Looks like we did it, sugar tits!"

Lorna gave him "The Look" again. "What'd I tell you about callin' me that? If I wasn't so damn wore out, I'd open up an extra-large, hot 'n spicy, chunky style jar of whup-ass on your skinny hide!"

"Sorry, *booger bits*," joked Craig. "What say we go drop this big, brown turd in the mud?"

Lorna slapped her hands together and hollered, "Sounds like a game plan, Coach! Put me in!"

11

They drove until they hit Old Richmond Road, a two-lane relic a few miles down from the trailer. Craig pulled over to a soft shoulder and put on the parking brake, leaving the engine running.

"Let's git 'er done," Craig said.

Lorna, now back to her perpetual state of crankiness, replied, "How very original. You should sell that line to a comedian."

Craig shook off the insult, as he had done many others like it. "Hop in the back and we'll slide this sucker out."

They crawled into the truck bed and pushed for everything they were worth. The chair felt like it was fighting them every step, but Craig and Lorna's will proved greater. After one final shove, the evil object toppled off the tailgate and landed in the dirt.

While Craig struggled with the busted latch on the tailgate, Lorna sprinted to the truck cab like Honey Boo Boo chasing down an ice cream truck. Soon, Craig joined her and they took off like a scalded dog.

"Woo-wee!" whooped Craig. "I feel better already! Why don't we have ourselves a little celebration?"

"Amen to that! When we get back, I propose we take us a big ol' snort of some firewater."

"I heard that—hellooo Nyquil!"

Except for the time he'd threatened to kill himself, Craig had never seen Lorna happier.

12

A few hours after forgetting that NyQuil is a medication and not a beverage, Craig and Lorna fell into bed. Although stoned from the great, green syrup, Craig was struggling to fall asleep. Lorna, on the other hand, was dead to the world, her C-PAP humming quietly on the nightstand. *At least her facemask will keep one of her ends from snoring,* Craig thought.

He watched the ceiling fan rotate, using his mind to see if he could make it look like it was moving in the opposite direction. As midnight morphed into the early morning, the *whup-whup* of the ceiling fan—coupled with his nervous exhaustion—lulled Craig to sleep.

13

*A soft hum coming from the living room awakens Craig. He gets out of bed, trying not to disturb Lorna. He feels uneasy, but his mind compels him to investigate.*

*As he walks down the short hallway, the sound becomes a melody that both haunts and allures him. He cannot turn away from it.*

*Craig enters the living room and sees the chair resting under the window as if it had never left. He should tremble with terror; instead, a warm wave of serenity washes over him. The awful object that had earlier repelled him is welcoming him again. All he wants, all he desires, is sitting before him. He has only to go out to the tool shed and find the hacksaw and a large screwdriver.*

## 14

Donald was heading back to the cabin after inspecting the construction site. His retirement from the firm was just a few happy steps away. He was ecstatic when he and Kathy had pulled the trigger on the place near the lake. He could already feel the sun on his back, the rod in his hands, and the fish on the hook. The ding of the dash-mounted cellphone interrupted his reverie. He glanced at the screen and saw that it was Terry, the project supervisor, calling him. He punched the hands-free button and answered. "Hi, Terry. Let me guess: Carnihan's not on board with the plan."

"Wow! You must be psychic. Listen, he wants to sit down with us and—"

"Terry, let me call you back." Donald ended the call, then slowed down to get a better look at the brown leather chair on the side of the road. With some uneasiness, he recalled that a gruesome murder/suicide had taken place not too far from here.

He parked his truck, then got out and approached the discarded item. "This thing's in pretty damn good shape," he said. "Welcome to the new man cave!"

The lightness of the chair surprised him as he lifted it and carried it to the rear of his truck. "This ought to be easy enough," he said, as he set the chair down. He was about to drop the tailgate when he noticed something flapping on the plush headrest. "Say, what's this?" It was a small, damp piece of paper. On it, someone had written, **TAKE!**

# IT CRIES AT NIGHT

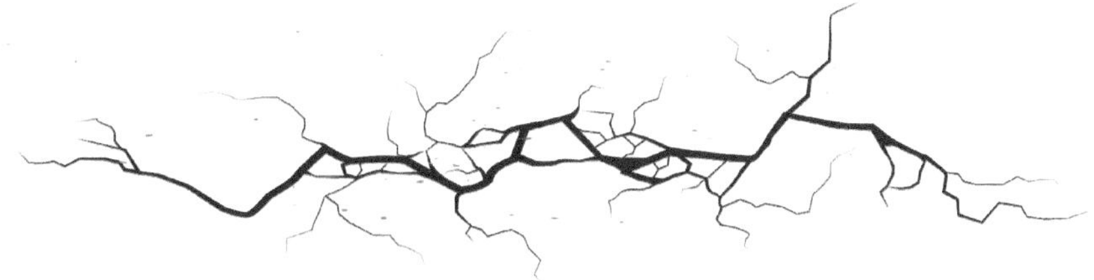

1

Cara's life was pinwheeling at the edge of a cliff. Soon, it would plummet into an endless freefall.

The new baby that Kevin and she had expected to unite them failed to survive its first breath. The infant was going to be an answer to Cara's silent prayers for a healthy baby girl. When the doctor informed them that Cara couldn't have kids anymore, Kevin left. Like a dissatisfied customer, he exchanged the damaged product he'd initially purchased for a better, more reliable one. Unfortunately, Cara ended up being the broken item and Elise was the better option.

Cara didn't have a husband, child, or life anymore. The daughter she'd dreamed of having would never feel her mother's warmth, nor hear her lullabies. She was alone in a quiet McMansion with an empty nursery. To occupy her free time, she watched television and emptied several cardboard boxes of wine from Costco's fertile vineyards.

One day, bored, Cara curled up on the pricey leather couch Kevin made her get. Setting her glass of wine on the coffee table, she picked up the remote. "So, what's rockin' on Netflix? There's always somethin' good, right? She skipped past the TV shows and movies that didn't interest her and looked for something more intellectually stimulating: documentaries.

The first few selections didn't impress her: *History of The Rolling Stones* "Before my time."

*The Roman Aqueduct System* "Who cares?"

*The '70s in Review* "What were we thinking, then?"

She scrolled through several titles until she found one that had potential. The promo pic showed a man assembling a doll. The title was *Birth of the Synthetic Child*.

"Hello. What's this one?" Cara read its synopsis.

*Skilled artists create them. Collectors buy them. Parents without children interact with them. This documentary looks at the world of realistic, interactive dolls.*

Cara clicked on the documentary, took a sip of wine, and got comfortable.

In the opening scene, a young woman was sitting in a nursery. Everything was in slow motion. She was wearing a flowing white gown and seated in a rocking chair. The soft sunlight streaming in through the room's window cast an ethereal, golden-hued glow. The woman was cradling a newborn. A gentle swirl of calming mood music permeated the setting.

A scene with a man sitting at a worktable came next. The artisan was weaving hair into a doll's scalp. Sequences of him inserting eyes that opened and shut, along with bending the doll's joints into lifelike poses, followed this.

"These are the highly skilled artists who meticulously create realistic babies," the narrator said. "The infants are so rich in their detail that doll collectors buy them by the dozens. Many psychologists claim synthetic replacements can often be therapeutic for women who have lost a child or who cannot conceive."

Next came somber interviews with young couples who'd lost an infant. Their poignant stories moved Cara. She held back a cascade of thick tears as she found her heart overtaken with sympathy. However, listening to their happy testimonials about having welcomed a synthetic child into their lives brought about another emotion: hope. Cara noted the company's name: New Birth.

*Whaddaya think, girl?* She opened a middle drawer in the coffee table, pulled out a pen and notepad, and jotted down the company's name. Then she laid the information on the coffee table to rest while she gave the idea some thought.

2

After a few days, Cara decided to put an end to her self-pity. Before she could change her mind, she marched into Kevin's former home office and fired up the PC. Her hands paused over the keyboard. "Oh, just do it!" she ordered herself. She googled the company's name and watched the computer's small colorful wheel spin until it located New Birth's website.

The main page displayed a full-screen picture of a sleeping infant nestled in a crib. Cara flipped through a few dozen photos before stopping at a picture of a female doll. Its face, with its look of pure innocence, was mesmerizing. Its fingers were curled and delicate, just like those of a real infant. Enthralled, Cara ran her fingertip over the image, tracing an imaginary line around its bright, open eyes and dark strands of auburn hair. She remembered the soul-deep smiles of the young couples in the documentary. She told herself that she wasn't purchasing a toy—she was searching for a daughter. *I know it's weird, but...*"

Cara moved on to the site's checkout page. She read all the purchasing information as quickly as possible; to her, they were simply words on a page. She was eager to get to the critical part: bringing the baby home. At the end of the agreement, New Birth suggested that customers complete a complimentary birth certificate that accompanied each doll, its purpose being to add an emotional element to the experience. The document requested the name of the newborn. Cara didn't expect this formality. She sat with her lips pursed in thought.

Then it hit her: the storage box in the attic. It contained a shortlist of names that she'd packed away, along with the other baby items she could never bring herself to throw out. *The name on the list that caught my attention—what was it?* She closed her eyes until it popped out as if it were born. "Aimee. Your name is Aimee."

Based on the company's shipping schedule, Cara's chosen model was unavailable and it would take a minimum of six weeks before they could ship the order. Therefore, the package that greeted her the next morning caught her off guard.

3

Cara wasn't expecting any deliveries, yet there was a small cardboard box at her feet. She searched her mind, making certain that she hadn't forgotten a previous purchase—she hadn't. Someone might have sent her a gift. *Who'd send me a present out of the blue? My birthday's not til November.* There wasn't a return label, only her mailing info. An idea sprang to her mind, and she beamed. "Oh, wait. It can't be the doll. Oh, but I bet it is. I wasn't expecting you for a while, she said to the box. I suppose this early arrival qualifies you as a preemie." Trembling with anticipation, she took the item inside.

Cara toted the package into the dining room and placed it on the table. Then she went into the kitchen, retrieved a pair of scissors from the catchall drawer, and prepared herself to meet her mail-ordered daughter.

Cara thought of a shallow grave when she looked down at the packing peanuts. The thought chilled her. She began clawing to rescue the infant from its cardboard casket. She placed her hands under its arms and yanked it out.

"Well, here we are, you and me. Sooo... howzabout the nickel tour? This is the dining room where we dine. Through there is the living room where we live. And this doorway leads into the kitchen where we... kitch." At the last line, Cara giggled until she snorted. "Oh, excuse me. I haven't heard that sound in ages." She studied the face of the rubber child. "I'm insane, aren't I? Well, if we're gonna do this, let's go all in."

Although awkward at first, she cradled the doll in her arms and began swinging it gently back and forth. Then, looking at its clothes, cringed. "Only a man could pick this outfit. We've got to remedy this once we get you settled in. Let's check out your room."

She carried Aimee upstairs and entered the nursery. Everything was just as she and Kevin left it after they'd decorated. The pleasant morning sunlight cascaded in, minute dust particles dancing rhythmically in its warm rays. It reminded her of the happy young mother in the documentary.

Cara sauntered to the rocking chair next to the window, easing herself and the new infant down into its soft comfort. With Aimee's head resting on her shoulder, Cara rocked for several minutes before laying the doll inside the crib.

Cara stopped and turned. An unexpected peace fell upon her, as hope wrested joy from her marred spirit, returning it to her again and again in endless abundance. Life and love filled her, the closed door of her heart fully open, fully free. She smiled. *Welcome home, baby girl.*

4

Cara devoted herself to taking care of the doll. Feedings, baths, and nursery songs filled the time in a way that lounging in front of the TV couldn't.

With Aimee snuggled in a papoose, Cara shopped for clothes, toys, and bottles to add to the baby supplies already stored in the attic. She bought formula, as the anatomically correct model could pretend to urinate. Likewise, its eyes and mouth opened based on its position, making feedings possible.

The approving glances of the passersby encouraged and amused Cara, as they seemed to enjoy the believable sight of a doting mother carrying her child.

Shortly after returning home, Cara placed the bags of baby items on the dining room table, removed one of the new pairs of pajamas, then took Aimee to the nursery.

After dressing Aimee, Cara took a picture with her phone to see how the sleepwear looked. "Ooh, momma's girl looks so cute," she cooed. "I'm gonna get some formula for your tummy, then sing your favorite lullaby. But first, I give you the greatest kiddies' band on Earth: The Wiggles!" She turned on the cd player and left.

Cara went downstairs and began warming some formula in the microwave. She swayed in time with the Wiggles, humming along with their upbeat version of "Itsy Bitsy Spider."

Abruptly, the song stopped midway through a verse. The house became still and silent, the lone ticking of the wall clock adding to its eeriness. Cara went upstairs to check things out.

The room was as she'd left it. *Was that the end of the CD?* She went to the dresser and saw that the player was in the off position. She pressed the play button, and the song picked up where it had stopped. *Must be defective.* Cara hit the stop button and went to the crib. "Did you tire of The Wiggles? I'm getting a little sick of them, too."

Staring into the crib, she noticed the onesie pajamas Aimee was wearing seemed to be too snug for her. "What's this all about?" Upon closer inspection, she discovered that the fabric around the wrists and ankles had shortened. "Hmmm, I could've sworn they fit. Next time, check the size, dummy."

Although she'd rationalized the CD and the pajamas, Cara still felt uneasy. To *hell with the formula—this tired momma needs to burn off some stress.*

Speaking to the doll, she said, "We'll just hold on to the formula and go to sleep, little Miss Thang." She bent down and kissed the sleeping child on her soft forehead. Then, keeping the nursery neat, she straightened the stuffed toys in the crib. "Sleep tight, Mommy's girl," she whispered before leaving the room.

Cara went downstairs and rode the Peloton for an hour. Afterward, she went to the kitchen, sliced a grapefruit in half, and sat down for a light lunch. When she finished, she returned upstairs to dress Aimee so she could take her to the park and enjoy some fresh air and sunlight.

As soon as Cara entered the room, she stopped. Aimee was sitting up, her head facing the door. Someone had scattered the stuffed toys across the floor. Cara shivered, as her imagination toyed with her. *God, please don't let anyone be up here.* She worked up her courage and stepped into the hall.

"Hey! Is anybody up here? I'm calling the police! Nothing stirred, but she stayed put. Cautiously, she checked upstairs but found no one. *God, I must be losing my mind.* It took a while for her nervousness to ebb. "Time to get out of this house and relax. But first..."

Cara was relieved to have the various-sized garments she had acquired for her biological daughter to fit into. After selecting a few outfits from the attic, she returned to the nursery and dressed Aimee. Then they went to the park, a mother and her child.

5

It was a warm June morning, the sun's rays bright but gentle. Cara was sitting on a worn park bench, pushing the baby carriage back and forth, humming with every motion. The sound of fresh summer air tickling the leaves of the surrounding trees, coupled with the joyful squeals of children on swings and merry-go-rounds, created a soothing symphony of life. *I'll bet the first sound you hear in heaven is the laughter of little children,* she thought. Someone called out, pulling her thoughts back to the wooden bench. "I'm sorry, what?"

Two benches down, a thirty-ish-looking woman was waving to get her attention. A younger woman was sitting to her right. "Down here," the older woman said. "I haven't seen you before. Judging by the stroller, I'm guessing you're a new mom."

"Yes, I am," Cara said. "I'm a first-timer. I take it you guys come here often."

"Yep, we're two of the regulars. I'm Cathy. I own the boy in the Paws Patrol t-shirt and the girl in the chocolate-stained jeans."

The younger woman leaned around her companion. "Hi, I'm Mary Beth. I'm an au pair for the wild child in the over-priced Baby Gap overalls. Hey, it was this job or dog-walking," she joked.

"Nice to meet you," Cara said. "I'm Cara. This is my daughter, Aimee."

"Welcome to our world," said Mary Beth. "Mind if we take a peek?"

Cara hesitated, concerned that the women would think her odd. "Gee, I don't know. She's napping right now. I don't want to wake her."

"We'll be quiet," said Cathy. "We promise."

Cara tensed, her nerves clawing at her stomach. "I don't know. Once you wake her, it's—"

"Don't worry," Cathy assured her. "We're experts at not waking sleeping children. How else will we have any peace?"

Mary Beth laughed, shaking her head in agreement.

Before Cara could protest again, the women approached her. They both beamed as they surrounded the stroller. For a few seconds, the authenticity of the doll fooled them.

Mary Beth was the first to notice. "What the...?" she said. "What is wrong with you? This isn't a real baby."

"Let me look," Cathy said, pulling back the thin pink blanket concealing the pretend child. Her eyes broadened, a combination of surprise and confusion. "Are you frickin' kidding me?"

Cara felt the heat of their judgment. "You don't understand," she huffed. "Look, I know this appears—"

"You need to go," Cathy said backing away, as if Cara were an axe-wielding maniac.

"All right, I just want to—"

"I mean *NOW!*" barked Cathy.

The lively park came to a halt as people watched the commotion. A man who'd been swinging his little boy looked in Cara's direction, suspicion blazing in his glaring eyes.

Cara rushed from the park. In the distance, she heard Cathy yell, "You freak!"

6

Cara walked around her neighborhood for hours, hoping the exertion would de-stress her from the humiliating incident at the park. Remembering the reactions of the park dwellers, she became angry. Who were they to judge her? Had they let go of a dream that would never come true? A life without a child? As darkness hovered in the distance, Cara was to the point of tiredness.

She entered the house, parked Aimee's carriage in the foyer, and carried her upstairs, giving her some comforting taps on her back. "Shhhh. It's all right now, sweet girl."

Cara switched out the doll's outfit for a fresh pair of floral pajamas. After singing and rocking her, Cara went to the kitchen and had a glass of wine.

She entered the bedroom, removed her cell phone from her purse, and checked her emails.

There was only one: New Birth. She opened the email, thinking it contained additional billing information.

*Dear Ms. Kincaid, We have an update on your order #62589. Our supplier has informed us it will be an additional two weeks before they can ship the product. We apologize for the inconvenience and deeply appreciate your patience. A representative will be in touch as soon as the product becomes available.*

*Most sincerely, Donna James Regional Sales Manager*

"That can't be right." Cara wondered if she should bother to correct their error. Would it be so bad to let them send Aimee a free sister? Her conscience won out. "No sense in letting them think they screwed up." She wanted to take care of the problem now, so she wouldn't forget.

*Dear Ms. James, Thank you for reaching out to me; however, there appears to be a mistake. I received my doll the morning after placing the order on June 9. Please cancel the shipment.*

*Sincerely, Cara Kincaid*

Cara hit send, then plugged the phone into the charger on her nightstand. After reading a few chapters of a James Patterson novel, she called it a night. She was reaching for the lamp when the phone dinged. She squinted her bleary eyes and saw she had another email from New Birth. "Why are they responding so late?" Then she remembered they were on west coast time. She opened the email.

*Dear Ms. Kincaid, Thank you for letting us know about the delivery. However, in correcting our oversight, I found that we have shipped none of those models for a couple of weeks.*

*I checked with our manager in Shipping and Receiving and he assures me that his records do not show a shipment of the order. To confirm the status of model H-236, he searched our warehouse but did not find any in stock. Also, we have no record of another model being shipped by mistake. We're not sure where the error lies. In the meantime, I'll cancel the delivery of your doll. Thank you for your patronage.*

*Gratefully, Donna James Regional Sales Manager*

"Don't say I didn't warn you." Cara felt the urge to look at the pictures she'd taken of Aimee earlier. Happiness warmed her as she swiped each picture until coming to one shot in particular.

Something looked strange about the pajamas, so she zoomed in. Confusion struck her when she saw it fit the doll. Her neck tingled. "Things are getting weird around here." Cara wondered if the newness in her life was making her forget things. She was ready to get up and take care of the issue, but exhaustion from the day had drained her of all her strength. "Tomorrow, crazy doll lady," she muttered, "tomorrow."

She returned the phone to its charger, switched off the light, and fell asleep thinking of Aimee.

7

Cara had been out for hours when a high, whiny sound woke her. She lifted her head from her pillow and listened. Silence. Believing it had all been a dream, Cara let her head rest on her pillow again. She inhaled deeply and let out a long breath, returning to sleep.

The noise woke her again. This time, she got up to investigate.

Cara opened the bedroom door, stuck her head out, and listened. Groggily, she attempted to determine the source of the sound. She considered the air-conditioning. Then she wondered if the hall's smoke detector was malfunctioning. A chill coursed through her body as she finally placed the noise. A baby was crying, and the sound was coming from the nursery.

Cara drifted dreamlike down the hall, following the wail. The closer she got, the more distressed the weeping became, unnerving her. When she arrived at the nursery's door, she reached for the knob but was afraid to touch it; her hand shook. She readied herself, then threw open the door. The room went silent. Adrenaline sharpened her senses, allowing her to think more clearly. *This is so, so crazy. You're just getting too caught up in this fantasy life.*

The weak glow of the pink elephant nightlight illuminated some of the quiet room. Cara crept to the crib and peeked in. The doll was lying on its back, its eyes closed. To ensure that she'd not taken leave of her senses, Cara poked the infant with her index finger, then snatched it back. She chuckled with relief when nothing sinister happened. "Time to cut back on the ol' vino," she joked.

Then, "Stupid air conditioner. I'll deal with you tomorrow." She turned to leave. "G'night, kiddo."

"Mommy."

Cara stopped. An icy wave of goosebumps washed over her skin. Her lips quivered; her legs ceased to work.

"Mommy, take me."

Cara remained motionless, adhered to the floor by naked terror.

"Mommy. Mommy. *MOMMY-MOMMY-MOMMMEEE!*

Cara's piercing scream filled the haunted nursery. Horrified, she fled to her bedroom. She slammed the door shut and backed away, tripping over the corner of her bed. Falling backward, her head struck the nightstand, spiraling her down into empty darkness.

8

The morning sun streamed through the bedroom window and gradually made its way to Cara's face. She pulled herself up to a sitting position, her tired eyes blinking. She struggled to remember how she'd ended up on the floor. Cara winced as she touched the small lump on the back of her head. She enjoyed a brief respite from the previous night's disturbance before the memory exploded in her frazzled mind. "No, no, no," she mumbled. Once she collected herself, she set about doing the one thing that terrified her most: checking on Aimee.

The short walk to the nursery felt like a surreal and perpetually stretching journey as her uncooperative feet slid over the hall's thin runner.

her lungs. She peered inside, not sure of what might happen. The protective skirting obscured the view of the inner crib, forcing her to move closer. Frigid sweat moistened her gown.

Cara looked inside at the doll. With its clothing ripped away, it resembled a watermelon that someone had tried to force into a banana peel. Aimee had grown at least a foot taller. The soft tufts of her auburn hair were now fuller and longer.

*What in the world is happening?* She considered running from the house, but she'd already convinced enough people she was crazy. A public outburst about haunted dolls would land her in the psych ward.

*Oh, God. I've gotta do this. I've gotta know for certain.* Cara took three quavering breaths, then picked Aimee up, lifting her to face level. She jerked when its eyes popped open. "Aimee?" she whispered to the toddler.

"Yes, Mommy?" it said through lips that moved stiffly, like a ventriloquist's dummy.

Cara gasped in surprise. Trying to remain composed, she talked as calmly as she could. "What do you want from me?"

"I need new clothes, Mommy," it replied in a tender voice. "I'm feeling cold. Oh, and I'm hungry. *Very... huuun-greee...*" it growled.

Cara didn't want to panic; she was afraid of what might happen if she tried to run away again. Her voice shook as she spoke. "Tell you what, sweetie. You... you just lie back down. I'll g-get you some breakfast and find something to fit you. Then... then we'll shop for some n-new clothes."

She returned Aimee to her crib and backed out of the room, fearful of turning her back to the possessed toy.

Cara went to the kitchen—*where we kitch*—she remembered. This time, she didn't laugh. What could she feed the doll? Would it want solid food? She remembered a box of Honey Nut Cheerios in the pantry. After pouring some into a bowl, she laid it on the highchair's tray.

Though her legs wobbled, Cara negotiated the staircase, each step propelling her to the room where the haunted doll sat waiting, hungry. Alive.

Once there, Cara began dressing Aimee in a bigger outfit. Tense with terror, she expected the thing to scream at her or grab her arm.

With Aimee now clothed, she carried her to the stairs, holding her away from her body as though she were toting a wild, flailing animal. *If this thing talks to me while I'm going down these stairs, I'm gonna fall to my death.*

Cara was glad that Aimee was still small enough to fit in her highchair. *How am I supposed to feed solid food to a doll?* She pulled in a trembling breath. "Can you chew your food, Aimee? Would you rather Mommy fed you some formula?" The doll didn't answer; its lifeless eyes stared into Cara's. She waited for a response, but none came.

*BING!* The doorbell sent a zap of adrenaline through Cara's body. Her quickened heartbeat thumped in time with her desperate breathing. Despite her fear, it occurred to her that opening the door might provide her with a brief opportunity to escape. She waited for her breaths to slow before speaking. "It's okay, baby. Mommy will be right back."

As if reading her thoughts, Aimee said, "Don't you run away from home, Mommy. That would make me so sad... *and angry.*"

Cara shivered. Could the doll somehow follow her? Was it able to strike her dead with a single murderous thought? Was any of this real? She was too terrified to risk escape. Still, she yearned to experience the real world again—the one where humans were humans and dolls were dolls. "Mommy's not going anywhere... I-I promise."

Cara trotted to the door and peered through the peephole.

Standing on the stoop was a young African-American woman dressed in an attractive, thin- strapped summer dress. Cara didn't recognize her. With escape now out of the question, she decided it was best to ignore her and return to the kitchen. Still, she craved a taste of normalcy, if only to ensure that she wasn't suffering from a psychotic episode. Cara didn't want to rouse Aimee's suspicions, so she prepared herself before answering the door.

"Oh, hi," the woman said pleasantly. "I hope I didn't bother you in the middle of something."

"Uh... no, not at all. Um, who are you?"

"I'm so sorry. My name is Evelyn. And you are?"

"Cara... Cara Kincaid. I'm sorry, but what's this about?" Her voice quavered, her nerves betraying her.

"Well, first, hi there, Cara. I'm a member of Macedonia Baptist Church down on Broad Street. I'm just visiting our neighbors in the community to invite them to our worship service. May I ask if you're a believer?"

"You've no idea what I've come to believe these last few days," Cara said, a sob getting away from her.

"Is everything okay?" asked Evelyn. "You look pale, sweetie. Maybe I should come back another time when you're—"

"Oh, no!" Cara yelped. She needed to get a grip on herself, or the woman would leave her alone with whatever was waiting in her kitchen. In a more relaxed tone, she said, "I mean, please come in. I'd be happy to have a visitor. Things have been a bit unsettling lately. With you being a person of faith, I'd love to get your perspective on something... supernatural."

Evelyn felt uneasy. "Oh, I don't think I should offer any advice on—"

"I'm so sorry. I can see that I've made you uncomfortable. It's a lot to ask of a stranger, but I can use a friend. I need you to—I mean, I'd *like* you—to stay for a minute. You can meet my daughter."

"Well... okay," Evelyn said with some hesitation.

Evelyn entered the house and looked around carefully, as if she might trigger a trap. "So, how old's your child?"

"Right now? About two, I think. Just follow me. She's in the kitchen eating some Cheerios."

"Oh, yeah; kids your daughter's age sure like to nibble on some Cheerios. Say, what'd you mean when you said you 'think' she's about two?"

"She grows in a hurry." Cara tried not to appear frightened. "Come on. She's just in here."

Aimee was sitting in her highchair, older and more developed. Her clothes were cutting into her body. She looked about four years old, her hair nearly shoulder length. The bowl of cereal was empty.

Evelyn stood next to Cara, speechless. She stared at the faux child, then moved her eyes to observe Cara. She couldn't help thinking that she might be one of those unfortunate individuals who find themselves in the wrong place at the wrong time. "Sooo... this here's your daughter?"

Cara's eyes grew moist, her lips struggling to keep another sob at bay. "Evelyn, let me ask you a serious question, and in return, I'd like your most candid and heartfelt answer."

"'Kay."

"Do you think it's possible to love something into existence? Seriously, think about it. The Bible says that God breathed life into a mound of dust and created humankind. See, I wanted a baby very much, so I bought this online. Since yesterday, she's gone from being a infant to a preschooler. You think I'm crazy, don't cha, Evelyn?"

"Well, just let me say—"

"Oh, it's okay. I'd think I was bat crap crazy, too. So, in answer to my question..."

Evelyn constructed her response carefully. "I think... I think with God, all things are possible. But listen—Cara, right? You might want to talk to someone else. I could have my pastor put you in touch with somebody who could help you deal with this."

Cara exhaled nervously, shaking her head, then locked eyes with Evelyn. "Come with me. I want to show you something. Don't worry, I won't attack you or anything. I just need to know if I'm the only person who thinks this is real."

Evelyn hesitated.

Cara pressed harder. "Please, just let me show you something on the computer. It's the site where all of this began. Just look at it, for my sake. Please, Evelyn."

"Okay. Show me the site. I'll help you if I can."

Cara walked to the office with Evelyn trailing behind her. Stepping behind the desk, she turned on the computer. When she arrived at the New Birth website, she waved Evelyn over.

Cara flipped through the images until she came across Aimee's. "Okay, this is the place where I bought it."

Evelyn pointed at the screen, her brow furrowed. "So you're saying that this," then pointing toward the kitchen, said, "grew into that?"

"Not only that. Here, check this out. See? Just below the image? It says the company's warehouse is out of stock, and that it'll be weeks before they get any more in. Evelyn, she arrived the day after I placed the order—the very next day. Where did it come from? Not from New Birth. They swore they never sent her. Evelyn, with God as my witness, that baby appeared out of nowhere and came alive. It cried at first, then it started talking, and now it's almost ready to start kindergarten. Do you think you can help me understand what's happening here? I've been through a lot in the last year or so. I lost my baby, and my cheating and self-serving husband left me for another woman. And now—"

A crash came from the kitchen. Evelyn ran there first, with Cara just behind her.

A four-foot-high doll with a sinister grin, wearing the tattered remnants of its prior clothing, was standing in front of the overturned highchair.

"I gotta get out of here!" Evelyn yelled.

"No! Evelyn, stay with me!" Cara's desperate pleas echoed through the foyer as Evelyn ran from the house. "Evelyn!" she hollered again, to no avail. Cara realized she was on her own and would have to save herself. She needed to act fast before the doll became dangerous.

Desperate and terrified, she slammed the front door and ran back to the kitchen. Her immediate plan was to grab the doll, throw it down the basement stairs, and lock the deadbolt. She hoped it might buy her enough time to figure out a safe way to destroy it.

Upon reaching the kitchen, Cara stopped so abruptly that she skidded and fell. Then she screamed.

9

Evelyn was still distraught when she returned to the house later with Reverend Jones. She hoped he didn't think she was having a nervous breakdown, or worse, high on drugs. She was relieved when, after hearing her rambling account of the events, he agreed to help her.

Evelyn followed Reverend Jones to the front door of the house she'd fled in terror. Her breath hitched when he rang the doorbell. "I hope you'll believe me, Pastor. I'm telling you, there's some sort of devil's play going on in this house. Please don't think I'm crazy. I promise you, I'm not. I know I'm not!"

"Evelyn," Reverend Jones interjected, "I never said that you're crazy. I know something happened to you this morning. I just want to sort this out. Look, if it's any consolation, I once—"

Someone unlocking the door interrupted his train of thought. When it opened, Reverend Jones smiled and said, "Hello, ma'am. I'm Reverend Michael Jones from Macedonia Baptist Church. One of my flock—Evelyn here—said that you might require some help. May we come in?"

"Now's not the best time, Reverend. I'm in the middle of cleaning up a mess in the kitchen."

"I see. Maybe we could stop by when it's more convenient, Ms...."

Evelyn's face became a petrified mask of horror as the woman with long auburn hair answered, "Aimee. Just call me Aimee."

# YOU NEVER CAN TELL

1

*R**ing! Ring!* sang the doorbell.

"Okay, he's here," Sara said, through breaths of excitement. "Please, everyone, be on your best behavior."

"Sara, relax," said her father, Bill. "He isn't the first boy you've brought home. Everything'll be fine."

"Yes, sweetie," said Connie, her doting mother. "Tonight will go smoothly; we promise. Right, Bill?"

"I'm not making any promises yet."

"Oh, Bill, don't make this uncomfortable for Sara."

*Ring! Ring!* the doorbell repeated.

"Okay, here goes," Sara said. She took a breath, straightened her necklace, and opened the door. "You made it!" she squealed to Mark, her new boyfriend.

"Sorry I'm a little late, but I missed the turnoff to get to your house. When you said you guys lived a little off the beaten path, you weren't kidding."

Sara had met Mark at a high school church retreat two weeks prior. She'd noticed him watching her during the daily activities but was too shy to return his gaze. After keeping his distance for a couple of days, Mark approached her. Whereas Sara was quiet and timid, he was friendly and confident. It wasn't long before an awkward first conversation grew into taking long walks after meals. By the end of the retreat, it was as if they could read each other's minds. He learned about her favorite bands and authors, and she about his favorite sports and hobbies. It surprised Sara that she'd found another companion so soon after her last relationship. It hadn't ended well.

"Come on in," Sara said. "My parents can't wait to meet you."

Bill and Connie had stationed themselves in their tasteful and immaculate den. An oil painting of Jesus—who looked more like a hippie from the '60s than a laborer from the Middle East—adorned the mantle. The hopeful smiles beaming from their cheerful faces were matched only by the sheen from the clear, plastic furniture covers that kept a healthy distance between the upholstery and other people's grime.

"You ready for this?" Connie whispered to Bill.

"Sounds like Sara isn't the only one who's anxious about tonight." Footsteps drew closer. "Okay, showtime."

Sara clasped Mark's hand and walked him into the den. Clearing her throat, she announced, "Mom, Dad, this is Mark."

Mark gave a sheepish smile. "Uh, hello, Mr. and Mrs. Blanc. Thank you for having me over tonight."

Bill extended his hand to Mark, who shook it firmly. "Hello, son. When Sara told us about you, the missus and I said to each other, 'We have got to meet this boy'. Please, come on over and have a seat. We'd love to hear more about you."

"Thanks. I'm looking forward to getting to know you guys, too. To be honest, Sara hasn't told me much about you."

The admission embarrassed Sara. "That's why I invited you over, goofy—so you can meet them. Let's sit on the couch."

After everyone was comfortable, Bill said, "So, Sara tells me you both attend the same high school. That right?"

"Yes, sir. We've likely crossed paths in the hallway at least a hundred times and never noticed each other. I'm glad we finally got to meet."

Sara looked into Mark's eyes, a subtle smile tugging at the corners of her mouth. "Me, too," she gushed.

"So, where do you go to church, Mark?" asked Connie.

"Grace Community Church on Broughton Street. It's not a big congregation, so we're pretty close-knit."

Bill chimed in. "I guess Sara told you we're members of Holiness Pentecostal. You passed the little white building a couple of miles back up the road; nothing fancy. We're pretty close-knit ourselves. Tell me, what do your parents do for a living?"

"Mom works from home; my dad runs a meat packing plant."

"Oh, really? Which one?"

"Hollis Meats off Interstate 40."

"Oh yeah, I drive past it on my way to the shop. How's business been?"

"Not too good. Everybody's feeling the pinch these days. Meat's been hard to come by; expensive, too. May I ask what you two do?"

"Same as your folks, more or less," Connie replied. "I'm a stay-at-home mom, and Bill here is the best darn taxidermist in these parts."

Bill chuckled. "Oh, now, Momma, don't go bragging on me. You'll embarrass all of us."

"Well, young man," Connie said, "I hope you like veggie lasagna and garlic bread. I made *pleeenty!*"

"You don't need to ring that dinner bell twice!" boomed Bill.

As they traveled to the dining room, Mark inhaled the pleasant aroma wafting from the kitchen, a combination of cheeses and herbs. "That sure smells good, Mrs. Blanc. We don't eat a lot of vegetarian dishes at my house; we're more the meat and potatoes type. Dad thinks because he's in the meat business, we oughta eat it all the time."

Sara caressed Mark's shoulder. "Nothing wrong with that. It's great to fill up on protein; keeps you lean."

At the dining room table, Mark pulled Sara's chair out for her before taking his place.

"Take note, Bill," Connie said. "That's how a gentleman treats a lady."

"Duly noted, sweetheart. How's about I play a little footsy with you under the table instead?"

Sara moaned in embarrassment. "How's about the two of you knock it off? Mark doesn't know you well enough to tell when you're joking."

"As your father said," Connie answered, 'Duly noted.' " Then, to Sara's momentary relief, she changed the subject. "Mark, would you care to lead us in prayer?"

Sara blushed. "Mom, please, don't put him on the spot like that."

"Oh, it's okay," Mark said. "I'd be honored."

Everyone closed their eyes and bowed their heads. "Dear Lord, we thank thee for the bounty put before us, so that we might use it in accordance with thy perfect will, and for thy glory. Amen."

"Amen," added the others.

"Don't be shy about digging in, Mark," Bill said. "As we like to say around here: 'The Lord helps those who help themselves.'"

Connie snickered; Sara did not. "Oh, Daddy, no one finds that funny."

"I think a little levity mixed with faith is a good thing, don't you, Mark?" Connie said.

"Of course. As St. Teresa of Avila said, 'Lord, save us from gloomy saints!'"

"Here! Here!" Bill bellowed.

Connie shot her husband a glare of disapproval. "Now that we have all Bill's silliness out of the way, let's talk about you some more. What are your plans after high school?"

Mark chewed his lasagna and considered the question. "Dad's pretty adamant that I follow him in the meat packing business. I figure I can make a better living learning a trade than I could from a degree in Gender Studies or Elizabethan Poetry."

"Oh, I don't know," Connie said. "I think there's something to be said about expanding one's intellectual horizons, but I understand what you're saying. It's important to help carry on family traditions, as long as it doesn't hold you back from realizing your dreams. Are you and Sara in the same grade? You look a little older than sixteen."

"Sara's a year behind me. I'll be graduating in June."

"That's exciting. I guess Sara has a thing for older men. A couple of former boyfriends were older, but not by much. Have you ever seen a dead body up close before?"

Mark was the only one to stop eating. "Excuse me, ma'am?"

Connie took a sip of her tea. "I asked if you've ever seen a dead body up close before, dear."

Mark put his fork down and looked at everyone. "I-I'm not sure what you mean by that. Do you mean a human corpse?"

Sara giggled. "Well, of course, goofy. What other kind do you think?"

Mark's stomach was churning, his vision blurring.

"You okay, son?" Bill asked.

Mark was swooning. "Is there something... something in my food?"

Sara giggled again. "Honestly, goofy, we put in your tea. It would've made the lasagna taste horrible."

"It's true," Connie agreed. "Do you remember that time we put it in... oh, what was his name?"

"Barry," Bill said. "I think it was Barry."

Sara nibbled her garlic bread. "You're both wrong. His name was Gary."

"Oooh, that's it!" Connie said. "We put it in Gary's meatloaf. That was disgusting."

Bill grimaced at the recollection. "Threw up all over the table. Gee-ross!"

Mark panicked. "I need to... need to—"

"Oh, use your words, Mark," Sara said with an air of impatience. "You need to what, leave? Just say, 'leave' already. God, you've become annoying. And when are you gonna pass out? Mom, are you sure you put enough Zolpidem in his tea?"

Bill, too, had become impatient. "Oh, for pity's sake!" He got up, went into the kitchen, and grabbed a skillet. Upon returning, he knocked Mark out with a blow to the back of his head.

"Timber!" Bill yelled.

Mark's eyes rolled back, and he fell forward, landing a perfect face plant on his plate of warm, cheesy lasagna.

2

Mark stirred a while later. He squinted and saw three gauzy figures standing near him. His mouth was dry, as if he'd been sucking on cotton balls. He lacked the strength to lift his throbbing head. There was a chair underneath him. He tried to move, but something was holding him against it. A rope?

"Oh, look. I think he's coming around," a female said.

Someone lifted his chin. "Yep, he's rejoining us," said a man. "Spread the tarp while I prepare the instruments."

Mark heard a whooshing sound and felt a breeze as something flittered in front of him. Somewhere, metal tinkled on metal. Other people were in the room, but their images were hazy. His vision cleared, and he could feel his body again. His bleary eyes washed over the semi-dark room comprising cinder block walls. The air was damp and stuffy, the floor hard like concrete. Was he in a basement? "What's... goin' on?" he slurred.

"Maybe we should start killing them outright," suggested Sara.

"Hey, you're the one who likes to hear them scream," Connie reminded her. "Why else do you think we bought this place way out here in the boonies?"

"I figured it was to hide the cars."

"That was the practical part of the decision, dear. But we also considered how much we like to see you happy."

Sara's face lit up with joy. "Oh, you guys!"

A chill rushed through Mark, as he realized his dilemma. "What are you going to do? Sara, for God's sake, what's happening?" He got his answer when he noticed they had decorated the room with the stuffed corpses of young men.

They had posed one of them, smiling and waving, his fake glass eyes a chilling black. Another had his hands positioned on his hips, peering upward. He looked like Superman, standing proudly before the American flag. They had arranged a few other taxidermied bodies in similar states of leisure and nobility.

Mark's bounding pulse throbbed in his neck. "Oh, my God! Is this a kill room?"

"You betcha," said Bill. "As you know, I'm a taxidermist."

"A taxidermist with a *biiiig* difference," Connie added. The three of them laughed at the odd and humorous remark.

"You people are soulless psychopaths!" Mark shouted.

"Well, when you say it like that," Connie sniffed, "who wouldn't think so, Mr. Smarty Britches?"

"Okay, so Mark," said Bill, "here's what's going to happen. I'm gonna hook you up to an IV of my special blend of muscle relaxant and formaldehyde. Your heart's going to be going a mile a minute, pumping the fluid through your system—that's another reason we want to keep you awake. Once you're ready, I'll cut you loose and lay you on the tarp. The next step involves removing your insides and flaying your arms, legs, and neck. Then I'll take this stiff wire and... well, you'll figure it out soon enough."

"No, please don't," Mark begged. "Sara, do something."

"Oh, don't be such a crybaby. It seems as if all you boys want to do is sniffle and beg like hungry puppies." She stepped into the outstretched arms of one of the dead boys and hugged him. His eyes were sealed; his lips forever pursed for a kiss. Sara lifted her face and pressed her lips to his, smearing her tongue all over his waxy mouth. Then she turned and winked at Mark. "Jealous?" she snickered.

Mark turned his head from the gruesome act and retched. "You won't get away with this. I told my parents where I was going."

"Oh, please," Connie sneered. "I can search this entire property looking for a lost item, but if someone's done a clever enough job of hiding it from me, I'll never find it. Just ask one of these boys."

Mark's eyes widened with horror; his voice quivered with fear. "It wasn't supposed to happen like this!"

Bill pushed the metal IV pole toward him, a clear bag of soupy, white liquid dangling from its hook. He stroked Mark's hair. "Oh, son, how else would it have gone down?"

Using his legs, Mark lifted his chair and sprang at Bill, clamping his teeth around his nose. He held onto it like a hungry crocodile, twisting his head back and forth, causing the cartilage to tear and bleed. Bill released a high-pitched howl when Mark ripped the mangled nose from his face.

Blinded by thick, squirting blood, he staggered backward and crashed into a small portable table, sending a metal tray lined with surgical instruments clattering to the floor.

The horrific sights and sounds of the brutal assault immobilized Connie and Sara.

Mark exploited his brief opportunity to escape. Standing as fully as he could, he used his body weight to smash the chair against the wall behind him. He twisted free of the ropes and grabbed a large knife from the floor. Then he charged Bill, slashing his throat so deeply that his head flopped backward on his neck, making him look like an open can of gore.

Mark turned to Connie and Sara, both still stunned and frozen. Connie looked at the sharp, bloody knife and trembled. "Now, dear, take it easy. There's no need for more violence. You can lock us down here and go call the police. We won't put up a fuss, will we, sweetie?"

"N-no," Sara stuttered. "Remember what you said, honey? 'It wasn't supposed to happen like this'. Isn't that what you said? Well, it doesn't have to happen this way either."

Mark's body relaxed as he lowered the knife. His face was expressionless, his eyes devoid of pity. "You're right; that's what I said, 'honey'. But I think you misunderstood my meaning."

He lifted the knife and stabbed Connie in her stomach several times, twisting and pulling with each rapid plunge.

Connie looked surprised and confused as she watched her contents spill out and slide down her legs. "Well, I'll be darned," she chirped. Then she fell forward, her eviscerated body making an audible squish as it hit the concrete floor. A crimson pool spread out from underneath her, encircling her hollow frame.

Sara shook as a wet spot grew on the crotch of her pants. She whimpered in terror as she began backing away. "Mark, please. You don't have to do this."

"No, I don't, but there's a lot of guys out there who'll be glad I did." He grabbed Sara's arm and yanked her onto the tarp. She struggled against him while he held her in place and stabbed her eye, producing painful, ear-splitting shrieks. When he withdrew the knife, pink goop oozed from the open socket like cascading jelly. Then he drove the weapon deep into her remaining eye. Sara convulsed as she gulped in the coppery air. Mark delivered the final deathblow by slamming the blade hard into her mouth, shattering her front teeth. The thin strip of razor-sharp steel slid over the surface of her tongue, slicing a thin path to the back of her throat.

Its eager tip came to a grinding halt when it broke through the back of her skull, producing a soft, wet crack. Sara's limp arms twitched, and her legs gave way. Mark held onto the knife's handle with one hand and lowered her mutilated corpse with the other one.

He looked around at the carnage, as well as his blood-soaked clothes and body. "It's gonna take forever to scrub this mess off," he sighed. Then he reached into his front pants pocket and retrieved a cell phone. He speed-dialed a number and a man picked up.

"How'd it go?" the voice asked.

"I won't lie to you, Dad; this one didn't go as planned. You won't believe the freaks these people turned out to be. They kill teenaged boys and stuff 'em like dead animals."

"Seriously?"

"Oh yeah; you should see their collection."

"I thought you did your homework on this girl. You said you watched her at school. Didn't you learn anything when I had you follow her at the church retreat?"

"It's like I told you: She's a loner that nobody notices. She's part of a small, church-going family—you know, meek little lambs. Her parents are middle-aged, so they shouldn't have put up much of a fight. Seemed like another easy kill, but I guess you never can tell what folks are hiding, especially the religious ones. Am I right?"

"Yeah, especially us *religious ones*," cackled Mark's dad. The two of them laughed long and loud at the obvious irony.

Getting back to business, Mark said, "The bodies are in the basement. You and Paulie can pull around back with the refrigerated truck. I'll unlock the door."

"How big is the mess? I don't want to be there all night with bleach and rags."

"Actually, they were kind enough to provide us with some plastic tarp. It's neat as a pin down here."

"Well, okay then. We'll be there in about thirty minutes. You know, son, this wicked economy had me worried. Thankfully, God has rewarded our faith and trust. We should be grateful for this divine provision of fresh meat."

"Amen," Mark said.

# CRAZY GOD LADY

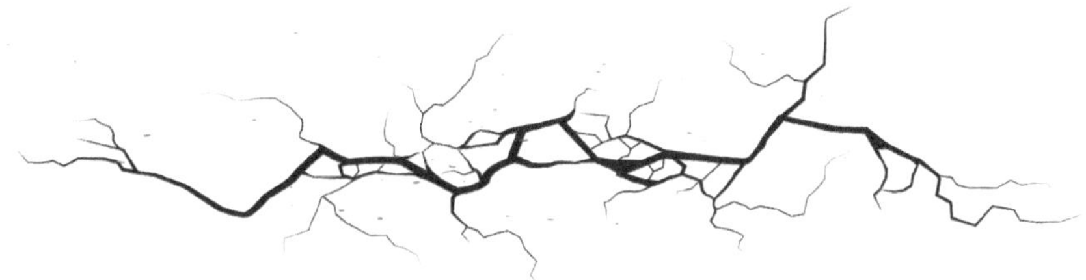

1

"**B**eware of Crazy God Lady in apartment 11-A," Max told Dale, the new maintenance guy.

"Why? Is she dangerous? You'd tell me if she was, right, Max?"

The crusty old complex manager picked through the ashtray on his chaotic desk, fished out a butt with a smidge of life left, and lit it with the dwindling cigarette between his lips. In a husky voice ravaged by decades of smoking, he croaked, "Nah, she's creepy but harmless. Still, I'd keep things short and sweet with her. You can never tell when somebody's mental fan belt is ready to snap. Don't waste time or the owner's money on repairs; he is one cheap S.O.B. If you can't fix it with duct tape, WD40, or picture hanging wire, put 'em off till they get fed up and move out. Toolbox and maintenance requests are on top of the file cabinet. Have fun!"

Dale wanted more clarity regarding his job duties. Instead, he was getting the old, *Here's your hat, what's your hurry?* business. He would've preferred to be back doing what he knew best: hanging sheetrock. But with the recession stopping new construction, he had to take whatever he could. Here, he was putting Band-Aids on long-term problems at a low-income housing complex called Forest Oaks.

"What are you waitin' for?" Max bellowed. "Those crap-clogged toilets ain't gonna unplug themselves!"

Dale took the beat-up toolbox and the clipboard holding his marching orders and left.

Once he was out of range of Max and his unadulterated indifference, Dale perused the day's assignments. "Let's see... we've got Landry, Joseph in D-9: squealing garbage disposal. Then it's Higgins, Ruth in F-3: clogged bathtub drain. Ugh, those things are nasty."

Dale thumbed through the rest of the work orders, stopping at a familiar address. "Evans, BeBe in none other than 11-A. Well, nice to meet you, God Lady. Seems you have a faulty thermostat. No way Monopoly banker guy is gonna spring for that."

Of the seven residents Dale visited that day, he'd only made one happy. Two had stood over him complaining about the sorry state of the apartment complex; three had yelled at him for not fixing their problems. That left the tenant who'd demanded that Dale give him his driver's license, so he'd know where to find him when he got his gun back from his cousin.

When late afternoon finally reared its head, Dale was ready to call it quits. But before that happened, he had three more glorious souls to attend to. The next maintenance request jumped out at him. "Hey, it's Crazy God Lady's turn. Can't wait to meet you, sweetheart."

2

Dale knocked on the door of 11-A, preparing himself to be greeted by someone odd.

"Just a moment, please," a feminine voice called. "I've got to figure out how to get this door open."

Dale's chin dropped to his chest. "And so it begins," he moaned.

Someone fumbled with the locks, and the door opened. An elderly black woman peeked out through the wedge of opening. "Can I help you, son?" Her manner was kind, her smile warm and genuine.

"Are you Ms. Evans?"

"I am. Are you lookin' for my daughter, BeBe?"

"If she's the one who placed this maintenance request, then yeah. Is she in?"

The woman opened the door. "Come on in, sugar. I'll get BeBe."

Dale wiped his feet on the ragged welcome mat and entered the apartment. He was struck by the overpowering smell of old dinners. Dusty furniture that hadn't aged well filled the cramped room. A stuffed cat with a missing ear was sitting on the floor next to a stained recliner. Dale cocked his head and thought, *Nah, that's not weird.*

"BeBe!" the woman hollered. "The maintenance man is here!" Turning to Dale, she said, "Let me show you the thermostat."

Dale trailed after the old woman as she shuffled along at a snail's pace. *C'mon, c'mon,* he silently pleaded. Finally, they reached their destination. "So, what's the problem, exactly?" he asked. "The form only says that the thermostat isn't working."

"It's gotten awfully warm and stuffy in here," said the woman. "BeBe needs it cool."

"I'll see what I can do," Dale said, setting his toolbox down on the dull, dirty carpet.

A nearby door creaked open, and a sweet scent of strawberry incense wafted through the room. A grin traveled across Dale's face as he inwardly announced, *And here she is, kids. I give you… Crazy God Lady!*

He didn't know what to expect, but it wasn't the person gliding toward him with an aluminum walker. The tall, thin woman was of indeterminate age with deep brown skin. Two large circles of cold cream decorated her cheeks, making her look like a clown with no sense of style or talent. She was dressed in brilliant white attire. A spiraling turban adorned her head; elegant gloves covered her arms up to her elbows. The lenses of her wrap-around sunglasses were pitch black, making her eyes impossible to see, impossible to read.

Dale thought she looked odd, mysterious, and silly. He deliberated before engaging with her. *Whatever you do... don't... laugh.* He gave himself a couple of beats before beginning. "Hi, Ms. Evans; I'm Dale. The apartment manager sent me here to check out your thermostat."

"You don't need to explain it to me," BeBe said dismissively. "I knew you'd be coming today; I have a sense of such things."

Her haughty tone annoyed Dale, who smirked and said, "Yeah, me too. I have a sense that's what it says on the form. Wanna tell me what the thermostat's doing or not doing?"

"It's not working at all," Bebe complained. "I must maintain a temperature of precisely seventy degrees; otherwise, I can't fully observe my universe."

Dale refrained from rolling his eyes but not being a mouthy smartass was well beyond his ability. "So at seventy-one, you're blind as a bat, universally speaking."

An uncomfortable silence engulfed the room. Dale couldn't see BeBe's eyes, but he felt the heat of her indignation burning into him like an ant under a magnifying glass.

"Oh, dear Lord," the old woman murmured. "You've done gone and done it now, boy."

BeBe scowled and pushed her walker toward Dale, intimidating him. He stepped backward until the wall said, *Whoa!*

The woman stood to her full height, looming over Dale. "You don't know who I am, do you? That's understandable—only my chosen do. I need it to be that way. If anybody else discovered my true identity, it would ruin my plan."

Dale wanted to be on the opposite side of the door. However, since he was stuck inside the strange apartment, he figured he might as well play along. "Your plan, huh?"

"Yes, my plan. Let me ask you: Are you aware of the floods, forest fires, and other natural disasters that have worsened over the years?"

"I guess so."

"Those aren't just a series of random events; they are of my making. I am God."

Dale narrowed his eyes. "You mean, 'God' God?"

"No, that God is dead. I am his reincarnation. My purpose is to observe and then decide."

"Decide what?"

"Whether I'll allow my universe to continue to exist."

Dale was interested, amused. "When did you turn into God? You said you were reincarnated?"

BeBe turned from Dale and began prowling the room. "A few years ago, I fell down those stairs outside—busted up my head pretty good. Soon after, I began having visions. I saw angels, demons, fire, and oblivion. As cosmic perception invaded my consciousness, I had terrible headaches. I was speaking in tongues and couldn't sleep. I didn't know what was happening to me. My husband wanted me to see a doctor, but he couldn't understand that my transformation was beyond human knowledge."

Dale struggled to keep a straight face as BeBe prattled on.

"Once God relinquished His infinite energy to me, I rose to a new level of existence. When I shared my divine purpose with my Earth family, they all laughed at me; they were doubters. But as they witnessed my spirit evolving, they became fearful."

"That's nearly interesting," Dale quipped. "By all means, continue."

"My children told their school counselor they were frightened and embarrassed of me. He sent a social worker here to my temple. When she threatened to remove them, I ordered her to leave before my wrath consumed her and her evil ilk. Not long after, my children left with their Earth father. If only they had stayed—the magnificent gifts I would've bestowed on them."

"You can still send them a gift card," Dale teased, each of his words oozing sarcasm.

Ignoring the slight, Bebe resumed her story. "Sadly, I had to accept that I'd become a god without subjects. So with wisdom and purpose, I summoned my Earth mother to attend to my needs; her devotion is holy. She's keeping me hidden from the infidels until my time of judgment comes."

Dale turned to BeBe's mother to gauge her reaction.

She shook her head as if to say, *It's the loony bin I'm keeping her hidden from.* Snickering, she leaned close to Dale and whispered, "I guess I'm Earth Mother, but you can call me Mavis."

Given BeBe's blasphemous statements, Dale wondered if he should get out of the apartment before the real God pressed the smite button. Crazy God Lady was shaping up to be one of those difficult tenants he'd wait out. In the meantime, he needed an escape plan. He pretended to rummage through his toolbox. "Listen, I don't think I have the right tool to fix your thermostat. I'll be back when I find one."

"But you hardly looked for it," observed Bebe.

"Yeah, well, it ain't there," joked Dale. "I'm surprised you didn't already know it was missing. This darn heat must still be screwing with your psychic signal."

"Yes, I suppose you're right. That makes it even more important to remedy the problem. I'll tell you what, Dale: If you fix the thermostat soon, I'll grant you one miracle."

"Oh, that's all right. I don't need any miracles right now."

"Are you sure? I can heal broken bodies, bring prosperity. Why, I can even raise the dead."

"You sure about that? 'Cause I'm looking at an invalid who's sharing a cheap apartment with a dead cat."

Mavis giggled under her breath.

"My powers aren't available to me; that would be self-serving," BeBe explained. "But I can bless others. We'll have to keep it to ourselves, of course; otherwise, I'll give myself away."

Dale wrestled with a yawn, as BeBe's entertainment value continued to dissipate. He looked at Mavis, who was peering down at her shuffling feet. It seemed as though she, too, was longing for a wrap-up.

"I'll chew on it for a while," Dale said. "In the meantime, I gotta get going: so many repairs, so little time." Then he thought, *and so little interest.* He got to the door quickly. He couldn't recall having the desire to kiss one more than he wanted to now.

3

By the week's end, Dale was ready to give Max his two-weeks' notice. Frustration and exhaustion had filled him to the brim. Thinking of his plight, he thought, *I'd rather live out of my truck and eat nothing but bologna sandwiches.*

He looked at the list of impatient tenants demanding to see him, if only for them to have someone to yell at or threaten. As he flipped through the stack of forms, something curled around his ankles—a cat. "Get out of here!"

As the cat fled, Dale noticed its missing ear. *I've never seen a cat so banged up before. Only that dead one in...*

Dale wondered if the stress from the job was making him skittish. He had a lot of work to do, so he gave himself a short mental pep talk. *Just be cool, my man. The animals around this dump are as damaged as everything else is.* Feeling a tad better, he went about his duties. However, as the day dragged on, uneasiness began clinging to him like cold oil.

## 4

A few days later, Dale was sitting on one of the rotting picnic benches next to the complex's decrepit playground. "Those poor kids. They oughta hook 'em up to an IV of tetanus vaccine," he remarked to himself. His mood sank further after he looked inside his crumpled brown lunch bag. He'd prepared himself for the minuscule budget he'd be living on after he quit by eating bologna sandwiches for lunch every day. "Speaking of crappy," he groaned.

He was choking down the cheap, dry bread when he heard a siren. Soon, its wail was rolling through the complex. Dale wasn't concerned; the place had its share of fights, drug deals, and burglaries. He finished his lunch and headed in the ruckus's direction.

Dale found an ambulance parked in front of Building 11. *Good thing the action's here,* he thought. *Crazy God Lady can walk over to whoever's messed up and heal them.* Then he saw the door to BeBe's unit open and thought, *Uh-oh! Hope she hasn't killed anybody.* He waited along with the ever-growing group of curious residents. Dale turned to the man standing next to him. "Any idea what that's about?"

"Shoot, I don't know," the man replied. "It's either that whack job or her mama. Probably the old lady. If it was the whack job, they would've taken a straitjacket in with 'em."

After a while, the EMT's carried Mavis out on a stretcher. She looked unconscious but alive. Her IV bag swung from side to side, as they toted her down the rickety stairs and into the waiting ambulance.

When the vehicle drove away, the crowd of gawkers dispersed, leaving Dale alone. He wondered if BeBe needed a ride to the hospital. He considered offering her one, but his mind catapulted the idea from his head. The number of work orders he needed to complete was something he thought about. However, his conscience suggested that he at least go up and see if BeBe was okay. As he ascended the cracked, warped steps, he told himself, *If it's going to be an ordeal, just wish her well and leave.*

Dale knocked on the door and waited. Nobody was on the other side when it opened. Despite his apprehensiveness, he peered inside the apartment. The sight stupefied him.

BeBe was in the kitchen, too far away to have opened the front door. She was humming an eerie melody and stroking the resuscitated cat. She looked at Dale and smiled. Her stained, broken teeth made her look like a feral animal.

"Oh, hello there, Dale. You ready for that miracle yet?"

Dale's jaw fell ajar; his tongue was as dry as sawdust. As soon as enough warmth returned to his body, he turned and ran, leaving BeBe to her worries and her creepy feline.

Dale stopped a short distance later to catch his breath and cull his thoughts. How had Crazy God Lady been able to open the door? Had she been cradling a once-dead cat? A chill climbed the steps of his spine as his heart danced in his chest. "Time to get out of here; this crap's insane."

Despite the waiting tenants, Dale skipped out and went home to do some heavy drinking.

5

The following morning, Dale tracked Max down and gave him his two weeks' notice. He took care not to mention the previous day's scare. "I know it's kind of short notice," Dale explained, "but things aren't working out the way I planned. The stress is getting to me."

"I saw this comin' from a mile away," groused Max. "If it ain't one thing, it's two. All right, then. Just finish what you can, and I'll notify the owner we need another warm body down here."

Max pulled a small flask from his hip pocket and took a couple of big swigs.

"Should you be drinking this early in the day?" asked Dale.

"Hey, it's eight o'clock somewhere," Max declared. He gave a parting burp and staggered away, giving a wide berth to some large imaginary object in his path.

Dale was relieved that his departure was official, leaving him in a good mood for the rest of the morning. He was unscathed by the crude and personal epithets hurled at him by the inhabitants of the dysfunctional complex, as if his soul had flown too high for their offenses to reach. He only allowed the swirling chatter to affect him once when he overheard Mavis had died from complications related to her high blood pressure.

*Her daughter's a laughing loon,* he thought, *but the old woman was sort of sweet. Can't help wondering what's gonna happen to Crazy God Lady without her.*

6

By late afternoon, things were winding down. Dale had fixed the leaking toilet in 7-G and was heading back to drop off the paperwork and toolbox. The shortest path took him alongside Building A. The thought of Crazy God Lady returned to him, as he walked past her apartment, giving him the willies. Looking up at the open window, he saw movement. He stopped to get a better look. His face blanched when he saw Mavis close the curtains.

Dale's lungs refused to pull in air. A part of him feared the ghost might see him, stealing his soul with a single glance. Fueled by terror and adrenaline, he sprinted to the office.

As soon as he arrived, he threw open the door, leaned in, and tossed the toolbox and clipboard toward the filing cabinet. Then he fled as though his sanity depended upon it. Then he fled as though his sanity depended upon it.

On his way home, he returned to the liquor store. The fright had made him a thirsty boy again.

7

As his tenure with the complex dwindled, Dale avoided walking near Building A. Although it had happened days prior, he still broke out in prickles of fright whenever he recalled the dead woman's image in the window.

On his last day, Dale was attempting to repair the cooling coil on a refrigerator. As he labored in vain, he thought of the classic song by Queen, "Another One Bites the Dust." After pronouncing the appliance dead, he began quietly packing his tools, hoping to avoid a verbal nipple twisting from the resident. He paused when he overheard the man talking on the phone.

"I'm tellin' ya, Reggie. Shawna said she could've sworn she saw Mavis pickin' up the mail outside BeBe's door. I told her she needed to get off the pipe. People are just takin' that voodoo daughter of Mavis' too seriously."

*So, it wasn't my imagination*, Dale thought. The realization only added to his horror.

The tenant—Rogers was his name—overheard Dale filling his toolbox. "Listen, I gotta go. That useless repairman's gettin' ready to leave. I need to make sure the fridge got fixed."

The loud noise of the angry man stomping toward the kitchen interrupted Dale's thoughts. He steeled himself for the fury guaranteed to follow his bleak assessment of the refrigerator.

"Oh, I *know* you ain't leavin' me with a busted fridge!" yelled the man.

"No, sir, it's not that," Dale said. "It's just that I need to order a new part. It should arrive in a few days, tops." Dale knew Max would never place the order, but he reasoned that after today, he'd be long gone from the land of the lovable losers and its odd inhabitants—including their pets.

After completing his final assignment, Dale returned to the office to tie up any loose ends with Max before leaving for good. He discovered the crotchety old man sitting at his desk listening to a baseball game through a scuffed-up radio on top of a filing cabinet. Wispy clouds of blue smoke filled the cramped office, adding to the dry stench left by millions of cigarettes smoked over the years. Dale stared at the man who oversaw the dumpster fire called Forest Oaks and felt a twinge of pity. Poor Max seemed like someone who looked back on his life forlornly, knowing that it had whipped him.

"All done, boss," Dale said. "Guess this is where we shake hands and part ways."

"Not so fast, my friend." As Max spoke, the ubiquitous cigarette adhered to the corner of his mouth bounced around like an orchestra conductor's baton. "Before you go be-boppin' out of here, we've got one more request to tend to. You didn't think you'd leave early on your last day, did ya? I need you to take one final beating."

"Max, I'd rather smear my privates with honey and go looking for hungry bears."

"Come on, kid. You can handle it. It's the *laaast* one."

Dale's shoulders slumped, his mouth drooping into a frown of disappointment. "Okay, whaddya got?"

Max formed a devious smile. "Well, my boy, you are going out in style! It's for 11-A: Crazy God-Lady. Please, hold your applause till the very end."

Dale's form flushed with fear.

"She wants you to check out that stupid thermostat again," Max continued. "Just give it a quick once-over to shut her up. Then tell her the new guy'll handle it. See: it's easy peasy, lemon squeezy, George Jefferson married Weezy."

As Max laughed at the witty remark, a wet ball of phlegm lodged inside his hitching chest, causing Dale to grimace in disgust. The old man coughed so forcefully that it sounded like he was trying to hack up exact change. The sickly puddle made it as far as his throat before he swallowed it, sending it back into his tobacco-ravaged lungs. "Whoa," he said proudly. "That one's a keeper!"

Returning to his instructions, he said, "Now, where was I? Oh, yeah. Get this whack job off my back and outta my life. Now would be good."

"Max, listen… listen," Dale stammered. "I'd rather not take this one on. Can't you wait and give it to the next guy? You sent me there on my first day. It'll be a great way to break him in.

Come on, Max. Please."

Max shook his head, making it clear to Dale that his idea was a no-go. "Kid, it's only three in the afternoon. Technically, you're on the clock for another two hours. Just knock this one out, and I'll cut you loose early."

Dale had no desire to enter the domain of the self-professed god again. And if Mavis was traipsing about, he didn't want to see her.

Sensing Dale's hesitation, Max put the pedal to the metal with his coercion. "I'd hate for the main office to hold on to your last paycheck because you clocked out before your scheduled time." Then he played his last card by challenging Dale's manhood. "You ain't spooked by Crazy God Lady, are ya? Ha! What a sissie!"

The words hit Dale hard enough to make him ponder his decision. *You know that you'll always regret not meeting this head-on. Just go, and face your fears. There was no ghost, is no ghost, and will never be a ghost.* However, much like the residents when he peddled his spiel, he wasn't buying it. He wanted to be done with the place, so he went along to get along. "All right, I'll do it. But when I'm done, I'm done. That's the deal, Smokehouse."

Max looked impressed. "Smokehouse—I like that one. See, you have some backbone, after all. Seriously, kid. Take one for the team, and I'll give you the best reference in the world."

Dale forced a disingenuous grin. "Gee, thanks, Max." Grabbing the toolbox, he headed out the door.

Behind him, he heard Max yell, "Don't let Crazy God-Lady curse ya, dipwad!"

8

Dale waited a few minutes before knocking on BeBe's door. Despite his earlier boost of courage, he regretted his decision. As he rapped on the door, the bologna sandwich rolled around in his stomach. Suddenly, the front door flew open as if a violent gust of wind had struck it. Again, there was no one there. He hesitated to enter. "Hello? Ms. Evans?"

From the entrance, Dale watched the bedroom door open. BeBe, dressed head-to-toe in her ethereal ensemble, pushed her walker into the living room. "Yes, Dale. Come inside and close the door."

Panting with every footstep, Dale entered, closing the creaking door behind him. He waited before speaking, hoping his voice wouldn't betray his nervousness. When he was ready, he said, "I'm sorry, ma'am, but I still don't have the part to fix your thermostat."

"I thought you said it was a tool you required."

Dale felt unguarded. "It's a part *and* a tool. Listen, a new guy's starting on Monday. The stuff to fix it should be here by then."

Bebe cocked an eyebrow in suspicion and drew closer to Dale. "It's too warm in here for me to know if you're lying. Perhaps she can get the truth out of you."

A stiff hand gripped Dale's shoulder from behind. He quaked as he turned his head.

Mavis peered into his eyes, displaying the warm smile he remembered from their first meeting. Nothing about her appeared ghostly; she was simply alive again. Frigid blood gushed through Dale's veins like glacial water.

*MEOW!* A throaty growl rising from the floor drew Dale's eyes downward. Seeing the resurrected cat turned his flesh to stone.

BeBe addressed Mavis, her voice seeming far away, like a whisper from another room. "Earth Mother, is this man lying to us?"

Mavis continued smiling, as she nodded her head to signal yes.

BeBe became enraged. "You've lied to your god for the last time," she snarled. "You have been indifferent, dishonest, and disrespectful. What should I do with you, infidel?"

Dale's body threatened to faint. He wanted—*needed*—to leave. He turned toward the door but seeing Mavis standing there with her eternal grin changed his mind.

The cat serpentined through Dale's legs like a thick snake, making him jerk and back away.

His gaze bounced between Crazy God Lady, the walking corpse of Mavis, and the hissing, one- eared cat.

He took a few steps backward, tripping over a cardboard box. He dropped through the empty air, arms pinwheeling. There was a loud crack as Dale's head hammered the wall behind him, snapping his neck. Unable to move, breathing became difficult. From his shoulders down, he was a lifeless hunk.

BeBe moved her walker until she stood over him, a look of satisfaction on her dark face.

You should have fixed the air conditioning. I would've granted you a miracle. I still can if you repent of your transgressions."

Fear and desperation flooded Dale's emotions. He could sense his life drifting from him like a vapor. He appealed to the woman who could raise the dead and heal the broken. "I'm so sorry for everything I did to offend you. *Please*. I want to live."

"I forgive you. But you need to understand that resurrection has its rules. First, you must die; then, you will face my judgment. Now speak the truth this time. Do you believe I have the power to raise you? If so, you have my promise of renewed life."

Dale looked at the woman whom he'd ridiculed, realizing that he had judged her harshly, ignorantly. "Yes, I believe. I..." Nothingness.

9

Dale yanked air into his body. He felt weak and drowsy like he'd awakened from an all-night bender. As his mind returned to life, he recalled recent moments from the world he'd left: working with his hands, fixing lights, and holes in walls. Then an image of Crazy God Lady invaded his memory. She'd promised him something, but a promise of what? Life? It was life… and healing. He smiled as he wiggled his toes and drummed his fingers. "Well, whaddya know? That loony tune's the real deal," he said.

Dale tried sitting up and bumped his head. Despite his eyes being open, he couldn't see anything. His searching hands probed the darkness. *Where am I?* he wondered. Confused and alarmed, he cried out. "Hey, God Lady! Where are you? Ms. Evans?" Dale waited for a reply. When no one answered, he began picking through myriads of explanations. *Maybe I'm dreaming. I might be in limbo. What if I'm alive, but…* His body sweated pearls of ice as he grasped what had happened—and it was awful.

A heavy horror seized him, as he realized Crazy God Lady had kept her word. He'd been raised him from the dead, healed. However, there had been judgment involved. Dale began sobbing. Trapped in the eternal blackness, he could just make out the sound of rain hammering his grave.

# THE GIRL IN THE WALL

## 1

"Donnie, when are we gonna stop? I'm tired, and I need to pee."

Shannon and Donnie, her sometimes boyfriend, had been driving for hours. They'd left Georgia for Arizona two days earlier and still had a ways to go. The trip was more of a desperate escape than a journey toward new adventures. Donnie was deep in debt to the wrong people, and losing his job hadn't helped. It had been rough going for a while until he learned that hope and hard work were no match for dumb, blind luck. He'd talked to a cousin who had a friend that might have some construction work in Scottsdale. Donnie had nothing to lose except the thumb that his bookie, Ramone, threatened to take in place of his gambling debts. He hoped that a change of scenery and a fresh start might do him some good, and save him some appendages. So, Donnie packed a few of his favorite belongings, such as Shannon, and hit the road.

He prayed that the iffy motor in his worn-out 2010 Ford Mustang would last the distance.

He hoped Shannon would, as well.

Twelve hours in, Shannon needed a break if only to have somewhere to throw up. She was sick from the exhaust fumes leaking up through the filthy floorboard and regretted the thirty-six—ounce bladder-buster soda she'd gulped down around hour ten.

"Seriously, Donnie, I need to stop somewhere."

"Fine. We'll stop at the next motel. That make ya happy?"

"Yep: that, a commode, and a nice long shower."

No sooner had she spoken than they approached an exit on the interstate. A sun-bleached road sign displayed icons indicating that a bar, a gas station, and a motel were within a couple of miles.

Donnie followed the long, winding off-ramp to an empty stretch of two-lane road marked Highway 21. A sign posted at the confluence showed the motel was located 1.5 miles down on the left; everything else, to the right. Donnie headed toward the motel and glanced at the odometer to mark the distance.

As he drove, a horrid stench blew in through the air vents. It reminded him of untreated sewage.

Shannon crinkled her nose. "Oh man. What in the world is that?"

"Probably a bog or a pig farm nearby."

"It's too quiet out here. I'm gonna find somethin' on the radio." Shannon pressed the auto seek and watched station numbers flash by without stopping. "Great. We're so far out in the boonies you can't pick up anything."

"Just grab one of them CDs and pop it in."

"If I have to listen to any more Jason Aldean or Foo Fighters, I'm gonna jump out and walk."

"All right, but don't whine about how quiet it is."

Resentment lingered as they continued along the desolate highway. The road was dark: no streetlights, houses, or passing vehicles. Donnie strained his eyes against the night, unable to see beyond the reach of the headlights as creeping shadows swallowed their dim rays. A thick tangle of trees and tall grass closed in on either side. As they pushed on, a ghostly carpet of white mist rolled over the asphalt as if to welcome them.

"I don't like this," Shannon said. "It's creepy."

"Hey, you're the one who needs to pop a squat and get some sleep. Ya want me to turn around and look for someplace else?"

"No. I can hold it a little longer. Shouldn't we be there by now? The sign said it was only a mile and a half."

Donnie checked the car's odometer. "Hmmm."

"What's up?"

"Odometer says we should've been there five miles ago."

"Well, I didn't see anything with lights on. That sign's probably wrong. Just keep drivin'. I'll tell ya when I see somethin'."

Several minutes later, they still hadn't reached the motel. "That's it; I'm turnin' around," Donnie announced. As he looked for a place to make a U-turn, he saw a glowing light in the distance. As they got closer, he could make out a block of bright letters levitating in the soupy night air "Is that a motel sign?"

"Ooh!" Shannon chirped. "I think that's it! Thank God—my back teeth are drownin'!"

2

Donnie slowed and turned into the motel's parking lot. Fissures snaked across the ragged asphalt, whole chunks missing like rotted-out teeth. The motel was a drab, one-story, brick building with a neon sign above the door of a small office. Some of its letters were dead and gone, but enough of them remained to let Donnie and Shannon know they'd be spending the night at Miller's Motel.

Donnie eased the Mustang into one of the parking spaces nearest the door. He was about to kill the engine when something dark ran past his side of the car. "You see that?"

"See what?"

Donnie turned off the motor. "Stay here a sec. I wanna check this place out."

He got out and looked around the vacant lot. The air was hot and stale, abandoned by the wind. The fetid odor from earlier was stronger here. Although he didn't see anything unusual, the eeriness of the scene disquieted him. It reminded him of the feeling he would get when he boarded an empty elevator and a stranger stepped inside at the last minute.

"Is everything okay?" Shannon yelled.

Donnie gave the area another once-over. "It's all good—just a little White Line Fever. Come on, let's get checked in."

Shannon got out of the car and took a few steps before stopping. "Whoa. This joint looks like somethin' out of a slasher movie. If I wasn't so worn out, I'd pee behind a bush and keep movin till we found a Holiday Inn."

"Relax; ain't nothin' gonna grab ya." *At least, I hope not.*

3

As soon as they entered the cramped lobby, a sour scent of stale mop water and lemon air freshener encompassed them. One of the two fluorescent tubes inside the overhead light fixture flickered, creating a strobing effect. No one was manning the small Formica counter that served as a front desk. There was a closed wooden door a few feet behind it. "Hello? Anybody back there?" Donnie hollered. "You got customers up front!"

"Just a minute, please," a whiny voice answered. "Be right with ya." The door opened, and a short, chubby man in a white dress shirt appeared. The sweat-yellowed fabric worked in tandem with overburdened buttons to restrain an overflowing belly. A plastic pocket badge with "Leonard" imprinted on it complemented the seedy ensemble. "What'll it be, friends?"

Donnie and Shannon took a step back to get out of range of the clerk's body odor, a noxious mix of armpits and halitosis.

"We'd like a room for the night," Donnie said.

"I believe we can manage that." Leonard reached under the counter and grabbed a plastic binder, from which a pen dangled at the end of a long string like a condemned outlaw. Placing it on the counter, he flipped through some dog-eared pages until he came to a blank one. He spun the binder around to face Donnie. "Just put your name and a phone number I can reach you at on that top line, please."

Donnie snickered. "You're kind of old school, ain'tcha? Don't you got a computer, internet access?"

"No service this far out," Leonard explained. "We don't see a whole lotta business; just the occasional one-nighters... like you two." His sly wink made Shannon uncomfortable.

"Yeah, I figured that much by lookin' at your parkin' lot," Donnie said. "What do I owe ya?"

"I dunno. Whatever you think's fair."

"Seriously?"

Leonard leaned over the counter and said in a hushed voice, "Look, the owner doesn't always come around, and you two look dog-tired. So how 'bout we do twenty dollars? Sound about right?"

"Sold!" Shannon declared.

Donnie laid a bill on the counter as Leonard retrieved a key from a hook on the wall.

"Here ya go: Room 11. Let me know if you need anything else. I'm Leonard, and I'll be here all night. When you go out, hang a left; number's on the door."

4

Shannon thanked Leonard, and she and Donnie headed for the room. Along the way, they swatted through swarms of moths orbiting around the bare light bulbs on the side of each door. When they got to the room, they rushed inside before the squadron of insects joined them.

An unpleasant smell greeted them: dank and pungent, a stink of pot and sex lingering from previous occupants. Donnie flipped a sticky light switch, and a lamp snapped on. The gaudy room looked like it hadn't been remodeled for a very long time. The furniture was worn, old, and cheap. Grimy shag carpeting accentuated fading, peeling wallpaper.

"So," Shannon said, "this is what a twenty-dollar room looks like."

Donnie surveyed the squalid accommodations and shook his head. "Don't you have to pee or somethin'?"

"You better know it, cowboy!" Shannon made a bee-line to the bathroom.

Donnie pulled back the tacky covers on the queen-sized bed, exposing a dingy, threadbare sheet. Though a bit road-weary, he felt a pulsing in his loins. There was something about being with Shannon in a cheap motel room. He stripped to his boxers, climbed under the covers, and waited for her to return.

The bathroom door swung open and Shannon walked out. She stopped and looked at Donnie lying in bed, a look of hope plastered across his grinning face. "You're kiddin', right?"

"Come on, babe. We can mess around and then grab a hot shower together. Speakin' of grabbin'..." He flipped down her side of the covers and patted the mattress.

"Donnie, I told you I was tired. I'm gonna get my bag out of the car, come back, and wash off. Then I'm goin' to sleep. Understand?"

Flushed with disappointment, Donnie threw back the covers and jumped out of bed. "Fine, then. You do whatcha want. I'm takin' off."

Shannon glared at him. "Where you goin'? I know good and well you ain't gonna leave me here in this twenty-dollar outhouse by myself!"

Donnie hurriedly got dressed. "I'm gonna find a bar. You take your stupid shower. I'll have some fun tonight—with or without ya!" He fished his car keys out of his jeans pocket and stormed from the room, slamming the door behind him.

Shannon didn't think he'd actually leave. When she heard the Mustang's engine revving, she panicked. The thought of being alone at the isolated motel filled her with dread. She ran from the room and headed for the parking lot.

Shannon arrived in time to see the red taillights of the car peering back at her like two devilish eyes. "Donnie Jackson, don't you leave me here!" He kept going. "Donnie, you're a dead man."

As Shannon sulked in the now-empty parking lot, she noticed a large shadow forming on the edge of the woods across the street. It floated across the parking lot like an ominous cloud.

Suddenly, all the night sounds ceased. In the quiet, Shannon thought she heard breathing. She spun around, expecting to see that creepy desk clerk behind her, but there was no one. As the shadow passed in front of the lone streetlight at the entrance to the motel, the light dimmed. Shannon furrowed her brow. The temperature dropped noticeably; she could see her own breath. "Enough of this mess." Shivering, Shannon trotted back to the room.

5

She locked the deadbolt and then closed the room's thick curtains. She looked through the door's peephole. "Geez, how'd it get so cold?" She wondered if her uneasiness about being stranded was playing tricks on her mind. *It's probably just a cold front.* Still, she couldn't deny that something felt different. Threatening. The mist was so weird. She waited, half-expecting a knock, or to see the mist wafting in under the door, invading her lungs, and filling them with dry, black dust. "Keep it together, girl. You're way overthinking this."

After several minutes, nothing happened. She inched her way to the window and peeked through the slit between the curtains.

There was nothing outside. Just the parking lot. She allowed herself to relax a bit. "God, I need a drink, but a hot shower will have to do."

Shannon was about to look around the room for her toiletries bag when she realized it had accompanied Donnie to the bar. "Thanks, jackass," she hissed through gritted teeth. She made a silent vow to never let him see her naked ever again. Shannon removed her cell phone from her back pocket and tried calling him. But as Leonard had said, there was no reception. "Well, that's just great? Guess I'll just have to make the best of this dung heap." Shannon looked at the ancient tube television sitting on the dresser, wondering if it still worked—it didn't. "This suuucks!"

She plopped on the bed and stared at a brown water stain on the ceiling. She amused herself by attempting to figure out what the pattern reminded her of, as though she were taking a Discount Rorschach test. *Hmmm. It kind of looks like a cross between a bird and a star; that or a plop of poop.*

*thump thump* The noise came from within the wall. "Must be mice," she muttered.

*thump* "Hello? Hello?" The voice was faint, a whisper in the air.

Shannon sat up.

*thump thump* The knocking traveled from the bathroom. Shannon shivered. The combination of the mist, the cold, the curious tapping, and the disembodied voice was making her apprehensive. *Easy, girl. Let's go in there and get to the bottom of this.* She slid carefully off the bed, and stood motionless, concentrating. "H-hello?" she murmured. Shannon was hoping there'd be no response; that she could chalk everything up to frazzled nerves. Hearing nothing, she remained still, quieting her breath. The profound absence of sound made her think of being underwater. Seconds ticked by.

*thump thump* She tensed. The dull rapping emanated from the other side of the wall. She tiptoed closer.

A muffled, child-like voice penetrated the sheetrock barrier. "Can you hear me? Please, say yes."

Shannon chuckled. "Oh my gosh; it's only a little girl."

"Did you say something?"

Shannon considered whether she wanted to start a conversation with the mysterious child.

What might the little girl's parents think if they caught her communicating with a stranger? *Bless her heart; she's probably lonesome and bored. Just keep it short.* "What's your name, sugar?"

"I'm Melissa. Who are you?"

"Hi, Melissa, my name's Shannon. I guess you're my new next-door neighbor. I didn't hear y'all pull in. When did ya get here?"

A brief pause. Then: "A while back."

"Really? We just got here. Was the weather actin' up when you arrived? It was doin' somethin' freaky earlier."

"I don't remember. Can you keep me company?"

Shannon hesitated. Now that she'd satisfied her curiosity, she didn't want to get hooked into a long conversation. "I'd like to, honey, but I'm gettin' ready for bed. Nice talkin' to ya, though."

The child said nothing more. Shannon assumed that she either had gotten bored or feared he parents busting her.

Shannon went back to the front room and lay down on the bed again. She closed her eyes, allowing the stillness to relax her.

BOOM! BOOM! BOOM!

Shannon popped up. She took a moment to catch her breath. *Who's watchin' that brat?*

BOOM! BOOM! BOOM!

"That's it. I've had enough crap thrown at me tonight." Shannon sprang from the bed and hammered the wall with her fist. "Hey! Why don't you people watch your stupid kid! I'm tryin' to rest over here!" Her outburst drew no reaction. "Yeah, you better keep it down," she mumbled.

*Growl... growl...* Shannon's hollow belly was complaining. "I wonder if there's a vending machine around this dump." She felt around in her front pocket and found a couple of dollars. With some effort, she managed to push aside the earlier weirdness in the parking lot. Releasing a heavy breath, she said, "Okay, here we go," and headed to the door. She stopped halfway when she heard a child crying.

Shannon followed the sound to the bathroom wall. It wasn't pained or a *whaddaya mean I can't watch TV?* sort of cry. It sounded mournful, frightened. Her annoyance turned to genuine concern. "Melissa, is that you, sweetie?"

The crying ceased.

"Melissa? Are you okay?"

"Please, don't hurt me," the small voice begged.

Shannon froze. *Who's she talkin' to?* Was the child in danger? She pressed her ear against the wall. Soundlessness filled the space within.

"Help! Shannon, heeelp!"

Shannon jumped back. She had no idea what the situation was next door. *I can't even call 911.*

"Noooo!" Melissa hollered. "Don't do it!" Something smashed against the wall, and Melissa wailed louder.

Shannon's instincts kicked in. "I'm comin', Melissa!"

Shannon bolted from her room, ran next door, and began banging on the door of Room 10.

Melissa was screaming; somebody was tossing furniture. "Hey! Leave that kid alone!" Suddenly, a blanket of quiet dropped. Shannon kicked the door. "You better open this door, or I'll knock it down!" She expected more yelling, but none came. It was as if someone had hit the stop button on a recording. Shannon was shaking with anger, panting from exertion. *What in the Sam Hill is happenin' in there?* She tried peeking in the window but couldn't see around the heavy curtains; no light bled through the narrow opening. She heard only cricket songs and the soft fluttering of moths' wings. She turned to the parking lot and realized there was no other car there. Her neck tingled. She wanted to get back inside quickly, to feel the comfort of light.

After securing the door, Shannon sat down at the round, wobbly table under the window to think. "I don't like this. Thanks, Donnie!" As angry as she was at him for abandoning her for the sake of his entertainment, she couldn't remember a time when she'd wanted to see him more.

"Shannon? Are you still there?"

Cold swept over her. *Don't answer her. Just ignore her, and maybe she'll go away.*

"I think he just left. Please, I need you," the child pleaded.

"Whoever you are, this ain't funny no more," Shannon said. "Leave me alone, or I'll call the cops!" *Or at least I would if the stupid phone worked.*

"But he's coming back!"

There was genuine fear in the girl's voice. Despite the strange happenings, Shannon wondered if she might be dealing with child abduction. Or, given her anxious state of mind, if there was a little girl at all. She couldn't be sure. *I think I'd rather be dealin' with ghosts.* But her conscience wouldn't let her rest.

Shannon went into the bathroom and stood at the wall. "Melissa, who's comin'?"

"The scary man. I don't want to be here anymore. Please, help me get out!"

Shannon's heart thudded. "Is there any way out of there?"

"No, I'm locked in. And there's no light."

She bit her bottom lip. She could use a chair to break open the wall and free the captive girl. But what if the man was still there? "Melissa, I'm goin' for help. You need to be very quiet. I'll be back soon."

"But I'm scared of the dark. I need some kind of light."

Shannon licked her dry lips. She knew she needed to bring help, but she hated the idea of leaving Melissa alone, crying in the black room.

"Shannon, are you there? He's probably close. Please, hurry."

"I'm thinking, I'm thinking."

"I have an idea. What if I dig a little hole on my side of the wall while you dig one on yours? That way we could meet in the middle. Then I can share your light."

Shannon considered Melissa's plan. It might give the frightened child some comfort while she went for help.

"Honey, is there anything in there you can dig with?"

"I don't know; I can't see anything."

"Just feel around. I'll look for somethin' over here."

Shannon searched the room quickly, hoping to find something small and breakable she could use to penetrate the sheetrock. Turning up nothing useful, she returned to the bathroom. "Melissa, did you find anything?"

"No. Did you?"

"No." Then a thought came to her. She scraped the decrepit wall and a wisp of white dust floated around her fingertip.

"Look, this sheetrock is old and thin, so we might be able to dig it out with our fingernails. I'm gonna scratch on my wall. When you hear it, follow the sound and start diggin'. Okay, get ready to listen." Shannon scratched the sheetrock at a height she thought a little girl might be able to reach. She paused to check on Melissa. "Did ya hear that? It's about four feet from the floor."

"Yeah, I heard you. I know where you are now." There was relief in Melissa's voice. "I'll start digging—here I go."

Shannon began chipping away at the drywall. As she suspected, the sheetrock was brittle, so she had little trouble breaking through. She poked her index finger into the hole and wiggled it around so Melissa could better locate her. "Melissa, feel around for my finger."

The child said nothing.

"Sweetie, did ya hear me? Feel around for my finger."

"Shannon?"

"Yeah, darlin'?"

"He's here."

Something grabbed Shannon's finger and yanked it with enough force to dislocate it from her knuckle. The pain was immediate. She jerked her disconnected finger back but the hold on it was too strong and made her skin stretch like a rubber band. There was a loud crunch as the digit's middle joint snapped upward. Shannon howled.

"You leave her alone!" yelled Melissa.

The attacker applied a tighter grip on Shannon's L-shaped finger and tugged the rest of her hand further into the wall.

"Let me goooo!" Shannon squealed.

Melissa was sobbing. "I can't make him stop!"

Shannon realized that if she were going to have any chance of rescuing Melissa and herself, she'd have to act quickly. Using her good hand, she punched a hole in the weakened wall and then grabbed the arm of her attacker. "Run, baby—ruuun!"

Another large hand seized Shannon's arm and began squeezing, its sharp nails puncturing her skin. She thrashed around like an animal in a trap. The needle-like pain in her arm grew as the fingers clawed deeper into her stinging flesh. She wailed when the hand fully penetrated her arm, taking hold of the bone underneath.

Shannon grunted as mind-twisting terror hammered at her. She put her foot against the wall for leverage and readied herself for the explosion of agony that was to come. As she pushed away from the wall, her arm made low, snapping sounds. Her nerve endings were on fire; screams burned her vocal cords.

Suddenly, the grip relaxed. Shannon flew backward and crashed against the opposite wall, nipping her tongue, the tang of blood coating it. She dropped to the floor and forced herself to assess the damage. Her arm looked like someone had filleted it with a dull knife. The bone in the middle joint of her index finger had ripped through the skin. A flood of thick crimson poured from the wound like an open tap. Small, white dots swarmed her vision. She tried crawling from the bathroom, but the blood and ripped tendons from her shredded arm made her slip.

CRAAACK...

The wall split from the holes down to the floor and pulsed outward. A tall, cadaverous figure in a tattered black suit pushed through the crevice like a malformed baby. The spindly horror had no eyes, just deep, black holes weeping maggots. Its nose was two horizontal slits from which a syrupy discharge oozed. With its drooping skin and long, gaping mouth, it looked like a caricature of a screaming corpse. It turned and lowered its bald head toward Shannon. "Come with meeee."

Shannon's deafening shrieks reverberated in the blood-splattered room. Shock overtook her ruined body, masking the pain. With the torment temporarily at bay, she tried crawling with her useless arm again.

The thing laughed, deep and gravelly, It grabbed Shannon by her ankles and pulled her toward the opening.

She dug the fingernails of her crippled hand into the tile. The broken finger turned around in the opposite direction, as the nails from the remaining fingers snapped in half. Shannon went into shock. "Momma... Momma... Momma..." she mumbled.

The thing threw back its head and screamed, a cacophony of terrifying sounds rushing from its throat. The labored breaths of the otherworldly fog, the ghostly whispers of the terrified girl, and every horrified victim before her were captured in its unearthly shrieks. It dragged Shannon's raw body over the hole's jagged shards, plummeting her into the world of shadows beyond the wall.

6

The phone on the counter rang only once before Leonard answered it—he never kept it waiting. He drew the receiver to his ear.

"It's done," said the voice. "Come." Leonard shook; he'd never gotten used to its haunting hiss. He allowed his nerves to settle before going into the closet and grabbing the mop bucket and rags, then headed to the room where the mess would be waiting.

7

A few hours later, Donnie swerved into the parking spot outside Room 11. Wobbly and reeking of whiskey, he jabbed around the door lock with the key, getting lucky on the fourth attempt. He unlocked the door and staggered into the room. Only the cheap lamp on the water-ringed bedside table illuminated it.

Shannon wasn't in the bedroom. Donnie glanced at the partially closed bathroom door. "Babe, you in there?" She didn't answer. Seeing the light peeking around the jamb, Donnie figured he still might have a chance to make things right—at least until he screwed up again.

He ambled to the door and knocked. "Darlin'?" She didn't respond. "Come on, Shannon. Don't be like that. I just needed to get away for a while." Donnie opened the door and looked inside. He groaned at the empty bathroom.

Where could she have gone? She didn't have a car! Maybe Leonard had seen her go.

Donnie was near the front door when he heard the sound.

"Donnie? Donnie?"

"Shannon? That you, sugar?"

"Don-eeee..."

*How the hell'd I miss her?* Donnie returned to the bathroom, looked behind the shower curtain, and found it empty. "Where you at, babe?"

"Donnie, I need you."

The muffled voice was coming from the other side of the wall. He went over and leaned his ear close to it. "Shannon? What are ya doin' next door?" When she didn't answer, he pounded on the wall. "Shannon quit foolin' around and get back over here! Look, I'm sorry I left ya to go drinkin'."

"Donnie? Can you hear me?" the voice whispered.

"Barely. Look, I'm tired of this crap. I'm comin' over there."

"Donnie, please listen to me. I-I need to be as quiet as possible. Come closer to the wall.

Baby, it's important."

Donnie pressed the side of his head against the discolored sheetrock. "Okay, what is it?"

He didn't have time to scream as the hands burst through the wall, grabbed his head, and pulled.

The phone in the grimy office rang. Leonard answered it on the first ring. He never kept it waiting.

# POP POP'S GUIDE TO A HAPPIER LIFE

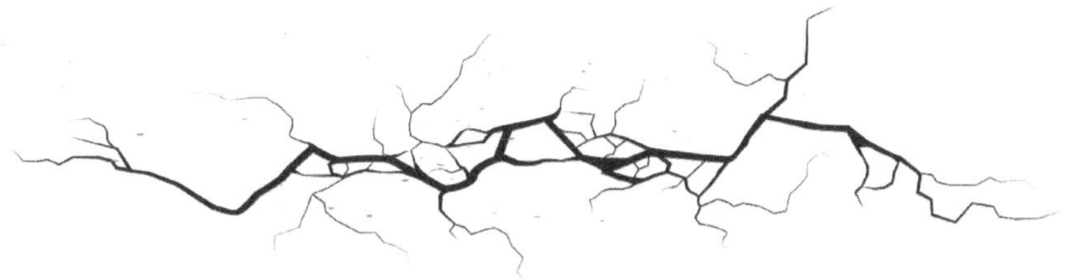

## 1

The scene at the funeral home was predictably somber. The harsh glare from the recessed lighting over Pop Pop's urn struck Carson as inappropriate and disrespectful. *He's my grandfather, not some archeological artifact on display,* he thought.

It'd only been a couple of days since his mother had found Pop Pop's body sprawled across his garden shed's floor. He'd had an iffy heart for some time. Still, Carson felt sideswiped by the suddenness of his death. Even in adulthood, he never stopped worshipping his grandfather.

Carson sat next to his stoic younger sister, Lexi, during the memorial service. His father, Lloyd Maxwell, was to her right with his typical *I-couldn't-care-less attitude.* Next was his sobbing mother, Monica and her brother, Robert. Their mother, Ruth, had been gone for over twenty years. The rest of Pop Pop's immediate family filled the remaining rows of padded folding chairs. The love of Carson's life, Sara, was behind him in the second row. He appreciated her more than he ever had. With Pop Pop gone, she was likely going to be the rock to which he'd be clinging.

The pre-service program featured photographs of Pop Pop at various stages in his life, projected onto a pull-down screen at the front of the small chapel. Seeing them made Carson aware that his aged grandfather had had a life before he came along. A soundtrack comprising soft instrumental music accompanied the slides. The series of lilting songs performed on piano and cello filled the reflective silence. Each number seemed to whisper, "He was here, but now he's gone—*forever*." As Carson stared at the decorative urn sitting on the ornate pedestal, the finality of it all hit him hard. He wept.

2

After the service, Carson exchanged hugs with his family, co-workers, and friends. He and Sara were heading to the funeral home's parking lot when Monica shouted after him.

"Carson, wait up!"

Carson turned to Sara. "Babe, can you give us a minute?"

"Absolutely, whatever you need." She gave him a quick kiss before walking to the car.

When Monica caught up to him, Carson said, "Hi, Mom. It's just too painful to stay, so I'm high-tailing it out."

"It's okay; I understand how you feel."

The thought occurred to Carson that as hard as it was for him to grapple with Pop Pop's unexpected death, it had to be much worse for his mother. He had lost his best friend and hero; she had lost a father whom she adored. Carson felt a twinge of shame for his selfishness. "Mom, I'm so sorry. I know I'm not the only one hurting right now. Are you going to be okay?"

Her smile was tender. "Yes, sweetie. It's you I'm worried about. You two were so close—as thick as thieves. I think he showed you more attention than he did me and your Uncle Robert combined.

Don't tell your sister or cousins, but he used to confide to me you were his favorite, not that the others would care. They spent time with him out of a sense of obligation; your visits were based on love."

Carson fought back the river of tears that were overflowing their banks again. "You think he knew that?"

Monica combed her fingers through the top of his uncooperative hair, a motherly habit that was hard to break. "Oh, sweetie, I know he did. But listen, you can call me anytime you feel the need to talk. I know I'm not Pop-Pop, but I guess I'll have to do for now."

She leaned past Carson and waved at Sara. "I'm sure Sara would love to be here for you, too. You know, I've always liked her. She just might be the one."

Carson grinned. "Far be it from me to disagree with one of my Mom's assessments."

"A wise decision." She kissed him on his cheek, turned, and walked away before calling over her shoulder, "He'd want you to be happy, Carson!"

"I know!" Then he thought, *I'm just not ready to begin yet.*

3

Soon, Carson returned to work at Reynolds, Reynolds, and Hayden, the law firm where he served as a paralegal. The insane amount of busyness was therapeutic. Going home meant dwelling on how much he missed Pop Pop.

His boss, Brian, kicked him out of the office when nine o'clock rolled around. "Come on, Carson. Go home and take care of yourself."

"Yeah, I think I'm done for the day."

Carson packed his things and left. He had to admit he was tired and hungry enough to go home to the apartment he shared with Alex, his on-again, off-again friend since college.

4

When Carson got home, he found Alex occupying the living room couch, playing one of his violent video games. Without taking a break from the action, Alex said, "Sup?" It was for him a rhetorical question.

"Just workin' my butt off, man," Carson replied.

"Yeah. Good. Quiet."

"Sooory." Carson plundered through the near-empty fridge, hoping to find something that was still safe to eat. Pickings were slim to none. "Come on, dude," he said. "It's your turn to get groceries. Looks like I'm having Coors for dinner. Thanks, Alex."

"Yeah, C. You're welcome."

"Same to you, dummy," Carson mumbled.

"Oh, hey, I almost forgot," said Alex. "An envelope came for you. It's on the counter."

Carson set his cold bottle of dinner down and picked up the large manila envelope. His name was on the front in large, black letters. There was no address or other identifying information, leaving him perplexed. "Who delivered this?"

"Don't know. It was just lying in front of the door like a Fed Ex package."

Carson turned the curious item over, inspecting it more closely. "'Kay, thanks."

"Welcome," Alex said, as he continued staring zombie-like at the carnage on the screen.

Carson took the beer and the envelope and went to his bedroom. He tossed his workbag on the bed and sat at his desk. He tore open the envelope and peeked at its contents. Inside was a single DVD, which he removed. He smiled as he read the disc's front: *Pop Pop's Guide to a Happier Life Vol. 1*. He recognized the distinctive scrawl. "Well, whaddya know? It's from Pop Pop."

He pulled his laptop from his workbag, set it on his desk, and fired it up. The computer stuck out its plastic tongue, and Carson fed it the disc. He nudged the tray and waited for the DVD to begin.

Carson recognized the setting immediately. It was the lush and colorful flower garden nestled in a beautiful, park-like area of Pop Pop's backyard. Beyond that, small fruit trees flourished. At its center was an open sitting area with two weathered Adirondack chairs. It was the spot where they used to sit and while away the time after they'd finished one of Pop Pop's famous chicken dinners—Carson's favorite dish, of course. Young Carson had sat spellbound as Pop Pop told him story after story about mythical characters in magical lands. When he was older, the talks turned to fatherly discussions about issues important to him: self-doubt, his emotionally disconnected father, girls, and life in general.

Now, Pop Pop was showing up when he most needed him. A warm wave of contentment enveloped Carson. Conflicting emotions filled him when Pop Pop appeared: deep longing, joyful surprise. Wearing his infamous, loud Hawaiian shirt, he greeted Carson with the phrase he always used on postcards and telephone calls.

"Well, hey there, buddy! I hope the sun's shinin' where you are. If you're watchin' this, you know that the second hand on this bad ticker of mine has stopped. I know you're sad, and that's okay. But just because we're not face to face doesn't mean that I'm not around. It also doesn't mean I have nothing interesting or helpful to share with you. In fact, I've prepared a series of… oh, I guess you'd call 'em life lessons. As you read on the front of the DVD, I'm gonna try to guide you toward a happier life. I'll talk about the useful stuff, you know, like we used to do."

"Like we used to do," Carson whispered.

"Consider this DVD an introduction of sorts. We'll begin the life lessons with Volume 2, so be on the lookout for it. Till then, I love you more than sunshine."

Carson tried to absorb what he had just watched. He wondered how many discs Pop Pop had prepared. Then it occurred to him that, for the first time in a while, he wasn't sad.

5

Two days later, Carson arrived at his apartment and discovered another manila envelope lying in front of his door. This one, too, had only Carson's name written on the front. He picked it up and went inside.

After he finished the sandwich he'd made, Carson took the envelope and retreated to his bedroom.

He readied his laptop, then retrieved the DVD from the envelope. As expected, the label read, *Pop Pop's Guide to a Happier Life Vol. 2.* Carson inserted the disc.

"Hey there, buddy! I hope the sun's shinin' where you are," said Pop Pop. He was still wearing his Hawaiian shirt and flashing his signature crooked smile. However, the rich greenery of the garden had faded. Dead leaves rained around him. The trees that were laden with succulent fruits now hung withered.

*How far apart did he shoot these?* Carson wondered.

"Carson, there are three things that help shape a man: the love of an honest woman, the loyalty of a good friend, and a willingness to do what's right. Today, I'm gonna talk about the first one: the love of an honest woman. It's crucial to have someone you can share your love and life with. But you've also got to be able to trust her. I think that's why I've never cared for that whore, Sara."

"Pop Pop!" Carson said in surprise. The harsh and crude description of Sara stunned him. A word like 'whore' ran counter to the gentleness of his sainted grandfather. It was a word that he had never uttered.

"I know this may be hard for you to believe, especially from your old Pop Pop, but she's not who you think she is. I need you to witness her debauchery and deceit. Prepare yourself, buddy."

The DVD cut away to a scene in an upscale bar. Sara was having drinks with an attractive thirty-something man dressed in an expensive-looking shirt and designer jeans. She was wearing a slinky red dress with a low-cut neckline that knew no shame. Despite the surrounding noise, Carson could hear what they were saying to one another.

"One more drink?" the man asked.

Sara, who seemed inebriated, said, "Are you trying to take advantage of me?"

"I don't know... am I?"

She leaned forward, whispering in his ear, "I sure hope so."

The man put his hand on Sara's inner thigh. She laughed, put her drink down, and began kissing him.

Then the scene cut to a motel breezeway. Sara and the man were kissing and groping one another. They stopped so the man could open the door. Sara wrapped her arms around his broad shoulders and pulled him into the room before slamming the door shut.

Carson felt rubbery, his breathing strained. "Oh, God. This can't be real. What is this?"

The DVD switched back to Pop Pop sitting in his decaying garden. His face displayed an angry expression that Carson had never seen before; it was unsettling. "Who is this person? Where'd he get this?" Carson wondered aloud.

"The who and where don't matter as much as what, the image said.

Carson was stunned when Pop Pop responded to his questions.

"I'm sorry you had to see this," the image continued, "but you need to understand that she's never really loved you. You're a joke to her—a toy for her amusement. Are you gonna let her get away with humiliating you, or are you gonna be the kind of man who doesn't suffer whores gladly?"

"Is this some kind of messed-up joke? How'd you hear me? Alex, so help me, if this is…" Carson felt anger filling him, making his face hot. "Okay, we both know the DVD is a fake. So, how'd you create my grandfather's likeness? He just died, you sorry piece of crap!"

Now it was Pop Pop's turn to look surprised. "Carson Tanner Maxwell! You better mind your manners, boy!"

"How the…? Carson said. *He's dead. The man's dead,* he reminded himself. He'd never known a time when he'd been terrified of his grandfather before. "If you're Pop Pop, why are you here?" he asked.

"Because you need me to be, remember? Because neither of us wants to let go of the other. And because I still have things to teach you. Carson, life is hard, and the truth sometimes hurts.

So, here's today's lesson: To have a happier life, you have to be able to trust a woman. If you can't, that whore is better off dead. Do you understand what I'm saying?"

Carson had no words.

Pop Pop smiled again. "Well that takes care of today's lesson. I'll be back with the next one soon. Till then, I love you more than sunshine."

"Hey, wait a—" Carson stared at the blank screen in disbelief. "No, no, no, this isn't right." He rewound the DVD to various points. There were still scenes with Sara, but static snow filled the frames where Pop Pop had appeared.

Carson ejected the disc from his laptop and tossed it into the wastepaper basket. *This is insane,* he thought. But what if…? He was unnerved and confounded. But he was also curious.

Carson looked at the DVD resting in the trashcan. After studying it for a moment, he retrieved it, returned it to its envelope, and placed it in the desk drawer with the first one. Then he set about finding out how the DVD had come into existence.

## 6

Later that evening, Carson called his mother. He'd practiced what he was going to say to her, but still the words lacked coherency. He felt unprepared when she answered on the second ring. "Hey, Mom, it's me. Do you have a minute?"

"I have all the time you need, sweetie. What's up?"

"Did Pop Pop ever mention anything to you about making some DVDs to send me after his death? Someone's been delivering some to my apartment. They're in a manila envelope with just my name written on the front. Do you know anything about them?"

"Are you serious? No, sweetie. I don't know the first thing about them. What's on them?"

Carson chose his words carefully. "On the front of the DVDs, it says, *Pop Pop's Guide to a Happier Life.* The first one was pleasant. Pop Pop was sitting in our spot in his flower garden. It hurt a bit at first, seeing him there and all. It was as though a part of him was still with me. But then it got strange."

"Strange? How?"

"It's hard to put into words. It's like his entire personality changed. I've never seen this side of him before. He became hateful. He called Sara a whore, and then—"

"Wait a minute. He called her a whore? Those were his exact words, a 'whore?'"

"Yeah, Mom—a whore. And this is the weirdest and most painful part. As proof, he shows me footage of Sara and some guy hanging out in a bar. They're all over each other. And then—"Carson's throat seized up, and his eyes became wet with raw emotion. "—and then they end up at a motel," he finished. "You can guess the rest."

"But Carson, how can that be? First off, despite how someone obtained that crude footage, I am so disappointed in Sara. But I promise you that whoever the man is on that DVD, he is not your

Pop Pop—not my dad. He adored you. It's not him you're seeing, sweetie."

"But Mom, it's definitely Pop Pop's garden. I can't understand it either, but I'm telling you, it looks like him."

He decided not to share the other part about his and Pop Pop's real-time conversation. His story was weird enough.

"This is a cruel and elaborate prank, or someone's stalking you and Sara," said Monica. "Why don't you call the police?"

"And tell them what, Mom? I don't have a clue what's going on. I just need some time to sort this out."

"Just be careful, Carson. Think about a private investigator; I'll pay the fee. And one last thing, sweetie."

"Yeah, Mom?"

"Talk with Sara."

7

Carson couldn't bring himself to watch the DVD again. The thought of viewing the images of Sara and her paramour made his stomach hurt.

When dinnertime arrived, Carson wasn't hungry. He tried working up the nerve to call Sara and ask for an explanation, but after thinking it through, decided against it. *This is something we need to work out face to face,* he thought. He grabbed the incriminating footage and headed to Sara's condominium.

Carson rang her doorbell several times, but she didn't answer. He peeked through a window, but the place was dark. He pulled his cell phone out of his pocket and called her, getting her voicemail. After a few more tries, he left a message.

"Sara, we need to talk—we need to talk *now*. I know, Sara; I know everything. Who is he, anyway? Look, just call me when you get this." He was about to hang up when Pop Pop's lesson entered his mind. "I'm starting to think I'd be better off if you were dead!"

Carson drove around for hours until his vision became bleary from exhaustion. He went home and crawled into bed with his clothes on. He dreamed of Sara.

8

The following morning, Carson struggled to get out of bed. The questions in his head tormented him. *How, Sara? How could you do this to me? To us?* He realized he couldn't afford to be late for work, so he showered, then got dressed.

Carson wandered around the kitchen in slow motion, looking for something to eat. He wanted something light on his stomach, so he prepared toast and coffee.

Alex entered the living area and sat on the sofa. Flipping on the TV, he turned to the local morning news. "Hey, C. How 'bout a coffee for your lazy friend?"

"Dude, you're helpless, hapless, and hopeless." Carson turned to the coffee maker but stopped when he heard the news anchor commenting on a homicide that had happened overnight at Heron Condominiums—the complex where Sara lived.

". . . say someone stabbed the young woman several times in her chest and abdomen. A police source has identified the victim as twenty-four-year-old Sarah McClendon. Authorities are asking anyone who may have seen or heard anything to call their anonymous tip line. Also, the parents of the victim are offering a reward to anyone with valid information that leads to the arrest and conviction of their daughter's killer."

A rush of nausea overtook Carson, and he vomited in the sink. Then he passed out.

9

Alex was standing over him, calling his name, when he came to. Carson felt the sore spot on the side of his head and found a small lump. He remembered the last thing he heard before he lost consciousness and felt dizzy again. He grabbed hold of the countertop and pulled himself up to a standing position. "Oh my God! Sara!"

"Carson, are you okay? I'm so sorry about Sara," Alex said. He walked Carson to the sofa, and sat down, putting his arm around Carson's shoulder. "Is there anyone I can call for you: your mom, dad, Lexi?"

"No!" Carson barked more harshly than he meant to. "Sorry. I know you're just trying to help. Good God, Alex, I was just at her place last night."

"Did she say anything about going out, maybe meeting someone?"

The question hit a nerve. Though it was difficult, Carson filled Alex in on everything that had happened. However, he changed his story to reflect that a mutual friend had shown him proof Sara had been cheating on him. He explained that he'd gone to her place to confront her, but she hadn't been home.

"I was so angry with her," Carson said. "I couldn't think straight. The worst part is the message I left on her phone. I told her I'd be better off if she were dead. Alex, what was I thinking?"

"Dude, there's no way you could've known. You need to take some time to process all of this. I'm right here for you. I'm not going anywhere."

Carson became more agitated. "I need to go to her. There's gotta be some kind of mix-up."

Before Alex could stop him, he jogged to the entryway, snagged his car keys from the wall hook, and opened the front door.

When he stepped outside, his foot collided with a manila envelope. His first thought was to toss it on the kitchen counter and leave, but the inexplicable pull of the package changed his mind. He picked it up and took it inside, his stomach knotting as he thought of its contents.

"Carson, what is it?" Alex asked. "Is that another one of those weird deliveries? What are they, anyway?"

Carson stared at the envelope. "Just go to work, Alex. I don't want to be bothered right now."

Alex looked hurt by the words. "Dude, just let me—"

"I said, just go to work!"

"Fine, man, suit yourself!" Alex grabbed his shoulder bag from beside the sofa and left.

Carson was uneasy about viewing the newest DVD; God only knew what horrors it contained. Instead, he spent the morning calling his family and friends and sharing the awful news. Like him, they, too, were in a state of shock and disbelief. Brian, his boss, told him to take as much time as he needed. But Carson had worked for him long enough to know that his kindness would only extend to a few days.

After he ended the difficult phone call to Sara's parents, he leaned back on the sofa and looked at the envelope. "What are you?" he asked.

Carson took the envelope to his bedroom and removed the DVD. He read the label: *Pop Pop's Guide to a Happier Life Vol. 3.* His hand tremoring with dread, he loaded it into the laptop and waited.

Just as he'd been on the previous DVDs, Pop Pop was sitting in his garden. His face was ashen and expressionless. The monochrome scenery surrounding him bore little resemblance to the lush and colorful place that Carson had known since childhood. This garden was devoid of vibrancy. The small fruit trees, rose bushes, and decorative shrubs were barren, their stark skeletons exposed under a deep gray sky. Then, despite the eerie setting, Pop Pop grinned, his happy-go-lucky demeanor returning.

"Hey there, buddy! I hope the sun's shinin' where you are. Would you look at this? We're already up to lesson three. Boy, howdy! That last one was a doozy, wasn't it? Listen, I know you're sad. Angry. Confused. I appreciate how much Sara meant to you, but it's better that she's done whoring around."

"Shut up!" Carson screamed. "Why'd you kill Sara?"

Pop Pop looked hurt by the accusation. "I didn't, buddy. I never laid a hand on her."

"Then who did? Tell me, or I'll start using these DVDs as Frisbees!"

"If you do, son, you'll never find out who killed Sara. I have to say: I'm perplexed over how quickly you've forgotten what you saw with your own eyes."

"I don't care about the creepy surveillance footage. This crap is over—no more peep shows!"

"Settle down now, buddy. You know old Pop Pop cares about you. That's why I've put together another life lesson. This one'll cover the second ingredient to a happier life: loyalty.

You see, just like a man needs an honest woman, he also needs a friend he can trust—someone who'll always have his back, no matter what. That brings me to Alex."

Carson's world of reality shifted on its axis. He responded to the thing that he worried might not be his grandfather. Barely controlling the fear in his voice, he said, "What about Alex? Don't you lay a finger on him, you hear me? Just leave him out of this."

Pop Pop leaned closer to the camera. His sparkling eyes turned hard, intimidating. He began speaking in a flat voice that gave Carson chills. "All right, buddy. Guess we're gonna have to do this the hard way again. Wanna take a peek at your. Best. Friend?"

The scene featured Alex sitting in a booth at a restaurant. He looked anxious, his eyes bouncing around the room. He pressed his cell phone to his ear. "Yeah, I'm calling about the murder of that girl last night. I know her boyfriend. This morning, he told me he'd caught her cheating on him and that it pissed him off. He said he threatened her. It pains me to say this, but he might be your culprit."

Carson felt the same sick knot in his stomach that he'd had when he viewed the footage of Sara. Though he upped the volume on the laptop, he couldn't hear what the other party was saying, only Alex's responses.

"There's a reward, right?" asked Alex. "Seriously, that much? I don't wanna give my name just yet." A brief pause. "Understood. His name is Carson Maxwell. He lives at—"

Pop Pop re-appeared, an expression of intense sorrow on his face. "I'm sorry he hurt you, buddy. The betrayal, the selfishness, the outright cowardice of that filthy Judas. Someone like that doesn't deserve to live. Your life would be happier without him. You see that now, don't you buddy? You deserve to be happy."

"I deserve to be happy," Carson said in a trance-like voice.

Pop Pop quickly perked up. "Good, then. That wraps up another lesson. I'll have another for you soon. Till then, I love you more than sunshine."

Numbness overtook Carson's body. *This isn't real. No way this is real,* he thought. The facts surrounding the past forty-eight hours turned in his fracturing mind. Sara's infidelity had brought about her death. He was concerned about what Alex's betrayal might bring. *What'd you do, Alex?* he thought.

Alex had sold him out for the equivalent of thirty pieces of silver. Carson feared the police might already be on their way to arrest him for suspicion of murder. He decided to get in his car and drive somewhere safe.

10

Carson took the back roads and side streets until he arrived at Pop Pop's house. He maneuvered his car up the narrow driveway that ran along the side of the property and parked inside the detached garage. Then he went into the house.

Carson entered the kitchen, got himself a glass of water, then entered the living room. He needed information, so he turned on the TV and went to the twenty-four-hour local news channel. He waited for the weather report at the top of the hour to end, so he could find out what the authorities had learned. Soon, the news anchor appeared and provided an update on the investigation.

"Today, police discovered a man's bludgeoned body in an alley off of Crescent Drive near First Street," said the news anchor. "They have identified the victim as twenty-five-year-old Alex Newsome of Forest Hills Apartments."

Shivering, Carson muttered, "Pop Pop, what did you do?" He continued listening to the report.

"Based on an anonymous tip earlier in the day, the authorities are searching for a person of interest. The individual is thought to have a link to Mr. Newsome and the stabbing victim discovered last night. In other news..."

Swirling thoughts filled Carson's mind. *Oh, my God. They'll take one look at his driver's license and figure out he's my roommate. They'll know he's the one who turned me in. What if they find the message on Sara's cellphone? The DVD's? What'll I tell them? This is bad. This is really, really bad.*

Carson went to the dining room to think. When he got there, he discovered a manila envelope waiting for him on the table. He hesitated before picking it up, wondering if he had the courage to open it. *Do I have a choice at this point?* he asked himself. Before he could change his mind, he quickly ripped open the envelope. Inside was a DVD marked, *Pop Pop's Guide to a Happier Life Volume 4.* He took it to the study at the back of the house and inserted it into the desktop computer.

Total blackness had replaced the once beautiful and tranquil oasis of calm. Pop Pop smiled, but it wasn't one of his warm, uplifting ones. Instead, he ghoulishly exposed his teeth, giving his expression a macabre and unnatural appearance, as though something sinister was trying to impersonate him. He began speaking in his usual top-of-the-mornin' manner. "Hey there, buddy! I hope the sun's shinin' where you are. As you can see, it's not shinin' so bright around here. I hope you're not too upset about Alex, but was I right or was I right?"

Carson was incredulous. "Do you not know what's happening? You put all of this in motion with your stupid life lessons.

Because of you, the police are gonna think I had something to do with Sara's and Alex's murders. If you care about me as much as you say, then make this right. Give me something I can tell the cops. Something they'll believe, such as who did it."

Pop Pop stroked his chin and nodded his head, as if he agreed with Carson. "Fair enough, buddy, fair enough. I told you if you hung in there, I'd reveal the monster who killed Sara and Alex. So let's move on to the last lesson I told you about: doing the right thing."

The scene cut to Sara alone in her bedroom at her condominium. As she was taking off her red dress, someone appeared in the doorway of the dark bathroom. Slowly, he stepped forward into the light. Carson lifted the large knife in the air and crept up behind Sara. She turned and screamed.

Abruptly, a different scene appeared on the monitor.

Alex put his cell phone away and left the restaurant. As he was walking past an alley, he stopped as if someone had called his name. He looked apprehensive. As he drifted down the path, he walked past a large dumpster. Carson rose from behind it, his face reminiscent of a dead-eyed psychopath. Gripping a short pipe, he followed Alex.

Carson felt disconnected from his body. "How did I... wait, no... it wasn't me, it was you. I don't know how, but it was you, Pop Pop. Tell me it was you!"

Pop Pop returned to the screen. "Buddy, the police have figured out where you are; they'll be here shortly. I know it's wrong to let an unfaithful woman and a treacherous man rob you of your happiness, but you've done a terrible thing, Carson. You need to own it. You need to do the right thing."

Desperation and confusion overwhelmed Carson. The faint line between reality and delusion became imperceptible, as rationality abandoned him. Succumbing to his madness, he convinced himself that everything that had happened was real. He realized that Pop Pop was only looking out for him the way he always had.

The weight of that love humbled Carson to the point of tears. "What should I do now, Pop Pop?"

A gentle look of patience spread across Pop Pop's weathered face. "Go to our place in the garden. There's one more envelope waiting for you. Go on, son. They're coming down the street right now."

Carson ambled out to the garden haven. The flowers were awash with Technicolor splendor. A rich canopy of fruit trees kept the harsh sunlight at bay. Sitting on one of the Adirondacks was the manila envelope.

*A howl of sirens screamed nearby, heading in his direction.*

Carson picked up the envelope. It was heavy.

*The sirens were on top of him. The noises of tires skidding to a stop and car doors slamming reverberated through the pleasant afternoon air.*

He opened the envelope, looked inside, and smiled.

*Many footsteps stomping on gravel rushed toward the back-yard. Loud voices, punctuated by the sound of wood exploding, echoed from the front porch.*

He pulled Pop Pop's .38 snub-nose revolver from the envelope and gripped it.

*Someone yelled, "Gun! Gun!"*

The feeling of a dozen wasp stings hammered his body, dropping him into a cold pit of infinite blackness.

11

When Lexi returned home after Carson's funeral, she was frazzled and distraught. The news Crews were making her family's lives a train wreck—they'd even been at the funeral. Her heart broke into more pieces as Carson's face filled her head. She couldn't comprehend how he had fallen so far, so fast. Despite everything he'd done, she missed her brother, yearned for him.

When she reached the front door, a large manila envelope on her doormat greeted her. She picked it up and saw that someone had written her name on it in large, black letters. Curious, she stepped inside to open it.

She went into her home office, sat down at her desk, and opened the envelope. Inside was a single DVD with the title, *Pop Pop's Guide to a Happier Life Vol. 1* scribbled on its face. She loaded the disc and sat back.

The screen flickered, and the image of Pop Pop appeared. He was sitting alone in his backyard paradise, wearing the old, tacky Hawaiian shirt she remembered with fondness. He smiled at the screen as if he could somehow see her sitting in front of him.

"Hey, Lexi, darlin'. I bet you're wonderin' why in the world this DVD is showin' up at your house unannounced. Well, fear not. I've got someone special with me here who's got some important things he wants to share with you." Pop Pop looked to his left and waved someone over.

Tears cascaded over Lexi's smile. She glowed as she watched her older brother sit in the Adirondack chair next to Pop Pop's. Carson looked into the camera, grinned, then said, "Hey, little sis. I hope the sun's shinin' where you are."

# MAGIC 8 BALL

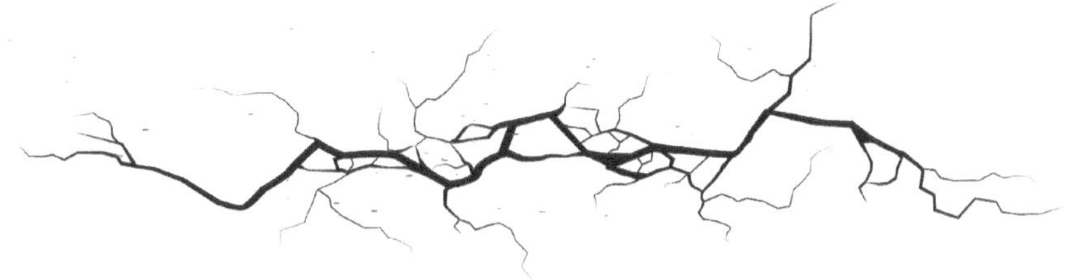

Stephen guzzled four beers, giving him a wicked buzz. But compared to his buddies, he was a lightweight. He had reached the age of twenty-five, a significant age by common standards, thus it was time to party. It thrilled him to have his best friends, Tyler and Evan, to share it with, bombed though they were.

"Geez, dude," Evan said to Tyler, "you're really throwin' back the highballs. You might wanna drink some water with 'em."

"I am. See? The ice in my glass is melting."

"Quit harassing the man," Stephen said to Evan. "I wouldn't be sitting here if it weren't for him. I'd be sitting over there with that hot babe in the Daisy Dukes and a tight Foo Fighters T-shirt."

Tyler sized up the girl in question. "That T must be 100% cotton, cuz that thang has *shruuunk.*"

"Yo, stupid," Evan said. "Isn't there something else you're supposed to be doing? Give you a hint: it rhymes with 'birthday present.'"

"Oh, nearly forgot," Tyler said. He fumbled beneath his seat and produced a small, haphazardly wrapped box, and set it on the table in front of Stephen. "'Kay, Stevie-Baby. We know how much you love to collect vintage toys and stuff. So, we did a lil' research and found somethin' special you said you'd love to get your hands on. And no, I don't mean Evan's mom."

"Hey!" Evan shouted. "Lay off my mom. She's the reason I've become the respectable drunk that I am today." Then, lifting his glass, said, "Cheers, Ma!"

Tyler sneered at Evan's inebriated outburst. "I apologize to you, Evan. How rude of me to speak while you were trying to interrupt. Where was I? Oh, yeah... *the present!* We got it from the private collection of some weird, rich snob out of Ireland. I know it's only the one gift, but it cost us a pretty penny, so ya better like it."

Stephen said, "Only one way to find out. "Here we go!"

"Wait!" Tyler shouted. "Let's add some measure of decorum here and give a proper intro. On the count of two—"

"Why two?" Stephen asked.

"Cuz, if we start at three, I don't know if I'll still be conscious by the time we hit one."

"I see your point. Please, continue."

"I surely will. On the count of two, we shout loud enough to generate concern amongst the other patrons... *in this establishment!*

"Sssh... keep it down, stupid," warned Evan.

"All right, all right," Tyler said, pressing his index finger to his lips in a shushing gesture."'Kay, yoush ready? Here we go."

Stephen's intoxicated brethren counted down in unison. "Two... one... *surprise!*"

Stephen ripped through the paper and raised the item to his face. He marveled at the genuine and well-maintained 1950s Magic 8 Ball, sealed inside its original box.

"Are you serious? Is this the real deal?" Stephen asked.

Evan chimed in to reassure him. "Does a bear crap what's left of you in the woods? Hell, yay-yuh!"

"Whoa, dudes," Stephen said. "There can't be more than a few original 8 Balls in this condition. Should I open it? It might kill the value. I can't decide."

"Nah, go ahead, rip in, and enjoy it," Evan replied.

Stephen restrained himself from being impulsive and tearing into it like a pit bull on a pork chop. "If it's okay with you guys, I think I'll wait and decide later. Wow, you two are the best."

"We know!" they screamed, as they generated concern amongst the other patrons in the establishment.

Another beer and an Uber ride later, Stephen was back in his apartment. He was still deciding if he should open the box. "Like I'm ever gonna get rid of this sucker. Besides, I wanna be its first customer."

Stephen plopped onto the couch like a bomb from a warplane, almost flattening his sleepy cat, Melvin. He opened the box's lid and removed the prized collectible. He was filled with joy as he gazed upon the object of his pleasure. He asked the simple yes or no question, "Will I ever be rich?" He shook the 8 Ball, flipped it over, and waited for the pre-written, random answer to bob to the surface of the dark blue water. He was neither delighted nor discouraged by the response.

*NO*

"Okey-doke, Mr. Magic 8 Ball: Will I ever meet Ms. Right?" He shook the ball and turned to the bottom to read the meaningless answer.

*DEFINITELY NOT*

"Dang, dude," Stephen chuckled, "that's just mean." Being drunk and in a silly mood, he continued. "Okay, all-knowing 8 Ball, let's try a harder one: What's my cat's name?" The response took Stephen aback.

*MELVIN*

After a brief silence, Stephen squinted his eyes and asked again. He shook the ball for a few seconds and then held it in his hands to prepare himself. When he was ready, he turned the toy over and read its reply.

*MELVIN*

Stephen jumped from the sofa, causing the 8 Ball to fall and roll beneath the coffee table. The unexpected commotion caused Melvin to shriek and sprint towards the bedroom. Stephen paced back and forth, rubbing his hands together. "Omigosh... omigosh... omigosh."

Once Stephen pulled himself together, he appealed to the small part of his brain that wasn't drenched in alcohol. It occurred to him that his so-called buddies might've rigged the toy to produce the unexpected answers. He could envision them parked nearby, roaring with drunken laughter. However, despite his best reasoning, he couldn't figure out how it could be possible for them to pull off something so complicated. How could they anticipate what questions he would ask? And if they could, how could they hear him outside of a hidden microphone in his apartment? He figured the theory was too fanciful to be true.

Stephen took in a few deep breaths, like he was going to bungee jump. Then he fished the Magic 8 Ball from under the table. He clutched the globe and perched himself on the sofa's edge, pondering his next question. It was based on something nobody knew. "All right, Magic 8 Ball: What magazine did I keep hidden under my mattress when I was in junior high?"

*JUGS-A-PLENTY*

Stephen's body felt as if it were closing in on itself as he read the ball's spot-on answer.

His hands were shaking, making it difficult to grip the oversized billiard ball. His heartbeat thumped in his ears as he cupped his hands to his mouth and hyperventilated into his palms. He wanted to throw the toy out the window to the parking lot below, yet he hesitated. *What if...?* he wondered.

Stephen started thinking about how accurate the answers to his personal questions were, and the positive outcomes they could bring. Interest replaced his fears as he looked into the amazing possibilities for his future. *Which stock should I buy? What lottery numbers should I play? What's the PIN of a rich person?* He breezed through all the questions but kept receiving the same reply: *ASK ANOTHER QUESTION*

Upon realizing that the object would not grant his selfish desires, Stephen retreated to fare more pedestrian. "Will I get a raise soon?"

*NO*

"That's cool; I can deal with that. Let's get to a good one: Will I die soon?"

*YES*

Stephen's mouth went dry. He hesitated before asking the next question. Although he dreaded the response, he pushed himself to ask, "When?"

*TOMORROW*

Stephen's pulse rate sped up as he stared at the frightening response. His breath quaking with nerves, he posed the next logical question: "What's... gonna happen to me?"

*EXPLOSION*

"*Explosion? Where?*" Stephen gripped the ball and shook it as if he were trying to strangle an attacker. Then he turned the toy over.

*WORK*

"Oh, God! Are you telling me that my building is going to blow up?"

*IT IS SO* Stephen pressed forward with the next question: "Will any of my co-workers die with me?"

*YES, DEFINITELY*

"Oh no... how many?"

*EVERYONE*

"That can't be right. For the love of mercy; Becky has a kid on the way!" Stephen rubbed his right temple as if pushing the awful information into his brain might help him better understand the magnitude of the tragic event. "All right, just tell me this: Will this huge explosion cause any collateral damage?"

*IT IS CERTAIN*

"How many more dead?"

*EVERYONE*

Stephen sat upright on the sofa, every nerve and muscle in his body strained with tension. He looked down at the toy. "You're saying there's going to be a deadly explosion tomorrow, and it'll be powerful enough to kill everyone in and around my building? Will it be a terrorist bombing? A gas leak?

*NO*

"Then what? Tell me! *Specifically,* what's going to explode?" He was about to shake the Magic 8 Ball, but before he did so, the tiny triangle bobbed to the inky surface on its own and displayed the terrifying truth.

*EARTH*

# SPEAK OF THE DEAD

Deputy Waylon Dupree winced when the first wave of thunder shook his patrol car. It was low and rumbling as if the earth beneath him were crashing through the canopy of asphalt to take hold of him. The heavy rain came soon after. He struggled against the high winds to stay on the road. *Add in some of that telekinesis and telepathy stuff and you got yourself somethin' right out of a Stephen King novel.*

At twenty-one, Waylon was the youngest deputy in the Bidwell County Sheriff's Department in Weldon, Mississippi: population 109 1/2. It used to be an even 110, but Mervin Garnell had gone and gotten his legs lopped off while trying to dislodge a raccoon carcass from his combine. As the rookie, Waylon had the sublime privilege of working the graveyard shift in a town roughly the size of your average Walmart.

*BOOM!*

"Lord of Moses! That wasn't no clap of thunder—that was a dadgum standin' ovation!"

It was almost two in the morning, and Waylon was dog-tired. The bottom had dropped out of the rain-heavy sky, and now he couldn't see two feet in front of him. He decided to be sensible about the whole exhaustion/biblical flood thing and find a place to pull over and grab some shut-eye. He knew of a car wash about five miles up the road on State Road 29, where he could swing into one of the outdoor stalls and nod off till the storm passed.

Waylon was well acquainted with the area. He'd grown up in the pinprick town of Blytheville. For well over a century, his kinfolk had filled the graveyards of Weldon, Blytheville, and nearby Buck Horn. His family's sweat and bones were in the soil of each of the small farming communities. Everybody knew each other; most were related in some way or another. As denizens of the peaceful, rural life, their biggest concerns centered around increasing their crops' yields and not accidentally coming on to their cousin in a bar. But there was also the unspoken yearning to run away from the land that absorbed its people like a sponge in a hurricane. The place never quite let go of you; it sure hadn't let go of Waylon.

Waylon took his time getting to the car wash—this wasn't the time for hot rodding. He pulled into one of the open stalls and killed the old Crown Vic's massive, 250-horsepower, V-8 monster motor. He sank into the well-worn butt crater bequeathed him by his lard-bottomed predecessor: the newly and thankfully retired, Big Mick Harvey.

Waylon was just about to cross over into Snoozeville, USA when the booming voice of Deb from Dispatch blared from the radio. The fearless female officer was a boisterous, hard-drinkin', rough 'n tumble kind of gal whom the boys at the department clandestinely referred to as Old Smokey. The name had come about because each of them claimed to have been on top of her at some point.

"Waylon. Oh, Waaylooon... Boy, are you asleep out there? Just grunt and let me know you're alive."

"I'm here, Deb. What's up?"

"I got a good one for ya. You 'member ol' Mabel Luckabee?"

Mabel was the stuff of legend in their neck of the woods. She was a mean, old cuss who never met a person she could tolerate or a deodorant she couldn't overcome. If cleanliness is next to godliness, then Mable was the antichrist. She was now well into her seventies and living alone in her raggedy, two-story farmhouse in Weldon. A widow by vocation, some of the townsfolks opined that her last husband, Ed, had passed away, not because of any mishap or disease, but because—like the other poor S.O.B.'s before him—he'd wanted to. Not long after, his Bluetick hound dog, Bucket Head, decided to go AWOL. Everybody figured with Ed gone, the dog must've thought, *Oh, no, you don't*, and taken off for parts unknown. Mabel was an equal opportunity offender. She hated everyone, regardless of race, creed, or species. Her scowling moonscape of a face filled Waylon's mind, making him grimace.

"What about her?" he asked. "Did she ugly away or somethin'? Durn woman looks like the love child of Steve Buscemi and Elma the Yak Lady."

"Don't know yet. I just got a call from Dorene, her nosy night-owl neighbor. Says she ain't seen her since Monday; that's two days ago. Dorene's tried callin' her, but she won't answer the phone. She also said the house lights have been on the whole time. I need you to do a welfare check. I know she's a pain, so just peek in her window and see if she's movin' around."

"Can't we just wait a few days to see if the buzzards are circlin' her house?"

"Come on now, Waylon. You and me both know two things: One, the buzzards won't go anywhere near her 'cause it might lower their culinary standards. And two, you ain't got nothin' better to do."

"Deb, the only thing worse than findin' that old hag alive would be findin' her dead."

"Well, if she is, her funeral's gonna draw quite a crowd."

"Why? Nobody can stand her."

"That's true, but you know what they say: 'Give the people what they want and they'll show up in droves.'"

"Fair point. All right, then; I'm on my way."

The rain had begun to ease off, but the thunder and lightning were still raising a fuss. Waylon was thankful for the graveled lane that led up to the Luckabee house; otherwise, he would have had to swim for it. After roughly thirty yards of potholes and low-hanging tree limbs, he pulled up to the decrepit, old place.

Waylon had been there a few times during his childhood to chuck rocks and cherry bombs. But with the storm still laying haymakers, the house looked more foreboding than he remembered. The lengthy shards of white paint, that the claws of time had carved away, made it look like a large potato that had gone a few rounds with an angry vegetable peeler. Its tattered roof sloped down to rusty gutters from which lush, rambling gardens of weeds flourished. Looming from the blackness, the eerie eyesore brought to Waylon's mind an exterior set from a Rob Zombie movie.

Waylon grabbed the small Maglite from his service belt, put on his plastic-covered deputy's hat, and jogged to the house's front porch. Its weak structural integrity gave him pause. *This porch makes me think of Mabel: old, nasty, and saggin' in all the worst places.* Waylon looked through the windows but didn't see anyone. He pounded on the door. No one answered, so he banged harder. "Mrs. Luckabee! Oh, Mrs. Luckabee! Sheriff's Department! Mrs. Luckabee, you in there?" When he failed to get a response, he tried the doorknob. Mabel had left the door unlocked, so he stepped inside.

Waylon walked through the house's main floor, calling the elderly woman's name, but all was still and silent. With each step, the sticky wooden floorboards groaned as if they were dying. As he went from one disheveled room to another, he was amazed and appalled at the amount of debris that Mabel had hoarded. There were several dozen unopened boxes from QVC, old clothes and magazines, dusty porcelain dolls, and other creepy items that might indicate someone wearing a skin suit was about to come at you with a running chainsaw.

"Giiirl, you are seriously messed up," he said. As he ventured further into the cramped house, a nostril-searing stench hit him square in the nose. "Woo-weee! Smells like feet, farts, and Fritos in here."

Waylon headed up the stairs to check out what he figured might be a bedroom, a bathroom, and—given the vibe of the creepy dump—a possible kill room. When he reached the second-floor landing, he heard a faint sound coming from one of the rooms. "Mrs. Luckabee? That you?"

He followed the noise to one of the rooms and found the door ajar. He pushed it open and saw Mabel lying on her bed. Dressed in a dingy, white nightgown, she was propped up on a pillow, staring at a small, portable TV located on a dresser near the bed's foot.

"Oh, hey, Mrs. Luckabee. You probably don't remember me, but I'm Don and Linda Dupree's boy, Waylon. I come by to check on ya. You okay?"

Mabel didn't acknowledge his presence in any way. She kept staring blankly at the TV as if it had hypnotized her.

"I'm sorry to bother ya, but I need to make sure you're all right. Are you... all right, I mean?"

Mabel continued ignoring him, so he walked between her and the TV. She kept looking ahead as if he weren't there. Waylon went to grab hold of her toes and give them a shake, but when he saw the thick, curled nails, he poked her foot with the hand-sized Maglite instead. *Note to self: destroy my flashlight.*

When she didn't respond, Waylon walked around to the side of the bed. He leaned in close to her and whispered, "Mrs. Luck-abeee." He pushed the side of her greasy head with the tip of his Maglite and she keeled over on her side."Judas on a tricycle!" Waylon felt for a pulse, but found none. Then he heard a faint scratching as Mabel's bottom lip began pulsing outward. He held back his sickness when two large, brown cockroaches exited her mouth. After pulling in a few deep breaths to quell his disgust, he pressed the talk button on his shoulder radio. "Deb? Waylon here. Pick up."

The radio crackled, and Deb's voice filled the room—too loud for Waylon's taste. "Sup, Waylon. How's the wicked witch of Weldon?"

"Why don't you ask her? She's standin' right here." He chuckled at poor Deb's expense.

"Oh... oh, sorry 'bout that, Mrs. Luckabee. I was just—"

"It's all right, Deb. She can't hear ya. She's deader than Kevin Spacey's actin' career."

"Oh, crap! Really?"

"Yep. In fact, you can call her whatever you want; she ain't comin'."

"Well, ain't you nice? Didn't your mama ever tell you to never speak ill of the dead? Though I guess we can make an exception in ol' Mabel's case. It ain't like she's gonna mind. Ya know, I don't mean the old gal no disrespect, but the only way I'm gonna be able to squirt a tear during this here tender moment is if I yank out a nose hair."

"Whatever. Listen, call in a—"

*WEEEE!* Waylon bent his head away from the radio's high-pitched whine. "Deb, are you there?"

"Way... where... can't... get out..."

Struggling to communicate with Deb, Waylon retreated downstairs in search of a better signal. "Deb? Can you hear me?" He was relieved when she answered.

"Yeah, I can hear you, but barely. You keep bobbin' and weavin' on me. Listen, I've already let Dave—I mean the sheriff—know about Mabel. I won't repeat what he called her. He's still on his fishin' trip, so he won't be there till almost sun-up. I also contacted the first responders down in Camfort, but they're at least a half-hour out. Said that the storm had caused some tree and powerline damage, so it may be even longer. Just sit tight until they arrive. In the meantime, I'm gonna need you to secure the scene and keep watch."

"Keep watch? You mean like in babysittin' a dead body till the meat wagon and the sheriff arrive?"

"Listen, Waylon. I know it seems like a big deal when you're new and all, but it'll be okay. Just make sure you don't disturb nothin'; the sherriff'll take care of the scene. Just go ahead and start your report."

"Geez, Deb. Of all the corpses to be locked in with on a stormy night, I had to draw Mabel Luckabee's." A low hum came over the radio. "Deb? Deb, you there?" Silence. Waylon sighed at first, then decided to make light of his predicament. He held the radio's mic up to his face and announced, "Well, hey there, all you night owls. You're listenin' to WAYN where the hits just keep ooon comin'."

Then, like a bad omen, the pounding rain returned with a vengeance.

Waylon went back upstairs to check out the rest of the second floor. He was happy to find that the upper floor rooms were not as cluttered and dirty as downstairs.

When he finished his exploration, he went into Mabel's bedroom, took out his cell phone, and snapped some pics for his report. Once he got that out of the way, he shut off the TV and headed back downstairs to look for coffee.

He was halfway down when he heard a loud click followed by the sound of the TV coming on. "The heck is that all about?"

Waylon re-entered Mabel's bedroom. The old tube television was on and Mabel's body was propped up on the pillow again. Waylon was unnerved and confused. *Say, wasn't she...* He watched the lifeless body for a few seconds. When it didn't move, he turned off the antiquated boob box, then walked to the door.

*CLICK.* It was on again. Waylon was adhered to the floor, afraid to turn around. He was relieved to observe that when he did—and with only a tad of guilt—Mabel was still dead as a brick. Waylon figured the mystery had a reasonable explanation, so he shifted into seasoned cop mode. He told himself that all he was dealing with was a prehistoric television, plugged into the wall socket of an old, rickety house with suspect wiring. *Piece-a-crap television. Thing's older than Moses's babysitter.* Waylon reached behind the TV and yanked its cord from the wall, then glared at the blank screen. "Now shut the heck up, or I'm gonna take out my gun and go *Scarface* on ya."

Waylon made his way down to the kitchen and began looking through the cracked, faded cabinets for some much-needed java. It took a lot of searching, but he finally found an ancient jar of freeze-dried coffee. The jar was sticky; the grounds clumped together like a rich, robust hockey puck. Waylon guessed that someone had likely purchased the brown muck sometime during the Clinton administration. *Has it come to this? Do I really need caffeine this bad?* Begrudgingly, he accepted that he did.

He turned his search toward finding a clean cup, as well as something in which to boil water. He flipped on one of the stove's burners and started digging around. When he saw a relatively clean mug, he lifted it as if he'd found the Holy Grail and sang, "Ta-da!"

There was a brilliant flash of lightning, followed by floor-shaking thunder. Then the power went out.

*Our Sweet Lady of Perpetual Nonsense, what now?* Waylon thought. Pulling his defiled Maglite from his belt, he went looking for the fuse box. He didn't have to look for long—there was one located inside the kitchen's walk-in pantry.

Waylon inspected the black briquette that was once the main fuse. *Deader than a mean, old woman in a farmhouse bedroom.*

CREEEAK... Dust and dirt trickled down onto Waylon's hat like grimy rain. The sharp noise came from the room directly above him: Mable's bedroom. His knocking knees betrayed his fear, as his breath retreated into his lungs, refusing to come out. On the one hand, he knew it was his duty to go check on things. But the other hand was telling him to grab the rest of his body and run like a crack-addled gazelle into the raging night. He settled the internal argument by siding with the more sensible hand. Waylon much preferred braving the torrential rain and sitting in his cruiser to staying in what he was rapidly coming to consider the redneck version of Hill House. In addition, he still needed to fill out a report. He was thankful that the paperwork was in the car, thus affording him a plausible case for reasonable cowardice.

When Waylon reached the front door, he tried the knob, but it wouldn't turn. Then, as if on cue, a sinister cackle bled through his radio, making his arm hairs stand on end. He began to fear that a powerful supernatural force might be at play. The idea chilled him. Taking a few steps backward, Waylon warned the silent crowd of imaginary gawkers: "Stand back, y'all! I'm fixin' to make a Waylon-shaped hole in this door!" Then an uncomfortable thought hit him. *Oh, for the love of Lucy! The guys at the station'll never let me forget it if I run like a little girl from a spooky, old house. Gotta tap into my inner Chuck Norris and handle this case like one of the big boys.* He drew what he could from his shallow puddle of courage and ventured back upstairs to inspect Mabel's bedroom again.

When Waylon got there, his first act was to locate the source of the noises. Confusion collided with unease, as he observed that nothing, including the recently departed Mabel, had moved. However, the lack of activity only served to make him more nervous. "Screw the guys. I'm done with this place."

As Waylon was leaving, the bedsprings squeaked, followed by the unsettling sound of somebody scampering away. He turned around and saw that Mabel was literally dead and gone. His skin tingled at the implications.

He shined his Maglite around the lightless room, praying that the formerly deceased woman wouldn't come running at him from one of the pitch-dark corners. Despite the massive storm bellowing outside, the world fell silent for Waylon. The weight of his dread submerged his entire mind in a cold, black pool of fear and disbelief.

"Where's Steve and Elma?" the scratchy voice said.

Waylon spun around several times, the flashlight's beam hopping around the room like a bouncing ball of light. Suddenly, bare feet slapped across the wooden floor as the thing rushed into the bedroom closet, slamming the door shut.

"Mrs. Luckabee? That you?"

The closet door creaked open halfway, and a shadowy figure crawled out. Its neck made a cracking sound as its head swiveled in Waylon's direction. Glowing yellow eyes peered up at him, numbing his quivering body. He focused a funnel of light on the thing dressed in a nightgown. Mabel's contorted body looked like a pretzel playing a game of Twister. Her breathing was quick and shallow, her frame heaving with every pant. As soon as the light settled on her crinkled face, she squealed and scuttled under the bed.

Waylon's twitchy hand rested on the butt of his service revolver. With great wariness, he plodded over to Mabel's last known resting place.

"Why don't you join me down here, Don and Linda's boy?" the voice growled.

Icy dots spread across Waylon's sweaty body like frigid spiders skittering on bare skin. Against his better judgment and basic common sense, Waylon lowered his head toward the floor. Alabaster arms shot out of the mattress, and gnarled hands seized him by his hat. Screaming, he twisted his head free of the ghostly grip.

Waylon sped from the bedroom and toward the staircase. After a few clumsy steps, his feet flew out from under him, landing him on his backside. Helpless against gravity, he tobogganed down the painful steps, farting loudly with each violent bounce.

Finally, his noisy hindquarters found the bottom of the stairs. After pulling himself up, Waylon returned to the locked front door. Grabbing the knob with both hands, he used all his strength to turn it, but his efforts proved fruitless. He pressed the button on his radio. "Deb! For the love of the Lord, please answer me!" The radio was still dead. His next idea was to try to break out through one of the windows.

Waylon ran to the living room and tried opening one, but it wouldn't budge. He pushed up on the next one. Same result. Desperate, he grabbed a small coffee table and hurled it against the window. It bounced off the glass like a tennis ball. He was about to use his gun to help improve his luck when a coffee mug went sailing past his head, shattering against the impenetrable window. He whirled around and saw the lower back part of Mabel's nightgown disappearing around the kitchen doorway.

Waylon yanked the gun from its holster, gripping it tightly in his right hand while holding the Maglite in the other. "That's enough, now! This is Deputy Sheriff Waylon Dupree! You better make yourself known!" There was a movement in the dining room. He went to investigate.

The dust from the many items stacked around the dim room flittered in the bright ray of the flashlight. Waylon's nerves were bouncing around inside him like a pinball. He steered the beam around the dining room.

"I hope you all show up in droves," the husky voice said.

"Quittin' time!" Waylon sprinted to the front door, where he fired every round in his gun directly at the doorknob, only to have them rebound off. His heart was racing as if it were qualifying for the Daytona 500. "Let me outta here! Whoever you are, please just let me go, and I'll jump in my squad car and leave right now!"

Footsteps emanated from the front sitting room. Waylon heard the crackling sound of a phonograph needle making contact with the vinyl. An old school, swing-style, dance number reverberated throughout the downstairs. He recognized the tune as one his grandma listened to whenever she decided to up the dosage of what she called her "happy time nerve medicine." It was an old Judy Garland song from the 1960s called, "Come On Get Happy." Soon, Judy's voice chimed in with a bouncy beat.

*Forget your troubles come on get happy/ You better chase all your cares away Shout hallelujah, come on get happy/ Get ready for the judgment day* Waylon raised his flashlight, holstered his empty pistol, and entered the dark room.

His body became one large icicle. The late Mabel Luckabee, her back to him, stood in front of a large, wooden stereo cabinet, swaying in time with the tinny-sounding tune.

"M-m-Mrs. Luckabee? M-Mabel, ma'am?"

She stopped moving and snapped to attention.

Waylon continued. "The station house sent me here to ch-ch-check on ya. You was upstairs dead, but clearly, you're feelin' better, so I g-guess I'll be leavin' now."

Waylon watched slack-jawed and bug-eyed as the moving corpse levitated and spun around to face him. He aimed the flashlight at the hag, accentuating her face's pallor. Her yellow eyes blazed with raw hatred. His mind was yelling at him to escape, but his body refused to cooperate.

He struggled to work up enough spit to speak. "M-m-Mrs. Luckabee, I just w-wanna leave and—"

*NOOO!* The shrill sound, coupled with the force of her voice, caused all of the first-floor windows to burst outwards. Her body flew through the air at Waylon.

He shrieked, then hurled the Maglite at her as hard as he could. Finally, his mind and body got on the same page, and he fled from the flying corpse. Waylon turned and ran straight for one of the paneless windows, launching himself like a twirling meat missile.

After landing on the front porch, Waylon rolled into the railing with so much force that his body busted through it and out into the yard. The violent impact made him look like a human bowling ball landing a perfect strike. Just as he was hauling himself up from the thick, brown mud, he heard a siren in the distance. *Thank-you-Jesus-thank-you-Jesus-thank-you-Jesus!*

The EMTs were the first on the scene. Dave, the long-suffering sheriff, was still on his way back from his ill-fated fishing trip. They found Waylon standing in the front yard, in the middle of the vicious storm, a thousand-yard stare in his eyes. The team couldn't get anything out of him, so they had him wait in the back of the ambulance while they dealt with Mabel.

After twenty minutes or so, one of the paramedics came down to grab some gear and check on Waylon, who was still shell-shocked. "You wanna tell me what happened in there?" he asked. "The windows are all busted out, and the place is a wreck. Was it like that when you got here?"

Waylon was regaining his wits. He realized that there was no scenario in which the paramedics—or anyone else for that matter—were going to believe him. Resigned to his peculiar predicament, he muttered, "Yep."

"Well, observations like that fall under your authority any-way," the paramedic said. "I'll just get on with my job, then." He began placing some items into a small vinyl bag. Before he left for the house, he turned and said, "As soon as we finish up here, I wanna take you in for a quick checkup. You look like you might still be in shock. Hell's bells on an Easter bonnet; I thought you boys were s'posed to be used to all this stuff."

He'd only taken a few steps when Waylon called after him. "Hey! Tell me somethin'. Where'd you find the body? Did ya see anything unusual?"

"Ya mean other than the house bein' beat to crap? We found her upstairs in bed. She was lyin' back on a pillow, starin' straight ahead—creepy as all get out. She must've known a blackout was comin', though."

"Why's that?"

"She had a small Maglite in her hand." Then he left Waylon alone to ponder his sanity.

*Am I crazy, or did I let my rookie self get so worked up that I started imaginin' things?* he wondered. *What a wuss!* Waylon had nearly talked himself down off the fiftieth-floor ledge of the Crazy Building when the radio in the front cab of the ambulance turned itself on. The sound of Judy Garland's mellifluous voice pushed

Waylon off the side of his mental skyscraper, as she crooned, *Forget your troubles come on get happy...*

# WHO IS THIS?

"Who is this?" asked the disgruntled voice on the other end of the line.

"What?" That was the only response Larson had to the unexpected question. He thought he had dialed the right number to his supervisor's office—my God, he'd dialed it a hundred times—but this time he hadn't.

"Your name; give me your name," the man insisted.

Larson wondered if he'd actually dialed the right number and if someone at the hotel was pulling a prank on him. "Uh, this is Larson calling for Bill."

"No. I mean your full name. Larson, *what?*"

Something about this guy felt very wrong to Larson; his voice was unnerving. He decided it was time to end the call, joke or not. He held the phone close to his face, then spoke directly into it. "None of your business, jerk!" Then he quickly pressed the end button. *Man, that was creepy*, he thought.

Larson had no desire to contact his supervisor after that. He only wanted to get his work schedule for next week, but he could do that later. Besides, his toddler, Jake, would wake up from his nap soon. He slept for two hours every afternoon; you could practically set your watch by him.

Larson worked nights at the Ramada Inn, while Caitlin, his wife, worked days down at the bank; they rarely saw each other. But whatever time they squeezed in over the weekends (if Larson didn't have to work) always seemed to make up for the week's separation. However, this weekend she was at her sister's place, helping her paint a bathroom while Larson watched the little guy.

Jake was nearly two years old. It wouldn't be long before he reached an age where Larson and Caitlin felt comfortable enrolling him in daycare. Then maybe Larson could go back to the first shift at the hotel. In the meantime, he was treasuring every moment with his first and only child.

*RRRING! RRRING!*

*Better get that,* Larson thought. *If Jake doesn't wake up on his own prerogative, he is one ornery little hombre.* He guessed it was Caitlin making one of her "You didn't lose our child, did you?" midday check-up calls. "Hello?" he said.

"Hello, Larson. Tell me something: what'd you do with all the money your mother gave you for charm school?" It was the man he'd hung up on earlier.

A mix of shame and fear overwhelmed Larson like someone had caught him doing something terrible. "How'd you get this number?"

"Ever hear of caller ID, 'jerk'?"

*Oh, bother,* thought Larson. He found it odd that he would think of those two words at a time like this. The comments came from one of Jake's *Winnie the Pooh* books. Pooh always said it when he found himself in trouble.

"Larson, we've got to stop meeting like this," the man said casually.

Larson broke off the call. His concern was not only for himself; he had a family to worry about as well. He sat down and began thinking of a reasonable way to manage the crank caller without making things worse. After all, this whack job had his number now. Larson was drifting toward the living room sofa when the phone rang again. He jerked as if a static shock had stung him. He answered it immediately, saying nothing at first; his nerves were too jangly. Then, as calmly as he could, said, "Hello?"

"Look, Larson, you're really beginning to annoy me. First, you call here and interrupt me while I'm—"

"Listen," Larson explained in his most apologetic tone. "I'm sorry if I interrupted you in the middle of something, okay? I just dialed the wrong number. That happens to the best of us every once in a while."

"Doesn't happen to me," the caller said condescendingly.

"Well, maybe not. But for those of us who aren't perfect—"

"You sayin', I think I'm perfect? Is that where we're at now, Larson? You psychic, all of a sudden? Let's have some fun, then. Right now I'm thinking of a number from, let's say, 1 to 50. No, let's make it 1 to 10. Tell me, Larson, what number am I thinking of?"

Larson's fear of the city's head cases was swiftly being replaced with hostility toward the arrogant loon he was talking with. "Look, pal, I said I was sorry. Sounds to me like maybe you've got more problems than a few wrong numbers calling. As a matter of fact, here's one more problem for you: I have your number, too." Larson fibbed a bit on that one, as his phone did not have that feature. "If you call my number one more time, I'll report you to the authorities. Then, when they take your phone away, you won't have to worry about any more annoying calls." He waited for another smug response, but none came. There was only a long silence. Larson figured that he'd better just end things, but the caller hung up first. He wasn't sure how to feel about how the verbal exchange had gone. These days, you never knew who you were dealing with. *How's that for city living?* he mused.

After a few minutes of sitting and no phone calls, Larson calmed down. He was just getting ready to reach for the TV's remote control when his phone rang again. Although it wasn't as startling as before, it still was enough to put him back on edge. He picked up the phone and, in a formidable tone, asked, "Yes?"

"'Yes?'" Caitlin said on the other end. "Who are you supposed to be, the butler?"

Relieved, Larson smiled despite himself. "Oh, hi, honey. I just thought it was someone else."

"Is Jake still sleeping? I didn't wake him, did I? Is that why you sounded so miffed? Did you think I was one of those telephone solicitors?"

"No. It's just that I had a freaky experience today."

Concerned, Caitlin asked, "What happened?"

Larson paused. Should he worry Caitlin unnecessarily over something that could be as trivial as some hothead he'd awakened from a nap? He decided he'd just leave it to lie and swiftly offered an innocuous explanation. "Oh, you know how weird some of those wrong numbers can be."

"Yeah, I suppose. I was only calling to check up on you two. Everything A-okay?"

"We're just fine, hon. Now get back to work, woman!"

"Love you," she whispered seductively.

"Love you, too," he cooed.

"Bye, sweets."

Trying to be amusing and annoying, Larson said in a love-struck voice, "You hang up first."

"No, you hang up first."

"No, you ha—"

Caitlin put a stop to the nonsense by hanging up first.

Larson's mood lifted. He went to make sure "Big Jake" was still alive like a lot of first-time parents do. He was relieved to find him blissfully asleep, his Donald Duck pacifier bobbling gently in his mouth.

Larson decided he could use some lunch, so he headed down the hall to the kitchen. The next fifteen minutes passed without incident. Then the phone rang again. Larson was willing to bet the ranch and the double-wide next to it that Caitlin was calling back to tease him some more. He would've lost that bet.

"Hello," Larson said, his tone more relaxed.

"Hi, Larson. It's me again. Listen, Larson, it's not as hard as you might think to get someone's address once you have their phone number, so you should really be careful how you talk to people."

Larson's anger rose. "Listen, idiot! I've had about enough of this crap! You show up on my doorstep, and I'll make you wish your old man had used better protection!"

"Oh, now, Larson," the man said in a conciliatory tone. "It's bad enough when you—"

"Hey, I've said all I'm gonna say to you, scumbag. You think you're so tough? Quit calling me up like a frightened little preschooler and come on over. I'll kick your smarmy—"

Larson's tirade ended with a soft click when the stranger hung up. Slowly, his anger turned to pride as he realized he had likely put an end to the malcontent. Still, he was a little ashamed that he'd allowed himself to be brought down to the level of a petulant dweeb.

A short time later, Jake awoke from his afternoon nap. Larson lifted him from his crib and held him tightly in his arms as Jake slowly eased back into the brave new world around him. "You'd have been pretty proud of your old man today," bragged Larson. "Nobody messes with us; do they, buddy?" As if to better prove this point, the rest of the afternoon passed with no additional calls from the stranger.

Caitlin got home a little earlier than expected, which was a good thing. She, Larson, and the baby could spend some much-needed and well-deserved time together before he had to start the night shift at the hotel. They enjoyed some leftover lasagna, as they caught up on the day's events. Once they were done, Caitlin and Larson settled down on the sofa and switched on the television. From time to time, they watched the apple of their eye exploring the vast frontier, otherwise known as the living room.

Larson had a satisfied look on his face that belied the mano a mano victory he had won earlier in the day.

"What's that for?" Caitlin asked with a curious smile.

"What's *what* for?" Larson answered with faux innocence.

"That mischievous grin that makes you look like a Cheshire cat."

"Oh, nothing."

"Just can the phony modesty. What'd you do?"

"It's really nothing," Larson replied, his ever-broadening smile betraying him.

"Larsooon," Caitlin whined. "Tell me, or else."

"Or else what?" he asked teasingly.

Caitlin leaned over to give him a playful slap on the face, but before she could, he relented.

"All right, all right," he laughed. "I'll tell you. Remember earlier when you called, and I told you that—"

"Shush," Caitlin said. "There's a news bulletin on."

Larson grabbed the remote and turned up the sound.

"The police arrested the serial killer known as The Torch a short time ago, just outside this apartment building," said the reporter.

Caitlin's mouth fell open, and she yanked in a frightened breath. "Dear God, Larson. That's our building." She upped the volume.

"It began when an individual, who was walking her dog, noticed a suspicious-looking man jogging east on Tyler Avenue," the reporter said. "According to her account, he was carrying a small canvas bag and a two-gallon gas can. She added he appeared angry and was talking to himself loudly. Thinking it odd, she called in a report to 9-1-1. When officers responded, the suspect began running. The officers caught him, and after a violent struggle, placed him under arrest."

Larson felt cold, immobile.

The reporter continued, as police officers ushered a growing group of onlookers behind a cordon of yellow tape. "The suspect, whom authorities have ID'd as Reuben Norse, was holding a family of four captive six blocks west of here. Eventually, the father, who asked not to be identified, was able to break free of his restraints and call for help. He described how Norse tied them up and gagged them before pouring gasoline on and around them. Norse then removed a lighter from his pocket, but before he could set the apartment ablaze, he received a phone call. The father observed Norse was extremely agitated while speaking with the caller. After a few more exchanges, Norse grabbed his canvas bag and the container of gasoline and stormed out of the apartment. Police are trying to ascertain where he was going and why."

"Geez, what a world," Caitlin muttered. "Thank God they finally caught that animal. It terrifies me to think he was right outside our building. Anyhow, what was it you were gonna tell me? Larson? Larson?"

# RAIN IN THE WITCHING HOUR

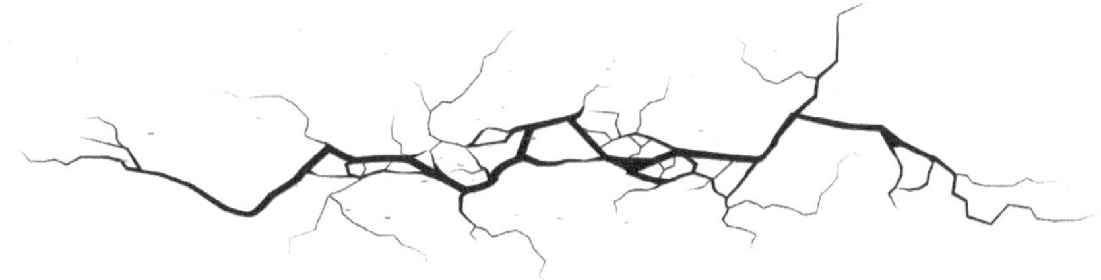

Rain poured down in unforgiving torrents. The windshield in Darius' Uber taxi was steamy despite him setting the defogger to full blast. Visibility was nil except for the blurry blobs of streetlights that intermittently illuminated the windshield. Darius was fighting to stay awake in the early hours. He had two options: Red Bulls or thinking about the headless bodies that had shown up over the summer. This was Atlanta, the big city, and there were some sick people out there. For all he knew, the rider he was going to collect was one of them.

"Continue following University Parkway for two miles," instructed the feminine voice on the app.

"How did I end up like this?" Darius lamented.

It had been his girlfriend Latisha's idea to have him work a second job. "I'm tired of livin' with your grandmama," she'd told him "Me workin' at the Dollar Tree, and you washing them cars for Antoine, ain't gonna get us any closer to gettin' out of here." She never said how she would do more to help pay for the move. But that was Latisha: getting drunk on wine while others crushed the grapes. This was one of those soul-searching moments for

Darius, as he questioned why he put up with her disrespect and self-centeredness. Perhaps it was his lifelong fear of confrontation that others had beaten into him that kept him chained to her. Or maybe he didn't want to be alone, allowing her to be his emotional insurance. Whatever the reason, here he was, putting miles on a fourteen-year-old Camry in a God-forsaken downpour in a part of town that wasn't safe in the daytime, much less at this ungodly hour of the morning. *Say, ain't this the witching hour?* he wondered.

"In one hundred feet, turn left onto Dryden Avenue," said the app.

Darius turned onto Dryden and headed toward the last street displayed on Google Maps.

"Turn right in thirty feet onto Blanch Street."

Darius slowed down as he drew closer. Struggling to see the street sign, he grabbed a rag from the glove box and wiped the condensation from the passenger side window. He craned his neck, trying to get a better look. "This ain't much more than an alley," he said. He looked at his phone's GPS; this was the right way.

The pummeling rain, together with the furtive look of this part of downtown, gave Darius pause. His instinct was to contact the fare and cancel the pickup, but he didn't want to hear the man's voice again. *There was something scary about it,* he remembered. *Something... dead.* After a pause for consideration, he turned down the dark, narrow side street.

Darius squinted through the streaks on the damp windshield. The street lamp was the only source of light. A vague figure was standing under it, alone and waiting. Darius drove up and lowered the passenger window. "Yo! You the guy who ordered an Uber?"

The person walked to the car, bent slightly, and peeped in at Darius, looking at him for an uncomfortable period. He remained mute as the rain dripped off his broad body. His fierce eyes locked with those of Darius, unblinking and indifferent.

Finally, Darius broke the silence. "Yo, I asked if you're the person who ordered an Uber." As each silent second stacked up, Darius became more wary. He was going to roll up the window and leave, but the mysterious man opened the rear door of the car and slid inside.

Darius turned to look at the stranger. He was wide and solid, perhaps a bodybuilder; it was hard to tell under his dark blue raincoat. A short, thick neck supported his enormous head, his straight black hair slicked back by the rain. When he breathed, he sounded like an angry bull preparing to charge. He ignored Darius, looking beyond the side window and into the wet darkness.

Despite his nervousness, Darius addressed the man. "Where is it you—"

"There's a site called Advantage Storage in the back section of Ansley Business Complex off Stratford Road near Pincott Boulevard. Do you know the place?"

*There's that voice again,* Darius thought. It was rough and deep, like the people who drink and smoke too much. "Yeah, I know it. But that's way across town. You okay with payin' for that much mileage?"

An ice cooler sitting beside the man drew Darius' attention. He wasn't sure why, but the object filled his stomach with a nauseating ball of dread. The man startled him when he spoke.

"The fare isn't a problem," the man said in a low, rumbling voice that sounded to Darius like deep thunder.

"Whatever you say, mister." Darius was afraid of turning his back to the man. A part of him wanted to get rid of the eerie stranger, but Latisha's voice kept rolling through his head: *I'm tired of livin' with your grandmama.* He threw the car into drive, telling himself to stop fixating on the man and the cooler. But as Darius drove, suspicion began snaking its way through his brain like squirming tentacles. *Something's not right,* he thought. *And it's not just the dark and the rain; it's something dangerous.* He pushed back against his unease by focusing on his senses. He felt the air from the defroster blowing its warm breath against the foggy windshield. He listened to the percussive rhythm of the swishing wiper blades coupled with the drumming rain. He observed the dancing, shifting shadows created by the roadside scenery. And he breathed in the coconut scent of the tree-shaped air freshener, swaying from the rearview mirror as it melded with the faded fragrances of its many predecessors.

Darius' eyes shifted to the rearview mirror. The man was scowling through the window as if he were angry at the night. Darius didn't want to antagonize his passenger, but he didn't think he'd be able to bear the half hour journey if he didn't engage with him. Who was he? Was he dangerous or simply odd? And what was in the cooler? The not knowing was already filling his head with images of psychopaths toting coolers containing body parts. But each time he opened his mouth to speak, fear closed it. Finally, he forced out the words before his brain stopped him.

"This rain is really something," he began. The man was silent. Darius pressed on. "Maybe what you need is a rowboat, not an Uber, heh, heh." The man continued ignoring him. Darius' eyes bounced between the road and the stranger's image in the mirror. "Sorry, man. I'll just leave you to—"

"Yes, it's a wet one tonight," the man interjected.

The unexpected response startled Darius, causing him to jerk the car a bit. He was relieved that the quiet stranger was content to communicate with him. Perhaps he could extract enough information to help him decide if he had anything to worry about. "It must be something important that got you out at this hour," Darius said.

The stranger shifted in his seat. "Does your Uber have one of those sliding glass partitions between you and the rider?"

The man's tone was intimidating. Darius gripped the wheel so hard he felt it give a little. "No, sir. There's no partition in this old car."

"That's too bad," the man muttered, his sarcasm clear. A few miles into the drive, he spoke again. "Pull into that convenience store up on the right. I can use some hot coffee."

"Sure thing," Darius said. He entered the lot and parked the car, but left the motor running.

The man opened his door but didn't get out. Instead, he leaned through the space between the two front seats until his mouth was within inches from Darius' head.

Despite the warmth of the man's breath, Darius felt chilled. It was wet and stale, smelling of... what was it? Dirt? Death?

"What's your name?" the man asked.

"It's Dari... Darius."

"Darius, are you the curious type?"

Darius' belly churned. "N-not particularly."

"That's good, Darius. That's good. So, listen.: Can I trust you with my cooler? It might tempt you to look inside. Can't do that, Darius. That would make for one nasty Yelp review."

Had the man just threatened him? The icy tingle passing through his body convinced him he had. When Darius finally spoke, his tongue was dry, and his words clipped. "I make it a policy not to bother with a fare's personal items. Don't you worry about me."

The man hesitated.

Darius held his breath.

Several tense seconds passed before the man spoke. "I appreciate your professionalism, Darius." Then he exited the car and went inside the convenience store.

Darius watched the man enter and make his way to the coffeemaker at the back before switching off the engine. His anxious breathing caused the glass to fill with fog, obscuring his view. He grimaced at his own scent; his shirt was wet with nervous perspiration. *What's the big deal about that cooler?* he wondered. *What's that weirdo got stored in there?* Darius wanted to know who and what he was transporting. The cooler would likely provide an answer. But did he dare to peek? The man had just put him on notice. What would be the price for disobeying him?

Darius used the fog to cloak the glass and mask his attempt at checking out the cooler. Despite the steamed up windshield, he could still see through the large store window. The man was behind three people at the checkout counter. Darius felt a mixture of fear and doubt, but he knew that if he didn't look now, he'd never discover the contents of the cooler. Judging by how slowly the checkout line was moving, he figured he might have a couple of minutes. "All right, let's get this over with before he gets back."

Darius looked at the storefront again—the man was now second in line. Who knew how long it would take him to return at this point? Darius braced himself, as if he were about to have a dislocated joint popped back into place. Though his insides felt gooey, he went into action. He leaned through the space between the front seats and reached for the cooler.

Darius let out an "oomph" as the tightness of the seatbelt pressed against his body, a consequence of forgetting to release it. Peering through the store's window, he watched the man hand the cashier money. Panic gnawed at him. Should he give the cooler one more try? He felt the weight of the decision pressing down on him. He unhooked his seatbelt and twisted around, extending his arm to its full length. His fingertips grazed the handle on the cooler, frustrating him. "Oh, come on," he grunted. He was breathing so hard that he became lightheaded. With one final lurch, he was able to hook his index finger around the handle. "Whew... gotcha!"

The jingling bell above the store's front door caused Darius to jump. Through the clouded windshield, he could see the man coming toward him. He quickly returned to his seat, his body shaking as he tried to hide his nervousness. Darius kept his eyes forward; he didn't want the man to see the fear they held.

The rear door creaked open and the sound of rain filled the car. The man dropped into his seat, his heavy size causing the Camry to bounce and sway. He closed his door and blew out a breath. "Man, this coffee's going to go down good."

Darius acted as if everything was fine and normal. *I need to say something casual,* he thought. *Something to put him at ease.* He realized the need to control the tempo of his voice—rambling might rouse the man's suspicions. "I hope you enjoy it," Darius said. "Cheers!" He started the car and reached for the gearshift.

"Hold on there," the voice from the back commanded.

Darius froze. "S-Something wrong, mister?"

The man leaned forward a bit. "Why is your seatbelt undone? Wasn't that way before."

Darius had no immediate answer. How could he have been so careless? *Run! Run!* his inner voice screamed. His left hand crept toward the door latch.

"I asked you a question, Darius. Why'd you remove your seatbelt? What were you up to?"

Darius' throat locked up, refusing to release words that might save him. He thought of movie scenes where a killer would pop up from a back seat and garrote an unsuspecting victim. His bones shook under his skin.

"Darius?" the man said.

Hearing the imposing man say his name made Darius' skin prickle. His jaw trembling, he muttered, "I was thinking of getting a coffee, too. I'll run in and grab one. I won't be a minute." He planned to use the opportunity to call for help. But what would he tell 9-1-1? *Hi. There's a spooky guy in the back of my Uber whose cooler is making me nervous.* Before he could decide, the man spoke.

"Why didn't you think about that sooner? I don't have time to waste. Get going."

Darius hesitated. Did he still have a shot at running?

"I said get going!" the stranger barked.

Darius reluctantly fastened the telltale seatbelt. *Just do what he says, and maybe this will all work out,* he thought. Then he said,

"Sorry, mister. As my girlfriend will tell you, I'm a bit slow on the draw."

"It's alright, Darius," said the man. "Just keep moving."

*Keep it together,* Darius told himself. *Don't make him suspicious.* Hoping to keep things relaxed, he said, "I guess I'm a little on edge. It's just one of those creepy kinds of nights: dark, rainy, and late. Gets a little spooky sometimes." He waited for a response, hoping the man might show that he believed his excuse. But the stranger said nothing. Darius glanced back through the rearview. The man was staring ahead, trancelike, his fingers drumming softly on the cooler's lid. Darius wondered which he feared worse: the man's cryptic voice or his grave silence. He returned his eyes to the dim, shiny street rolling under his car in slow, agonizing miles. When he gazed in the rearview again, the image of the man's leering face filled the mirror, startling him.

"Come on, Darius. Why don't you ask your question?"

*What's he talking about?* Darius wondered. "I don't know what you mean. What ques—"

"You know perfectly well what question. Please, don't insult my intelligence. Do you think I didn't notice when you were deciding on making a run for it back at the convenience store? I was on to your little act of feigned innocence right off the bat. You've wanted this ride to be over ever since I got in. Now ask the question. Ask about the cooler."

"H-h-honestly, mister, your business is none of my concern. I'm simply driving you to your destination. Nothing more. Like I told you, this night's got a creepy vibe to it, that's all."

The stranger lingered for a bit—although it seemed much longer to Darius—then relaxed in his seat.

When Darius stopped at the next traffic light, he glimpsed a car out of the corner of his left eye. He turned his head slightly and saw, to his relief and excitement, that it was a police cruiser. He hoped the stranger didn't hear his thumping heart and quickened breath. *I've only got a minute or so,* he thought. *How do I get that cop's attention?*

The stranger spoke, breaking his concentration. As if reading Darius' thoughts, he said, "You're tense again, Darius. Is it the cop car? Don't worry. He's not interested in anything going on over here. As long as you do nothing to draw his attention, he'll leave us alone. What do you think, Darius?"

The man had made his point. Still, Darius thought of rolling his window down and screaming for help. Maybe he could blow his horn or make a run for it.

The voice from the backseat interrupted his thoughts again. "It's getting late, Darius. Look, get me to the church on time and I'll throw in another twenty bucks for the effort."

Darius was silent, his mind filled with a jumble of thoughts as he tried to decide what he should do.

"Hey, Darius! Do we have a deal or not?"

When the light changed, the cop pulled away, making Darius' decision easier. "Yeah, sure, mister. We've got a deal."

Darius hoped he could keep the man calm long enough to think of something else. *This may be your last shot at this,* he told himself. *Make it count.* He planned to slide the Camry slightly to the right of the squad car, allowing himself just enough space to avoid the stranger's notice, yet enough room to jump free and run to the officer.

When he joined the cruiser at the next stoplight, he cautiously lowered his right hand toward the seatbelt latch. He set his mental timer and began counting down. *Okay... 3... 2... Dammit!* Darius didn't have a favorite color. But from that moment on, it would never be green. He realized he couldn't waste another opportunity on a red light escape; he'd have to devise another plan. *I got it!* he thought. Perhaps a young black male speeding past a cop would likely draw some attention. *Please, God. Don't let this cop be woke or stupid. I need him to pull me over.*

Darius checked the mirror to see if the fare was paying attention. The sight of the man staring nonchalantly through his window calmed him. This time, he didn't bother with a mental countdown. He pulled in a breath, his foot hovering over the gas pedal, ready to make the car roar. He steadied himself and slowly placed the ball of his foot on the top of the pedal. *Here we go!*

Darius watched helplessly as the policeman activated his left blinker and turned the corner, leaving him to face his predicament alone. He felt a sudden lurch in his stomach. It was like someone had put him inside a thousand-story elevator and cut its cable. His body slumped and his face slackened. In his disappointment, he didn't notice the Camry slowing down. The stranger's voice jolted him.

"Something wrong up there, Darius?" When Darius didn't respond right away, the man became annoyed. "Yo, Darius! You good?"

"Yes, sir," Darius mumbled. "It's all... good."

"Glad to hear it. Now pick up the pace. I want to get my business over with."

Darius drove wordlessly until they reached the entrance of the industrial complex that housed the storage units. He steered into the middle turn lane and switched on the blinker. Its steady ticking, along with the thudding rain, were the only sounds in the world. He waited, the complex looming in front of him, as the surrounding air grew heavy. His hopeful mind was nagging him, telling him he could still jump from the car and escape. But by this point, he was emotionally and psychologically drained. Besides, an athletic-looking guy like his creepy passenger would likely have little trouble running him down. Then what? There weren't any vehicles or other signs of activity. There was only himself, the possible psychopath in the rear seat, and the relentless rain that would drown out his screams and cleanse away any evidence. A part of him became angry with himself. Why hadn't he acted sooner to get rid of the man? Now he was out of options.

Darius thought of Latisha. Despite her mistreatment of him, he still loved her and hoped that she felt the same way. But reality hit him in his gut, pushing out the air and filling it with sadness. She'd grieve long enough to garner pity, then dump his belongings off at a thrift store the first chance she got. He wondered which was harder: dying in the darkness or living in self-contempt.

He remembered the mantra his old man repeated to him when he was teaching him how to fight off the bullies who were tormenting him. "The Lord hates a coward," he'd said. But despite the old man's efforts, Darius never found the courage to act. He had long ago resigned himself to his circumstances. *Lord hates a coward,* he thought as he hung a left and entered the complex.

The site was as large as four football fields. Steel structures with rusting roofs and clinging business signs took up most of the scenery.

"Where to?" Darius asked.

"Take the third right up ahead by the Advantage Storage sign. I'll tell you where to go from there," said the stranger.

After making the turn, Darius rolled past the units, wondering what was going to happen. He'd gone about twenty yards when the deep voice drifted from the backseat. "Pull up along unit #38."

Darius slowed, counting the unit numbers until he arrived at the one marked #38.

"Turn off the engine," the man instructed. "I have to take care of something, and I'm not sure how long it might take."

Darius did as the man told him. He put the Camry in park and killed the engine.

The man flung open his door and exited the car with a low grunt. "Don't go anywhere," he told Darius before slamming the door shut.

The man walked to the locked folding door of the unit and removed a key from his pocket. After opening the padded lock at the bottom, the man lifted the door until it clanged to a stop. He cast a look back at Darius, pointing his index finger toward the ground as if to say, "Stay right where you are." Then he disappeared inside, leaving Darius to his frantic thoughts.

Darius was nervously tapping his fingers against the steering wheel, a low and indiscernible tune escaping his lips. After a few minutes, the suspense was too much for him. "Screw it!" he said. "I'm looking in that cooler!"

Darius unfastened his seat belt and turned to the backseat. *Watch yourself!* he thought. He envisioned looking around and seeing the stranger running toward him. The cooler was directly in front of him. Anxiety closed in around him. His hands shook uncontrollably as he felt the fear settle in and around him. He paused, his breath catching in his throat. Darius shuddered at the thought of what dark secrets might lurk in the container. He braced himself for the answer. He stretched out his hands and eased them toward the cooler as if he were attempting to grab hold of a hissing snake.. "Okay, here we go," he whispered. Darius depressed the small button at the bottom of the cooler's handle and pulled back the lid.

"What the...?" The cooler was empty. Confusion clouded Darius' mind, accompanied by a sense of foolishness. His body unclenched as he released a deep sigh of relief. "Well then, what's he here for?"

The car door flew open, and an arm yanked Darius out in one rapid motion. He tensed with terror when he felt the big man's arm crook around his neck, constricting him like a python. As Darius struggled to free himself, he saw the attacker's reflection in the passenger side window. The only thing more horrifying than the look of sinister glee on the man's face was the machete he was clutching in his free hand. Blind horror like an electrical current shot through Darius' body as he realized, *It's him! Oh, God, it's that maniac!*

"You want to know what's in the cooler?" the man hissed into Darius' ear. "Your head."

The man dragged Darius toward the storage unit, grunting from the effort of restraining his victim.

Darius pressed his heels into the wet pavement, trying to slow down his attacker, but the slick surface prevented him from finding a foothold. He twisted his body, hoping to break free of the powerful grip of his attacker—his murderer. But the man had performed this maneuver many times on many victims and had always won the battle.

"Stop struggling, you little twerp," the stranger snarled, as he continued pulling Darius to his den of horrors. When he wrestled Darius into the unit, he exclaimed, "Behold my museum!"

Three six-foot shelves lined the walls, each one filled with plastic coolers similar to the one in the back of the Camry. In the dim of the low wattage overhead light, Darius could see small labels attached to each cooler—the victim's names, perhaps? His vision narrowed into a wide, black tunnel with a pinprick of light at the end. *Please, God—help me!* he inwardly pleaded.

As if to answer Darius' prayer, one of his dad's defensive maneuvers suddenly returned to him with the ferocity of a lightning bolt. Before his breaths could cease and his strength diminish, Darius threw his head back, smashing the killer's face with his skull. There was a loud crack as the man's nose crumpled. The unforeseen strike threw him off balance, causing him to loosen his grip on Darius' neck. Darius seized the opportunity to get out of the fight alive. With all his might, he pushed the man in the chest to make him tumble backward. If the tactic worked, the psychopath would end up on the ground, helpless against Darius and his adrenaline-fueled rage. However, the man was stocky and powerful. When Darius attempted to topple him, he stayed upright. "Oh, snap," Darius said, at his failed effort. He realized there was a reason none of the killer's other victims had lived to tell the tale: he'd physically outmatched them.

A thin line of blood trickled from the madman's nose. But he didn't seem to notice or care, looking more amused than outraged.

"I love it when they fight back," he chuckled. He raised his meaty leg and kicked Darius backward into one of the shelving units, sending some of its contents clattering to the concrete floor. One cooler popped open and the severed head of a woman skidded across the hard surface accompanied by scattering ice.

"Oh, dear God!" Darius screamed. Even if he somehow survived, he knew he'd never forget the look of horror on the poor woman's bloodless face.

"Your turn," the killer sneered, as he raised the machete to deliver the first chop.

Darius regained his footing and tried to run past the killer, only to slip on the spilled ice. Now he was prone on his back as his attacker stood over him.

"Well, aren't you the wascally wabbit?" the man quipped. He lowered himself onto Darius and raised the machete, preparing to sever his head.

Darius felt a surge of courage pulse through his body, providing him with the strength to resist. As the blade of the machete swung down, he jerked his head to the side, the curved iron narrowly missing him. A bright spark erupted when the blade contacted the concrete floor, stinging the side of his head. While the attacker's hand was low enough, Darius grabbed his forearm with both hands.

"Let go, you little prick," the man growled. Realizing that this victim would not go down as effortlessly as the others had, he began punching Darius in his face with his free hand.

Darius' right eye was swelling shut. He knew that if the man smashed his nose, the gush of the accompanying blood would pour through his nasal passage, then down his throat, choking him to death. Suddenly, he remembered another of his old man's sayings: "Hospitals and graveyards are full of those who tried to fight fair."

Darius latched his teeth on the arm that was holding the machete and twisted his head from side to side like a vicious dog. Warm, salty blood poured from the man's ripped flesh.

"Aaah!" the man wailed, before rolling off Darius. It was the opening Darius needed. With a loud grunt, he pushed himself up and climbed on top of the murderer, pinning his shoulders to the floor.

The sudden change of events dumbfounded the man. Glaring into Darius' angry eyes, he growled, "Not gonna happen, Darius; not gonna happen."

The old Darius might've believed the bigger, stronger foe. But this Darius had had enough shame... hidden anger... disrespect. He wrested the machete from the killer's hand and gripped it in his own. "Oh, but it's gonna happen, jerk off," he said.

"Wait!" the man pleaded. The cold merciless eyes that had made Darius shudder earlier were now filled with something his victims had felt: terror.

"Sorry, my man," Darius said, grinning. "Looks like I got you to the church on time—for your damn funeral." Then he slammed the thick blade against the deranged monster's skull, cleaving it almost in two, and filling the storage unit with the sound of cracking bone and one short, piercing scream.

Police cars, ambulances, and CSI vans lined up, making the lane of the storage units look like a staging area for a colorful nighttime parade. Inside the disarrayed and blood-smeared unit, detectives directed the forensics crew.

"Tell me something, Mike," the detective said to his partner. "Have you ever seen such a horror show?"

"Never, Eddy. And I hope I never do again," Mike muttered, as he watched CSI techs in protective gear examine the gruesome contents of the many coolers stored on the metal shelving units.

"I'm gonna go check on our hero," Eddy said.

"Make sure you ask him how he wants his name spelled on his Citizen of the Year medal," Mike replied.

"Don't I know it? The guy's a stud."

Darius was perched on the rear of an ambulance. Despite the blanket the EMTs had draped around him, he still felt chilled. The cloud-laden sky had finally shed its last drops of rain. *Oh, now you want to give me a break?* he thought.

An EMT climbed out of the ambulance and checked Darius' facial injuries. "You won't be winning *People's Sexiest Man Alive* anytime soon, but you should heal up fine. Are you sure you don't want to go to the hospital? You took quite a beating."

"Appreciate it, man, but I've had enough excitement for one night. If you're done, I'd like to just get the hell out of here."

Just then, Eddy approached the ambulance. He looked at Darius and grimaced. Then, turning to the EMT said, "Is he gonna be okay?"

"Yeah, he'll be fine in a week or two. If he could survive that psychopath, he can survive anything."

"Yeah, about that," Eddy said to the EMT. "Will you give us a minute?"

"Sure thing," he replied before walking away.

Once Eddy settled next to him, Darius asked, "Who is he?"

Eddy shook his head. "We don't know yet; there was no ID on him. And you made damn certain that dental records wouldn't be particularly useful," he chuckled. "We'll run prints. Psycho's probably got a rap sheet as long as my arm."

Darius' heart filled with melancholy. "And the victims?"

Eddy sighed, his heart aching in sympathy as he sensed Darius' sorrow. "As awful as it's been tracking this sick bastard, the hardest part is about to begin. How do you tell a person that the loved one they've been praying for ended up with their head in some freak's trophy case?"

An awkward silence lingered between the two men, who now shared a lack of hope for humanity.

"I have some questions for you, but they can wait till tomorrow," Eddy said.

"Yeah, let's do that," Darius replied as he pulled off the blanket and stood.

"Why don't you let one of my officers give you a lift?"

Darius thought the offer over. "Thanks, but I have something I need to take care of."

"I understand. But before you go, I gotta say you're one of the bravest people I've ever met. What you did in there... Let's just say that you are not someone to be trifled with, my friend."

Darius smiled and went back to the Camry. He situated himself, drew in a deep breath, and released it slowly into the night. His clothes were awash in crimson gore; he'd likely burn them.

He sat behind the wheel and watched two EMTs roll a stretcher with a black bag on top past him. The body within was huge, pushing against the material.

Warm confidence flowed through Darius. The guy had put up a good fight, but in the end, it hadn't mattered. He need not have been worried or afraid of the outcome; his old man had taught him well. He'd stumbled upon an inner courage he never thought he had. For once, Darius didn't feel like a non-person. He'd battled for his life and emerged victorious because his life was worth it.

He threw the Camry into drive and pulled away. He'd talk to the cops and the press tomorrow. Maybe. He didn't yet know how to tell his story. But for now, he wanted to get home. It was time for Latisha to move out.

# ABOUT THE AUTHOR

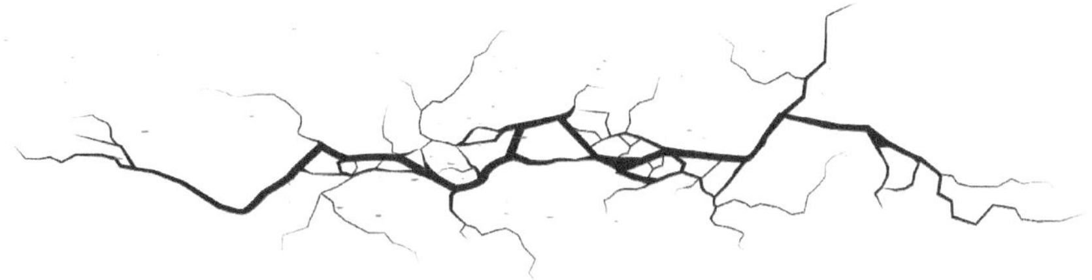

P.D. Williams is an author, composer, and multi-instrumentalist. His short horror fiction stories have been featured in several popular horror anthologies and e-zines. His works have also been broadcast on many national and international horror podcasts. He resides with his amazing family in North Carolina. For more info on the author, visit his website at pdwilliamsauthor.com.

# MORE CHILLS FROM VELOX BOOKS

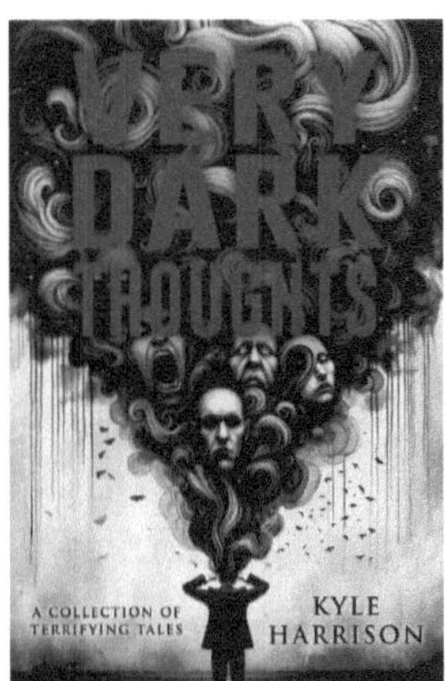

9 781963 107302